In Remembrance of Me
A December Killing

Peter Caras

In Remembrance of Me
A December Killing

By Peter Caras
© 2011 Peter Caras

Printed in United States

To my parents, Peter and Julia Caras.

ACKNOWLEDGEMENTS

I wish to thank my wife, Carin, for her encouragement twelve years ago to write this book; and to our sons, Brent and Christopher for their patience and understanding. Thank you to Anne Hicks, Wendy Allison, Ellie Kroesen, and Brenda Epley for their contributions. I thank Attorney Roger Reason and Tom Woronecki for their support and periodic review of the book. A special thanks to Kelly Smet and Attorney Jeremy Reppy for their invaluable assistance in the final editing, formatting, and printing of this book.

I have often said that my goal with this book is a modest one – that readers enjoy it.

PROLOGUE

Many cities and towns in four different states bordered Lake Michigan shores. The lake gave the area summertime amusement with its miles of beaches and endless water. Boats of all sizes sailed the lake, which facing north, looked like someone had drawn a straight line separating the lake from the sky. On a map the lake had the appearance of an appendage forcefully thrusting itself downward between Wisconsin, Michigan, Illinois and Indiana, where it stops. It was as if the steel mills in Illinois and Indiana, once mighty manufacturing giants, put up a wall of steel preventing the lake's encroachment into the two states. Soft, glistening beaches with microscopic sand, bordered by tall grass and trees, some dead and looking like driftwood growing out of the dunes bordered the Great Lake for miles. Though still beautiful in the winter, strong winds brought in colder temperatures and lake effect snow.

Throughout the year, many ethnic festivals served as annual reminders of the regions diverse populace, but less festive, traffic congestion, crime, corruption and pollution from the steel mills were daily reminders of the area's identity. Frequent train traffic with delays at railroad crossings caused many drivers to automatically turn their engines off until the gates lifted.

Despite the crime, corruption, brutal winters and bad economy, the population remained stable in the metropolitan Chicago area and for Westin, a town within the region.

Such could not be said for Westin high school, rather instability defined the school. Named after the town and its first mayor, the school once boasted a total student body exceeding 1500. Enrollment had declined in the last several years, a period marked by the hiring of Clinton Cantrell, its principal. Many parents argued that something was wrong with a school where the principal's own children failed to attend regularly. Cantrell had reason to be anxious, and declining enrollment was only part of the source of his anxiety. Some school board members and faculty believed their principal should have a Ph.D., like the other principals in nearby high schools. Others argued that his family was so dysfunctional that it impaired his ability to secure financing for the school, expand the curriculum and keep the faculty from leaving. Many felt he should have been a preacher; after all, he was an assistant pastor, had a bachelor of divinity degree besides his masters in psychology, and liked to quote scripture.

"The Reverend," as he was mockingly referred to outside of his presence by faculty and school board members, had cause for concern and anxiety—his family's mental illness and disassociation with him. Clinton Cantrell's worries grew as information about his family became more public. His wife, Bonnie, had been in an inpatient psychiatric unit several times in the last few years. The oldest son, Lenny, had often run away from home for days. Matthew Cantrell, eighteen years old and a senior at his father's high school, had an IQ of 180, but his truancy and disinterest in most of the school's subjects yielded only above average grades. Of greater concern to Matt's parents were his incorrigibility, drug abuse and association with Butch Roeder, a certified hoodlum known to police in all neighboring jurisdictions by his first name.

What neither the school nor the public knew was that the principal shed his academic demeanor when leaving school property. At home he was a warden, and his wife and children, inmates.

The community also knew little about Matt. Matt had plans; plans that would shock the peaceful town and indelibly stamp into the brain of every resident an unforgettable memory, and culminate in the most bizarre trial in the state's history. The crime and trial would draw national attention.

Matt slid down the top bunk to the cold, hardwood floor in his bedroom. He did not think of the room as his, since occasionally his brother Lenny would sleep there when he was not running away. Crammed with one chest, bunk beds and a sealed window during winter, a stale smell hung in the air, especially in the mornings. Without making any noise, Matt pulled on a pair of jeans and sweatshirt. The only light in the room came from a digital clock, which read 5:34 a.m. He left the dark room and passed the unlit Christmas tree into the kitchen. Matt liked it dark. He went to the refrigerator looking for some orange juice. His bare feet felt the cold of the kitchen floor. The light from the refrigerator illuminated his smooth ashen face, a face with no facial hair. He heard footsteps. The beating of his heart began to pound in his ears. His father turned on the kitchen light. Matt shielded his eyes from the sudden light, but didn't look up at his father.

"Where's your mother, boy?"

"Don't know."

"You don't know much, do you?"

"That's right."

"Don't get smart with me, boy. You may not get the pole anymore, but I'll take a belt to your behind anytime I want."

It was said that even the deaf could hear Clinton Cantrell. During school board meetings, public functions or in church, no one had to ask the principal to speak louder or to use a microphone. His large stature aided his booming voice. He had a dark face with crevices and sunken, oval shaped eyes. It was a face uncharacteristic of his profession and one seemingly not fashioned by a lifetime of good works and charitable thoughts.

Go to hell, Matt thought, but years of being tied to the pole in the basement and beaten, silenced him. He could only reply, "I've got to work on a school paper for next semester."

"Maybe a reform school paper. You need to read and study assigned school materials, rather than learning languages and reading books that will get you nowhere. Teachers say you sit and stare like a zombie. How do you think this makes me look as principal of the high school that you attend?" Matt said nothing, but that did not stop his father's attack. He was a pit bull. He puffed his chest out, crossed his arms in front, and said, "You're getting to be as useless as Butch. He'll be on death row some day."

Butch was Matt's best friend and lived a few miles away. They had been friends since the third grade.

Matt's fist tightened around the handle of the refrigerator door. His nails dug deeper into the palms of his hands. Matt wasn't sure what his father said. He had gotten better at blocking out the verbal assaults; yet, he could not prevent his heart from pounding and muscles from tensing. Matt had learned that the best defense to his father's attacks was to do nothing. He took comfort in knowing that vengeance would be his.

His father left the kitchen and Matt felt a chill but it had nothing to do with the thermostat setting or his father leaving through the front door.

With his father gone, it was time to get the hell out, time to do some damage. He called his friend, Butch Roeder.

"It's me."

"What time is it, man?" Roeder asked. Ten seconds ago he had been sleeping.

"I can't take it anymore."

"Still messing with you?"

"Nothing he says can bother me anymore," Matt said, fighting back tears. "It's time to implement the plan, bring everything, all the stuff."

"On my way."

Butch arrived in a pickup truck, year and model uncertain, and even reasonable people could differ as to its color. The truck looked like it had been assembled in a junkyard rather than an automotive plant.

Despite a temperature in the low twenties, Butch looked comfortable in a sweatshirt that once had sleeves. He liked to display as much of his body as possible. Football fans could count on Butch to remove his top outerwear during November and December football games. In the back sat Buck Shot or "Buck," the boys' jointly-owned black Lab. Like the truck, Buck had reached maturity years ago.

Matt let his friend into the kitchen. They nodded to each other. Butch smiled but Matt had to force a smile. Butch reached into his camouflaged cargo pants and took out some pills which he gave to his friend. As if by habit, Matt reached into one of Butch's other pockets and took out a bottle of cheap port. They both tilted their heads back and took a few large swallows.

With eyes barely opened, Matt's older brother Lenny stumbled into the kitchen. Butch offered the bottle to Lenny, who shook his head. The only thing in common between Matt and Lenny was their last names. Lenny looked like his father and both shopped at the big and tall store for clothes. Matt was less than six feet tall, and though a few inches taller than his mother, neither would ever be factored into any national obesity statistics.

"Ma here?" Lenny asked impassively.

"I assume she's with her friend because mom and dad fought last night. We're going Lenny."

"Dad thinks mom's gone a lot for someone who is sick."

"To hell with what the reverend thinks," Matt said, eyes narrowed, and with particular emphasis on "reverend." He liked referring to his father as the reverend, bestowing upon him what he believed to be an undeserved title.

Matt and Butch stepped outside. A gust of wind halted Matt and briefly took his breath away. The temperature and wind combined to make a brutal December morning, a morning better spent inside with a cup of hot coffee and a good book in front of the Christmas tree. The neighbors didn't mind the harsh December weather; after all, it was the Christmas season with lights strung along windows and gutters as proof. The complaining would start in January because it was the coldest month, the longest month, the month with the highest energy bills and slowest driving on slick roads. None of this concerned Matt or Butch at the moment. A killing would happen today and the friends' minds were not on comfort.

As they approached the truck, Buck jumped out and ran to Matt knocking him over. Matt got down on his knees and put his arms around the dog in a smothering embrace and started to cry. Buck licked Matt's tears and face. Butch turned around, not wanting Matt to see his eyes glistening with moisture. They had bought the dog from a widow whose deceased husband, a hunter, had always wanted some boys who enjoyed hunting to have the dog. Unfortunately, Matt's father did not allow dogs or any animals in the house. Matt loosened his embrace, looked up at the sky and seemed to say something. Butch paced uncomfortably. He had never seen his best friend so overwhelmed, had never seen him cry before. Matt's usual expression showed detachment, introspection. Butch had seen Matt enraged a few times following confrontations with his father. Matt took the sleeve of his coat and wiped his face, still holding the dog. Eventually, he let go and Butch called the dog back into the truck.

"I'll drive," Matt said.

"You sure, man?"

"I'm cool. Got the stuff in the back?"

Butch cast a look of disbelief at his friend, as if to say, hey, I may not have school assignments ready, but to do damage, you can always count on me. "We have everything," Butch said, echoing a popular advertisement via all media. Everyone in the county and adjoining counties knew the meaning of those three words. Eilert Kurtz owned a store, an unusual store, a bazaar, a store that never closed, not even on Christmas. In fact, it had everything. It might be difficult to find things with its cluttered aisles, but whatever you wanted, the store had. Eilert Kurtz bought, sold and traded. He once remarked that he never knew the extent of his inventory, nor the amount of his wealth. When a Super Wal-Mart opened a few miles away, Kurtz still prospered, while other stores saw their profits diminish. But, Eilert Kurtz would die today and the only thing he would own would be a vault in a mausoleum.

Matt drove through the first stoplight without stopping. He laughed, realizing what he had done.

"Partner, maybe I ought to drive," Butch said, but with no response from Matt. Instead, Matt talked about their plan while driving through another red stoplight. Butch thought there wouldn't be any plan if the cops pulled them over first.

The Cantrell family, along with a few other select families who were privileged to know Eilert Kurtz well, referred to his place simply as the "*property.*" On this land, Kurtz had his home, a haunted looking, old country farm house in need of considerable paint, and a place one would not expect a wealthy person to occupy. Kurtz's property included more than two thousand acres of woods, grass, weeds, ravines and four spring fed lakes containing the biggest bluegill and crappie anywhere.

Though only a short distance from the Cantrell home, the back entrance to the store owner's property was difficult to find during the day and impossible to locate at night. No street sign or entrance identified the property. One had to locate a large hickory tree that no longer reached for the sky, but rather leaned against two oak trees as if for support in its advanced age. Attached to a rusty gate with a reddish-brown, bulky chain wrapped around it, a sign read, NO HUNTING. Butch got out and opened the gate. Beyond the gate lay a narrow dirt road, barely wide enough for a vehicle, and littered with leaves, prairie grass, small trees and deep, uneven ruts. Matt proceeded about a mile and gradually the road disappeared. Foot-high harvested corn replaced the weeds and grass. The ride became rougher. Matt and Butch laughed as the truck bounced up and down over the field made tougher by the cold, hard ground. Matt drove to an area the size of a football field, but at least ten feet deep and looking as if a meteor had once smashed into it. The uneven ground made it difficult for walking. Matt got out of the truck and fell to the ground, lying there laughing. The drugs and port obscured his vision but he didn't care. Butch got out of the truck, staggered and fell, and likewise, also began to laugh.

Now why are we doing this?" Butch asked, looking puzzled, and perhaps for the first time contemplating the seriousness of what they were about to do.

"Five, yes, at least five reasons or motives as criminal lawyers like to call it," Matt said, as if commenting on the weather and without explaining the reasons, "and dad needs to feel some pain. Even though prosecutors don't have to prove a motive to get a conviction, juries want explanations for a crime. Butch, my fellow associate, we are going to commit the perfect crime. Assuming we are ever caught, the prosecution would have no DNA, no physical evidence, no fingerprints, nothing linking us to the killing. It's time partner."

"You know this legal stuff, don't you?" Butch asked.

"I've studied it a lot."

"What if he's not home?"

"He's home, so be ready when we get back."

"You do plan this stuff out, don't you?"

Matt said nothing and reached into his pocket for a small flashlight. With his eyes focused on Kurtz's home a few blocks away, and barely visible, it looked more gray and haunted than he had remembered, perhaps because of the low clouds and winter sky. A dense layer of leaves, pine needles and corn covered the path. He started to sprint, hoping his quick pace would silence his approach. Occasionally, he would step on a branch and hear it snap. The only other sound on the way to the house was the pounding of his heart against his chest.

Once there, he knocked on the faded gray, wood door. No answer. He knocked again, but no response. With his heart pounding and his face stinging from the cold, he repeatedly stabbed at the door with both fists. After a minute, the door opened about a foot and Eilert Kurtz filled the foot of that space. He had one hand on the inside door knob while tucking a shirt into his trousers with the other hand. It seemed as if Kurtz had been interrupted and didn't want any visitors. He looked at Matt with a questioning glance and spoke in an effeminate whisper.

"What are you doing here, Matt?"

"Mr. Kurtz," Matt said, making no apologies for his early visit.

"Go ahead and hunt," Kurtz said as he started to close the door. Matt's pale, glistening green eyes looked downward as he explained that Butch's truck had stalled.

"Well, give me a few minutes to put more clothing on," Kurtz brusquely said, slamming the door, leaving Matt alone on the wooden porch. After awhile, Matt was ready to knock on the door again when Kurtz emerged outfitted in a thick, brown, one piece bib overall.

"Where?" asked Kurtz.

"The crater area." They got into a late-model, tan Dodge pickup. Kurtz drove fast and neither spoke. They arrived at

Butch's truck in a couple of minutes and Kurtz proceeded to position his truck opposite the hood on Butch's vehicle. Leaving Kurtz's truck, Matt got out and opened the driver's door of Butch's truck, while Butch handed him a two foot steel pipe. Kurtz raised the hood of his truck and began connecting jumper cables to the battery. Matt approached Kurtz from the left with both hands clenching the pipe. He raised the pipe and brought it down against the left side of Kurtz's head as hard as he could. The victim fell forward over the battery and onto the engine. As the boys heard the sound of the crushing blow, a coyote howled in the distance. Soon other coyotes howled and even Buck responded. Butch yelled at Buck to shut up then got out of the truck, and with one hand pulled the victim off the engine and onto the frozen ground. He searched the pockets and found a new, leather bi-fold wallet containing $322.00, a drivers license, a barely legible social security card and a gas credit card. Butch remarked that the new wallet must have been a recent gift or purchase.

"Partner, I told you he carries money," Matt said.

Matt thought he heard the store owner breathing. He grabbed the pipe again, pulled it back over his head and down onto the right side of the face and head. He felt warm and couldn't focus his eyes. As he swung several more times, visions of his father flashed quickly before him. He looked down at the smashed skull and face. Matt's eyes widened and his face tightened as he delivered more strikes. These blows destroyed the face and skull making identity impossible. Matt brought the pipe up to his eyes to better see it in the dark. Buck started barking, breaking Matt's studied concentration.

"He's dead," Butch said, but Matt didn't seem to hear, and his eyes reflected the moment and the lack of feeling behind them. This was taking too long, thought Butch and the chances of discovery increased by the minute, but he felt reluctant to intervene. Buck took charge. He jumped out of the truck and ran into Matt, knocking him over, as if to stop the carnage. Matt put his arms around Buck and buried his head into the dog's neck. Butch pulled the dog away. Matt stared at his project and felt that it needed a little more work, but Butch stepped in front of him and motioned to the back of his truck.

"We have work to do," Butch said. Without any further talking, they grabbed two large pieces of wood from the bed of Butch's truck and placed them on the ground. The two pieces of wood had been previously notched out so that the smaller piece could be placed horizontally onto the larger vertical piece, both together forming a cross. After bolting the two pieces together, they grabbed Kurtz's body, placed his arms stretched out onto the smaller horizontal piece of wood, and his body onto the longer, vertical piece, securing him to the cross with cords, ropes and fasteners bought from stores in distant areas. With a flashlight they looked for the round post hole encased in a PVC pipe that they had previously dug out to a depth of three feet during the past summer. They couldn't find the hole, but eventually discovered that it lie underneath Butch's truck. They moved the truck a few feet, grabbed Kurtz and the cross, and on the count of three, tried to maneuver the cross into the PVC pipe but were unsuccessful. Unfortunately, the hole had filled up a little with debris and dirt since it had been dug out when the ground was soft. Removing as much debris as possible, they tried again. On their third attempt, they managed to twist and wiggle their project into the hole. Fortunately, Kurtz was not a big man, unlike Matt's father. Though short of breath and unable to talk, Matt signaled a thumb's up. Butch smiled, a job done according to a plan hatched months ago, and better than any work he had ever done on a school term paper.

"Time to go partner," Butch said.

"Kurtz's place first." Butch shot him an inquisitive look, but Matt paid no attention. They got back into the truck and drove to the house which was left unlocked.

Matt went inside and yelled towards the upstairs, "Ma, let's go."

CHAPTER 1

My job was to bring back to life the dead for a short period. For over thirty years, I prosecuted murder cases. There is no comparable job. In no other vocation or profession is one the voice of a deceased victim, the representative for millions of people, that being the state, yet on a smaller, but more personal scale, the advocate for the victim's family. I brought back the dead so that the public and more particularly, twelve people could see the deceased victim as a real person.

Surgeons can spend fifteen hours or more on a patient, but it's over with that day. In contrast, it takes weeks or months to prepare for a big murder trial and there's the trial itself. If there's a favorable verdict, the effort makes the reward greater. It's a high that no drug can equal. Even more rewarding is giving the grieving family a belief that justice was done and a sense of closure for their loss. All of this is done while the defense lawyer or defense team works just as hard against your case. It's a lot of work for a verdict that is not always favorable. In that instance, there is no high, but rather a feeling of exhaustion, disappointment and loss of time with nothing to show for it.

There aren't many prosecutors nearing age sixty who still prosecute. It's too stressful and the pay isn't great. The typical life of many prosecutors is to start the job sometime after law school, get about five years of invaluable trial experience and bolt for something lucrative.

I hadn't chosen that path. Call it wanting to put some vicious people away, to be the voice of a deceased victim, to speak for the state. Yet, what does it mean to prosecute someone on behalf of the state? Who in one part of the state knows or cares about a mutilated body in another part of the state? That aside, I have never experienced a greater "high" or exalted feeling than prosecuting, and more so when a favorable verdict is read. Many successful trial lawyers talk about this same high. This is the reward. This is what the job is all about but that would soon change.

I had planned to retire in June after having prosecuted violent crimes for three decades. Seniority and experience gave me the privilege of picking and choosing cases to prosecute. In the last several years that amounted to one or two big headline cases a year. For five years, I had also taught criminal law and criminology at the local two year college. Teaching gave me a diversion from prosecuting and the students liked the discussion of real cases, but I was ready to be done with that, too.

I had a lot of interests in life, though over half of them were either in remission or needed resuscitation. The piano for instance, near my study had at least six months of dust on it. Sometimes, I felt I needed two lifetimes to do all that I wanted, but work interfered with my hobbies and interests.

I got a lot of satisfaction assisting young prosecutors with their cases. Usually their mistakes resulted from a lack of preparation and the inability to anticipate what could go wrong at a trial. Some of them are not cut out for it. Anxiety, stress and low pay frustrate many of them. The adversarial nature of the job creates stress, along with the belief of the public that all defendants are guilty; thus, there is an expectation to win that creates additional pressure. In reality, prosecutors lose cases. They lose cases where the defendant is guilty. Sometimes they win cases, fortunately rarely, where the defendant is innocent.

"Dad?" my youngest son, Mark called to me.

"What?"

"In today's paper, there's a case for you."

"I'm retiring, remember? No more cases."

"Oh, of course, Dad," he said doubtfully. Didn't he believe my retirement news? He placed the papers next to where I was sitting, the local tribune on top of the Chicago Tribune. I couldn't help but notice the headlines.

On the front page of the tribune was an article by Randy Denny, a veteran court room reporter whom I had known for a long time.

```
BODY FOUND
HORRIFIC CRIME
NO SUSPECTS

By Randy Denny

The body of what is presumed to be Eilert
Kurtz, owner of a megastore bearing his name
was found yesterday afternoon on his property,
located in the unincorporated area of Morton
County at Grove Street, southeast of 22nd
Avenue.

The search for Kurtz's body began after his
son, Eilert Kurtz, Jr., became alarmed when his
father did not answer repeated telephone calls.
A neighbor, Ray Schiller, along with Eilert
Kurtz's brother discovered the body on the
victim's property less than a mile from the
store owner's residence.
```

I paused for a few seconds after reading part of the article. I was familiar with the area and had met Eilert Kurtz at prosecutor fundraisers. Everyone had heard of Kurtz and every home had some item in it purchased from his store. According to the article, the store owner had been retired and spent most of his time on his property, seldom visiting the store which had made him one of the wealthiest people in the state. His property consisted of over a thousand acres of wooded land, wildlife and a few lakes stocked with pan fish larger than any frying pan sold at the Kurtz store. I continued to read. The store owner had been brutally murdered and the Morton County Sheriff's Bureau of Identification Department had been on the scene since yesterday. A spokesman for the department declined to say much other than that the murder was heinous, uniquely bizarre, and would be thoroughly investigated by Detective Joe Matanovich and laboratory specialist Lawrence Meister. The spokesman also declined to speculate on the cause of death, saying that the investigation was ongoing and concluded with the usual comment that not all details were being released, nor were there any suspects.

"What do you think, dad?" Mark asked, light, creamy brown eyes wide open. Though tall like me, Mark had Mary's light complexion, while Nick, Jr., and I had dark eyes, almost black and an olive-colored complexion. He and my oldest son, Nick, Jr., were visiting in the area for a couple of days to see me and their mother Mary, who lived in a comparable condo across town. After almost thirty years of marriage, Mary and I divorced a year ago. She was unhappy and with no fault divorce it didn't matter the reason, any state of mind is grounds for divorce.

"I don't have the slightest interest, Bud." I called both of my sons, Bud, except when they were together. In my company, Mark laughed less, and had fewer smiles, making me wonder whether he blamed me somewhat for the divorce.

I sat in my study looking at the other condos across the lake. About half of them had Christmas lights and other seasonal ornamentation. Late autumn had performed its annual ritual of stripping the large oaks and hickories of their leaves, making the other side of the lake visible.

At home, I spent most of my time in the study. Two French doors showed the way into a room with an oak roll-top desk,

Waterford lamp, guest chair, file cabinet, two book cases, credenza and paintings. A few photographs of friends and family decorated the wide ledge at the base of two French windows. The study usually gave me comfort and security. Right now it didn't give me much of anything. Christmas had passed a few days ago, and overnight lake effect snow dumped four inches with predictions of an advancing snowstorm promising more white debris. I found winter depressing, but was it just me? I rationalized and concluded that if it was so great why weren't there large retirement communities in northern Minnesota rather than Florida or Arizona? Three seasons were enough. Did I need a fourth? After all, I hadn't been raised or taught to be greedy.

I put the paper down and resumed my thoughtful staring out the window. Several purple finches were eating safflower seed out of my platform feeder. Glad I'm retiring, I thought. It's an election year and my boss Ron, the Morton County chief prosecutor, will want a conviction with a VIP victim, assuming the killer is apprehended. He usually didn't have to ask me to prosecute the big ones. Like many prosecutor or district attorney offices in high crime counties, the majority of our prosecution staff was young with little experience in trying big murder cases. We had a prosecution staff of twelve attorneys, but only a few with much experience. One of them was ill, two recently left for higher paying jobs, and one took retirement.

I had been mentoring Anne Borsch or Spider, as the staff liked to call her behind her back because of her wide hips, thin limbs and dark clothing. Though conscientious, Anne did not have what I liked to call being "comfortable and smooth" in court. She hesitated too much at critical times, such as when trying to get an item into evidence or when cross examining a key witness. She also tended to wait too long to make an objection. Juries pick up on these flaws, especially when they contrast the prosecutor's rough presentation with the smooth flowing approach of a skilled defense attorney.

Unbeknownst to the public, seldom does the chief prosecutor or elected prosecutor ever try cases. Their functions are primarily political, administrative and ceremonial. It's his deputy prosecutors that prosecute the cases. In some states deputy prosecutors are called assistant state's attorneys or assistant district attorneys.

Though prosecutors get the publicity for convictions, it is not without the work done by the detectives and expert witnesses. These law enforcement officers and witnesses expect a conviction because they have sometimes worked hundreds of hours on the case, and are not happy when a defendant is found not guilty, particularly when the prosecutor is inexperienced. Likewise, the victim's family, though they may not formally demand it, are concerned when they find out the prosecutor for their loved one's case looks young enough to be in high school or college.

I had taken a few days off and didn't get to my office until the end of the first week of the new year. The prosecutors' office shared the same building with the courts, clerks and probation office. Veteran prosecutors had their own office. Eighteen offices formed a rectangle with the prosecutors on the periphery of this rectangle and the clerical staff in the center, mostly in cubicles. I occupied the second office on the left and had the same office since I arrived, though I shared it with another prosecutor for the first several years. Two large vertical windows faced south across a sidewalk, parking lot and grassy area, not exactly a postcard view. Light oak colored blinds were angled so that outsiders could not see in. Though a public employee, I did not care to be visible to the public or even my own staff. I always had my door shut, embracing privacy to the exclusion of the distraction of people walking past or stopping to say something. My desk had no files on it, but there were notes and requests from prosecutors and other office personnel for information or guidance on various issues.

One document grabbed my attention and ire. Chief prosecutor Ron evidently had not told Cindy, my paralegal, about my retirement. As she had been doing for years, she prepared a summary of the Kurtz killing, assuming, as usually happened, that I would get any case involving a relatively important victim or a highly publicized case. I jerked the phone off its cradle.

"Marsha, tell Ron I need to see him."

"He's not in now, Nick, but I'll let him know you called," replied Ron's secretary.

Cindy had put some time into the paper, so I figured the least I could do was read it. I had read nine of the eleven pages when Joe Matanovich arrived in his usual fashion without knocking on the door. He casually walked in as if it was his office. He looked towards the window with his beady eyes, completely unmindful of me and then took a seat. We stared at each other for a few seconds. He needed the time to catch his breath. I hadn't quite finished the summary. From the newspapers and Cindy's report, I knew Joe had been named chief investigator for the Kurtz killing. Joe and I had worked many murder cases. No one would ever accuse him of exceptional brilliance, but he did what I asked and he was thorough, albeit slow, and methodical. Even his speech was labored. A pulmonologist might suspect a respiratory impairment. A protuberant stomach had slowed him down in the last several years and his waist had grown from a size thirty-four to a forty-four. Though unsuccessful in losing weight, Joe took pride in not having lost any of his taupe-colored hair, which he had regularly cut short, especially the sides, Marine Corps style.

"I've always meant to ask whether you ever knock on a door before entering, or is this from some habit of breaking down doors to beat confessions out of people?"

"Go to hell, Nick. What do you Greeks know about manners and such? You know why we have AIDS?" I said nothing and continued to read Cindy's summary. He was determined to let me know the answer. "It didn't originate in Africa, but in ancient Greece."

I looked up at him with raised eyebrows. "Really? Why hasn't some scientist figured that out?" Before he could answer, I said, "Enough of the pleasantries, Joe."

"Are you interested in the Kurtz case? Definitely a big case, Nick. Maybe too big for you with your advanced age and diminished mental capabilities," he said with a smile.

I told Joe I wasn't interested in anything. He replied that that must be why I got divorced. I told him I was divorced because of one too many murder trials. Not many women would tolerate their husbands waking up in the middle of the night for years writing questions to ask witnesses, making notes for closing arguments, staying out till the middle of the night waiting for juries to come in with their verdicts. Besides, we got married too young. I was young and dumb. Now, just dumb. His grin concurred with that remark.

Joe felt I needed to pursue Cindy, my paralegal. I told him that for a homicide cop coming to this office all these years he wasn't too observant. Cindy wore a marriage ring but that meant nothing to Joe.

"Maybe in Poland they have some other kind of symbol for marriage. In the US of A its called a wedding band which to most people means something."

"Nick, let me tell you something. I'm smarter than you in these relationship matters. I've had several wives. Cindy likes you."

"Let's move on, Joe. Is there a purpose to your visit, sir?" When I wanted to end the garbage talk with Joe, I called him, "sir."

"As you know Nick, I've investigated hundreds of murder cases, but this is the most brutal, bizarre of all of them. Nick, how many cases have we had where the victim was beaten to death, face unrecognizable and put on a cross, crucifixion style?"

This was Joe's style. He didn't tell you anything, he questioned you.

"Crucified?" I asked.

"Yes, not nailed to the cross, but bound to it."

"Made of wood?"

"Yes."

"What type of wood?"

"I don't know yet."

"Joe, I'm retiring my friend, and I've told the chief that a couple of weeks ago."

"Why do you have a summary of the case?"

"Cindy didn't know. Ron evidently didn't tell her."

"Nick, I've got to tell you something. The chief and I talked and he needs you for one more case."

"I don't care what you guys talked about. I'm retiring in six months. You don't even have a perp and may never collar anyone on this case."

"Let's say we get the perp in the next several weeks or so, we could still do the trial before you retire."

"No, Joe." He looked down at the brown, expandable folder in his hands, papers sticking out of it from various directions. No effort had been made to organize the file or fasten the papers. He looked out the window and back to me. He blinked his eyes a couple of times. I waited for him to get up and leave, but he had the resolute posture of someone focused on getting something.

"Can you at least give me your thoughts on who may have done this?"

"Joe, I would think you should have some idea about a profile for these killers," I replied.

"You're the one who attended profile training at Quantico," he paused, "killers as in two or more, Nick?"

Ignoring his question because it seemed so obvious to me, I asked him to tell me what he knew.

He began by describing the victim, the crime scene and possible weapons. They took the usual photographs of the entire area and aerial photographs with a helicopter. Unfortunately, not much physical evidence had been secured. Joe figured some kind of metallic object like a hammer, crowbar or pipe was used to bludgeon the victim to death. The victim had a son, Eilert, Jr., and a brother, Bill. The son had become alarmed when his father didn't answer the phone for their weekly chat. He called his Uncle Bill, who with the neighbor, Ray Schiller, entered the house and found it vacant. A search of the premises yielded nothing, and they proceeded to search the back property and found the body and his truck near a large crater. The victim had on thick, brown bib overalls and nothing of value in his possession. According to Eilert Jr., a new wallet that he had given his father was missing. The son told Joe that his father always had at least several hundred dollars on his person. Because of the severe lacerations to the face and the misshapen skull, the victim could not be positively identified by the family or Ray Schiller, the neighbor of twenty years. Dental records and other evidence later confirmed the identity of the victim.

"You mentioned earlier my walking into your office without knocking. Why didn't you say something years ago?"

"How long was he out there?" I asked, ignoring his question.

"About a week."

"How far was his body from his house?" Now, I enjoyed asking the questions.

"Less than a mile."

"Did Kurtz hunt?"

"I assume."

"Did others hunt the property?"

"I think so."

"Tell me about his family."

"He stuck mostly to himself, though he did see a few women. Of course, he had his store which made him famous. He never actually retired, he just stopped going to the store, occasionally taking calls and giving advice to his managers and supervisors." Joe stopped. He leaned forward and put his left hand over his left knee. Either he was out of breath or didn't have any more information. His slow talking irritated me.

"What else, Nick?"

"Entry into the house?" I asked.

"No sign of any forced entry. I think most people would be scared to enter that creepy, old house. He had an insurance policy for the son for 500 K."

"Son have any close friends in the area, any with records? Check son's phone records."

"We're looking into all that, boss."

"Boss? If I was your boss, you would have been fired a long time ago." I knew I had been tough on Joe at times, but right now I didn't care about his feelings.

"Damn, that cold and snow are bothering you," Joe said. "Just because you're bigger than me doesn't mean I can't take your glasses off and whip your butt." I said nothing, but went over to the window and looked at a pair of juncos looking for food at the base of the crabapple tree next to my window. My gaze was broken by the intercom directing me to see the boss.

"Got to go and see the main man, Joe. No doubt he'll beg me to take this case."

"Good morning, Ron."

"How was your time off, Nick?" Ron asked, trying to muster a look of genuine interest, but failing.

"I would rather have been someplace warm."

Ron unloosened his already loosened tie. He leaned forward with hands flat on the desk. Photographs of Ron with the governor, other politicians and VIPs decorated the wall behind him.

"Nick I need your help," Ron said, wasting no further time. "As you may know, while you were gone, a prominent citizen, Eilert Kurtz was killed. I know you want to retire, and so do I. Nick, this is my last election. Assuming we get the killer, I also need him retired. I envision a retirement home with maximum security for the rest of his natural life. Then, I promise no more trials."

I didn't know how Ron had continued to get re-elected. He didn't look like a politician and didn't act like one. He had a weak handshake, didn't dress well and couldn't remember names. Maybe appearing apolitical was what the voters liked about him— that and his cuddly looking face and rotund stature.

He turned around in his chair and pointed to a summer photograph of himself and another man.

"Do you know who this man is, Nick?"

"Of course."

Ron raised his eyebrows, surprised that I knew the man whose face appeared on more television ads than anyone. The face of a man seared into everyone's brain in this part of the state by a blitzkrieg of television ads over many years, even though he no longer took an active part in running the store.

"Yes. He contributed a lot to my two elections and to those of the two previous prosecutors."

"Sorry, Ron. We have other prosecutors, and I have helped you and this office for almost half of my life."

"I know, I know, Nick," he said with a look of minimal appreciation and continued, "Nick, our list of experienced prosecutors is short," he said, lowering his head then raising it. "You know we've had two leave after they got their experience.

Of course, Lou recently retired. John is good, but not as good as you, and in any event, he's not well. That leaves Spider." Not known for his close association with the prosecutors, I was surprised Ron knew our name for Anne, but he didn't have to say anything about her. If a poll were taken among prosecutors and defense attorneys, the result would be that she was an adequate prosecutor, but neither exceptional, nor ready for a case that would likely draw national attention.

I got up to leave but Ron beckoned me to tell him my thoughts on the case.

"The likely perps are two or more individuals with at least one of them knowing Kurtz and having previously been to his property," I said, clutching the doorknob in an effort to leave. "This was planned in advance, perhaps months ago. A business connection or retaliation for something in the past is a possibility. Joe will need to look at any employees with a grudge or any that were fired, say in the last year or so." I wondered whether to say more but thought against it.

"I've seen that look before on your face and can tell that you would like to say more, Nick."

"It's a disturbing case, Ron. I wonder whether the perps were sending a message to someone. And with the planning that was involved, I suspect it could be a long time before the case is solved."

"A message?"

"It's clear they intended the body to be found." He looked puzzled, and I figured this was my time to get out of his office.

"Just think about it," he said, not wanting to give up.

"I have, Ron. There's no more trials left in me. I've done over 300 jury trials, most of them murder cases. That figure doesn't count trials prepared, but plea bargained out. I'm looking to transition into a new life. Until retirement in six months, as always, the staff can feel free to call on me to help with any problems and to give assistance to the person who prosecutes this case."

Silent, and with a glum look on his face, Ron dismissed me with a brief wave of his right hand.

I returned to my office and called Cindy, who came in and took a seat. She had started working here a few years after my arrival. She was in her mid fifties but looked much younger. I don't remember her original complexion since she frequently tanned and had a sunset, golden appearance. For some reason she didn't look older, like many people who had tanned and been exposed to the sun for years. She had titian or reddish-gold hair with sun streaked layers that flipped playfully on her shoulders.

"Thanks for the work on the Kurtz case."

"All for nothing, I hear," she replied.

"Why do I have a feeling I'm going to be inextricably woven into this case? I'm sick of it and don't even know much about it. There aren't even any suspects."

"Did you expect to do nothing for six months while you waited for retirement? And, I thought I would have been the first you would have told about retiring before telling anyone else," she said, hands on her hips, and eyes fixed on mine.

"You're right, I'm sorry."

"Joe left these for you with his apologies. It's material on the Kurtz case."

"Apologies? He probably had a smile, didn't he?"

"Perhaps a slight smile. Nick, we've worked on hundreds of cases together, right?"

"Of course," I said, wondering where she was going with this.

"Have I ever told you not to prosecute any case?" I said nothing, but nodded in agreement.

"I don't want you to be involved in this case."

"I'm not going to." Didn't anyone understand that I wanted nothing to do with this case or any case. I simply wanted to retire.

"You don't understand, Nick." I was getting a little tired of this and ready to go home.

"Why don't you tell me what I don't understand," I demanded, "and while you're at it Mrs. Wilkins, tell me how this case is any different from any of our other murder cases."

"Oh, it's Mrs. Wilkins, is it, Mr. Papais?" she shouted, cocking her head slightly to the right, her light, summer blue eyes narrowing into a cold stare, and bolting towards the door as she threw her summary on the floor. Then she suddenly stopped and turned towards me.

"You didn't read my summary, particularly the addendum, did you?"

"I read most of it, then Joe came in and that was followed by a visit to Ron's office."

"Had you read all of it, you would understand my concern," she said. She opened the door to leave.

"Please, don't leave. What is it I need to know?" She turned to look at me, eyes barely opened, and wet.

"The killer is challenging you personally, Nick. He's evil."

CHAPTER 2

Seldom are veteran prosecutors and homicide detectives alarmed by threats from felons or suspects. It's expected. Homicide detectives especially, will often tell a threatening suspect to wait his turn in line before attempting harm. Fortunately most threats are just that, threats. Cindy's disclosure concerned me because I didn't know the suspect, nor how he knew Cindy was my paralegal. She told me he had called her directly on her phone extension and with his voice muffled or distorted, told her that he would never be caught, and even assuming an arrest, that I, referring to my name, would never be able to obtain a conviction.

It had been over six weeks since the murder of Eilert Kurtz. Joe didn't have any suspects or persons of interest, basically nothing. He seldom talked about the case and must have realized that the perps were smarter than he had originally thought, and any ideas of a quick arrest were wishful thinking. I told Ron, my boss, that I would retire the first week of July and with no developments in the Kurtz killing, he wasn't in any position to ask me to prosecute the case. My duties were to counsel and advise prosecutors who needed help. Unfortunately for Joe, the press continued to hound him about new developments. Quickly tiring of that and to the media's dismay, Joe set up his voice mail to automatically inform any callers that the case continued to be vigorously investigated and all leads pursued.

Despite no case, a couple of weeks ago Joe had evidently entered my condo while I was gone, and left a copy of the file on my desk in the study for me to review containing his work to date.

He no doubt chose this method to seek my help because he knew I would say no to his face. Upset at his intrusion, I let the file lay for over a week and refused to answer any calls from him at home or at work. I also locked my door at work and told the staff I would not entertain any visits from him.

On a late Saturday evening almost two weeks later, and believing Joe had done his penance, I grabbed the file. Though disheveled and in no particular order, it contained an autopsy report, crime scene photos with descriptions written on them, witness statements, and a description of the physical evidence. A separate report included items sent to a lab for blood analysis, prints and DNA. Forensic evidence has solved many cases, but I'm from the old school of prosecution that puts a lot of trust in witness testimony, their credibility and the opportunity to speak about what they know. In this case it didn't matter since little evidence of any kind existed.

Besides questioning the son, Eilert Kurtz, Jr., Joe searched his phone records, work history, friends, bank accounts, etc. Joe's short stature did not give him an intimidating appearance, but his unblinking, steady gaze made people uncomfortable. His questioning was slow, often times repetitive. People got restless during Joe's questioning, if for no other reason than it took too long. During questioning, Joe would often have his right hand in his pocket, tossing coins around and creating a distracting noise. Whether this was habit or some kind of purposeful tactic, I didn't care as long as he gave me a good statement and an assessment of the person's credibility. Joe would type the statement on a portable typewriter immediately after the questioning. This further irritated people because of his prolonged presence and slow typing. His thick, stubby fingers made it difficult to use a laptop or keyboard accessory, yet he had no difficulty playing the piano.

The interview with the neighbor, Ray Schiller, yielded nothing. Years ago he and Kurtz had had a property dispute, but that eventually reconciled to the satisfaction of both parties. Though not friendly to one another, neither were they hostile to each other.

The file included some photographs and a black and white aerial photograph two feet across and a foot and a half high mounted on gator board. Writings and comments on the photo referred to things found and assumptions made. Arrows pointed to streets and compass directions. Detective Townsend had taken the aerial photo and had written the notations. A scene at the bottom left of the photo depicted a large crater area, some bushes and the notation, "body of victim found here." The next nearest notation read, "blood, hair and facial tissue" near the body. He described the wooden cross with various fasteners holding the body. The cross and PVC pipe were sent to a lab for analysis. Joe's report indicated that another vehicle had been at the crime scene, but fallen snow on at least two occasions since the victim's disappearance had affected tire track impressions. Though the height from which the photo was taken made it difficult to observe objects on the ground, the photo would still be admitted into evidence at trial.

I routinely advised prosecutors to admit into evidence as much as possible even if the information seemed not too important or helpful for the jury, since admission of evidence lets the jury know that a lot of investigative work was done on a case. This has to be done otherwise the defense team will use as argument what the police, prosecutor and the vast resources of the state have failed to do. Defense lawyers like to argue that a lack of evidence leads to a case not proven beyond a reasonable doubt. Prosecutors in the last ten, twenty years have an additional burden—overcoming juror's expectations of criminal evidence and trials as the result of a plethora of television programs focusing on forensic evidence. After all, would the jurors want to risk convicting a defendant on sloppy police work or on the failure of the state to procure all available evidence?

The scant evidence left me with some impressions, assumptions and questions.

Number one: Mr. Kurtz weighed 200 pounds and was five feet eight inches. It's not likely one individual could attach the victim to a wooden cross and place both into a pre-drilled hole. Two or more killers had to be working in concert.

Number two: What was Kurtz's truck doing this far from his house? Had he been taken at gun point from his home or did he voluntarily go out to the killing field with the killers? Did anyone accompany him in his truck? So far, the detectives could not lift any prints or other evidence from the truck.

Number three: What was the motive? Jurors want a motive. Robbery? True, robbery is often a motive with rich victims, but why wasn't he just robbed? Did he have to be killed? Was it to not identify the killers? Why wasn't he killed in his house? Was he abducted, taken to the field and robbed there? According to the son, a wallet he had given his father was missing and his father typically had several hundred dollars on his person. I believed that money and a wallet may have been taken, but only as an afterthought or as incidental to the real criminal intent which was to kill this particular person for some unknown reason. Legally, a robbery had been committed if anything of value had been taken from the victim. In most states this crime is called a murder during the perpetration of a felony. This meant that there would be at least a two count indictment: one charging murder and the other charging murder during the perpetration of a felony, to-wit: robbery. That combination could increase the penalty at the sentencing stage should the defendants be found guilty. But, robbery was not the reason for this killing.

Number four: Nothing was missing from the house and nothing disturbed according to the son and Joe. That may be true, but I felt somehow the house had some connection to the killing.

Number five: The cross and PVC pipe had some bizarre or occult significance or message. It also indicated significant time and planning.

Number six: Kurtz knew one or more of his killers.

Number seven: How did the killers arrive at Kurtz's property? I assume it had to be a pickup truck because of the length of the two pieces of wood. I further assumed that the PVC pipe had to have been put into the ground when the weather was warm.

Number eight: How many killers? Probably two. Most smart criminals know that the more individuals involved, the more likely one of them will talk to someone and disclose the crime to police.

Number nine: What tool or instrument was used to kill the victim? Dr. Loh's autopsy report revealed traumatic blows to the head and face, perhaps made by a metallic tool or pipe. Examination of the head, neck and face revealed multiple skull fractures, subdural hematomas, and splintered blood vessels.

Number ten: Age and race. The perps were white, age unclear. Generally, African Americans preferred quick shootings rather than long, planned out beatings. I believed the perps to be in their twenties or thirties because of the patience, planning and intelligence. I figured one or both individuals to be very intelligent and knowledgeable on criminal evidence.

Number eleven: Defense. If those responsible were ever arrested, what would be their defense? The most popular defense is simply that the state did not prove the crime beyond a reasonable doubt. It didn't matter whether the defendant did it or not: did the state prove that he did it. Similarly, the defense doesn't deny a crime, but simply that the state did not prove that this defendant committed the crime. Coupled with that argument is the alibi. The defendant could not have committed the crime because he was somewhere else at the time of the killing. Insanity defense? Well, as every trial prosecutor and criminal defense lawyer knows, planning negates an insanity defense because it often shows a rational mind, a thinking mind, a mind capable of thought processes, and planning undoubtedly occurred in this case. Yet, the insanity defense is successful on occasion despite thorough planning.

Number twelve: The previous assumptions meant nothing without the capture of the suspects.

It was taking too long to solve this case. Time works against apprehension of suspects in murder cases. Forensics may be helpful in obtaining a conviction, but it wasn't going to solve this case.

I heard knocking at the door and I assumed it was Joe. For a law enforcement officer, neither trespass, breaking and entering, nor privacy meant anything to Joe. After several knocks I let him in.

"What time do you have, Joe? My watch indicates 9:30 p.m. and not a.m."

"Sorry," he said, not caring much, I'm sure. "Have a chance to read the stuff?"

Determined not to let him off the hook easily, I asked, "Sorry about what, Joe? The breaking in of my place earlier, or the intrusion at this late hour?"

Joe's eyes fluttered and his lips moved as if he were talking. He smelled of alcohol and smoke, but he didn't smoke, so he must have been in the company of others who did.

"You look worried, Joe. Take your hand out of your pocket and stop jingling the change."

"Have a chance to read the stuff?"

"Yes," I said with an edge to my voice. I wanted to go to bed and not discuss my non-case.

Glancing at the piano, Joe asked, "When's the last time you played or dusted this?"

"It's been awhile, Joe."

"I won't keep you. How about a sonata before I leave?"

"You didn't come here to play Beethoven, Joe. What do you want?"

"I need some help with this case."

"I don't solve crimes, Joe. I prosecute those who commit them remember, or rather, I used to. It's only a few months until I retire."

"Nick, I'm getting heat to solve this case."

"Sounds like a personal problem, Joe. Have you sought pastoral counseling?"

"Go to hell, Nick!" Joe said, without looking at me and rushing to the door.

"Stop, Joe," I said. "Let's go sit in the study."

"Joe, I'm not sure what else I can tell you. From reading your file, it looks like you have done most of what we have discussed. I think you're just going to have wait for a lucky break. There's only a couple of neighbors near Kurtz's property and no one recalls anything unusual about the time of his disappearance." I paused then asked, "How many employees at his store, Joe?"

"About 450."

"How many did you interview?"

"About 450." I laughed, and he laughed a long, deep laugh.

"According to your file, no firings or suspensions in the last year?"

"Well, none that could be traced to Kurtz."

"I don't know." Joe took out a pen and a little red, spiral notebook.

"I read where the son gave you a list of Kurtz's closest friends, right?"

"He had a few friends, but the store was his main companion, his life, until a few years ago when he stopped going. He was odd, intelligent, eccentric, and preferred to stay on his property to be what he called a farmer. He grew crops and even had some farm animals. One manager told me Kurtz preferred to be called a farmer rather than a store owner."

"How many people signed the register book for the wake and funeral?"

"Oh hell, Nick there were over 2000 people who visited or attended the wake and funeral over the three day period."

"I know it doesn't help much, Joe, but the killer or someone close to the killer's family signed that register book." Joe's nod acknowledged agreement.

"You mentioned once that Kurtz dated a few women?"

"Again, not many, according to the son and brother."

"Of course, that invites a follow up question of how close was he to his son and brother." Joe said nothing, but started to shake the change in his right pocket.

"As you no doubt read from the file, I didn't come up with much with regards to hunters or anyone denied hunting privileges on his property."

"I don't think a hunter would go through this much trouble, Joe; yet, hunters take time to build tree stands to deer hunt and so forth, but I believe a hunter would have shot him, and with a weapon he didn't typically use. Let me ask you Joe, any unsolved crimes reflecting this type of imaginative killing or brutality?"

"None that I am aware of."

"Did he ever have any picnics at his property for his store employees?"

"I don't know." Joe started to shift a lot in the chair, eyes looking everywhere except at me. I'm wondering if he's thinking that maybe there could be more work that he could have done.

"What about people who may have worked on the property?"

"Work?" Beads of sweat formed on Joe's forehead.

"Sure, a lot of people like to help people out who own property in exchange for the right to hunt, fish, camp or picnic. You know, they might mow, pick up fallen branches, do repair work on the lake piers, that type of thing." Joe wasn't writing anything down. He just looked at me. I knew his method. He knew what he had to do.

Joe also knew that if we lost a case, I would blame it on him and his colleagues rather than the three Js: jury, judge or justice. I always felt and believed that a case to a large extent was made or determined before the first witness was sworn under oath; in other words, in either the investigation or jury selection phases.

"Joe, I'm not sure how you would investigate this, but there have been some vicious killings by school kids throughout the country in the last several years. I'm not talking about school shootings. These have been some high publicity cases. In a couple of those killings there were two kids involved." Tired, my eyes struggled to remain open.

"Quit yawning, it's only 10:00 p.m. So two school kids killing people outside of school. That's not totally unusual."

"Right, forget it. It's too speculative."

"No. I'm not leaving until you tell me more." He started to pace and his right hand reached further into his pocket, the jingling of the coins annoying me and keeping me awake.

"Some of those crimes have been particularly heinous and without a profit motive."

"Go on."

"The kids are different from each other."

"What are you saying?" he demanded.

"They're different, damn it. Don't you read true crime stories? One's a leader and one's a follower, or one's good looking and the other isn't; one's smart, the other is not."

"One chases skirt, the other doesn't, right Greek?" Joe said, his mouth grinning.

"I guess," I said, not too pleased with the analogy.

"It's time for you to go Joe," I said, exhausted. I began to gather my papers and stuff them back into the file.

"The son, Nick?" Joe persisted, unable to leave the son alone.

"What little I know is that the son and his father were close, no evidence of any hostility. The $500,000 life insurance policy is for burial expenses. Kurtz had real money."

"The son was assertive, bold; he didn't look mournful," Joe said, eyes widening. He pointed out defensively that he never said there was any hostility between father and son. I told him Cindy had already found that out. He didn't say anything in response because he knew Cindy could do some "investigating," though she only had a high school diploma and no investigative training. She was better than a couple of our real investigators or "ghost employees," as the staff liked to call them. Supposedly, we had two real investigators. I had actually never seen one of them and the other would make a cameo appearance a few times a year. They didn't even have to pick up their checks. The office mailed them out.

"The problem with this case is going to be motive," I said.

"If I may, Mr. Prosecutor, haven't you repeatedly said that motive doesn't mean anything?"

"What I have said is that the prosecution doesn't have to prove a motive, but the jury wants a motive. Let me ask you Joe, why such a gruesome crime?"

"Why is it gruesome? I've seen many horrible killings."

More questioning. "You keep questioning me, Joe, and I'm going to wonder if you know anything. This killing is not only brutal and gruesome, it's punitive and vindictive; it's savage. Those facial photos reflect horror and brutality. I think us, or rather you, are dealing with hatred, vengeance, psychosis or drugs or all of these. This is a killer who is intelligent and can kill with or without a motive. And with that Joe, it's time for you to go."

This time he didn't resist and was almost through the door when I yelled out, "You mentioned a couple of close friends, Joe. Who are they?"

"Well, there's a businessman friend that he fishes with once or twice a year in Canada, and the other is the principal of Westin high school."

A week passed uneventfully with the weather continuing to be the main news item. Record low temperatures and lake effect snow from Lake Michigan continued to punish the region. I took delight in the later sunsets, and knowing that spring was only a few weeks away and retirement in several months.

It felt good to be in my office one morning with little to do. A few minutes later Cindy came in looking cheerful and took a seat.

"What are you smiling about?" I asked. "Did you get a new job?" She laughed. It had been almost two months since she had told me about the phone call from the killer.

"You know what my big mistake was?" From the puzzled look on her face, I knew she had no idea what I was asking. "My mistake was not leaving this office years ago after I made my millions." We both laughed and stared at each other. Unlike many women, she had class. Most of the time she looked provocative, but not by design. We talked a lot when we were together with no topic forbidden. We would get so excited talking that we often interrupted each other. Our conversations were spirited, though seldom meaningful.

Unfortunately, Cindy had left the door open and the assistant chief prosecutor popped his head in and said, "Nick."

I, in like fashion, responded, "Jim." We never talked. The extent of our conversation was stating the other person's first name with no hello, good morning or how are you doing attached to the name. I think he was upset with me because he found out I didn't vote in the last election. He had told Ron, our boss, about it. Ron called me in his office after Jim's disclosure and proceeded to lecture me about how we needed to not just vote, but vote democratic. They could never understand my lack of interest in politics. I felt my main job was to convict violent criminals—to be in the trenches fighting it out against defense lawyers and sometimes inexperienced judges. Though Ron and Jim were both lawyers, they didn't try any cases. In some offices there's a division or tension between those that try cases and those who don't. One might say there is also a lack of respect or even open dislike between prosecutors who try cases in front of judges who have had little, if any, criminal trial experience. Most prosecutors hated trying cases in front of inexperienced judges. If the Judge was in doubt how to handle a problem or rule on a motion, he would almost invariably rule against the prosecution. After all, the prosecution seldom appeals its case, so it's easier for the judge to err against the state or prosecution than the defense, who will appeal an adverse ruling that may contribute to a finding of guilt.

My mind had drifted, but glancing at Cindy attired in a short black skirt and pink blouse got me refocused.

I got up to close the door to tell Cindy how much I would miss her after retiring, but I never got the chance. Almost immediately, Joe walked in without knocking, as usual, hand jingling change in his pocket and flashing his best grin at us.

"We got them."

Cindy got ready to leave, but I asked her to stay because she knew how to listen and investigate, besides I was only peripherally involved in the case and needed a distraction.

Joe began to question me, "Nick, who is likely to have done this?"

"I'm not interested in your questioning of me. I already gave you my thoughts on the case, so either tell me or get the hell out of here and I'll read about it in the paper."

"Papers know nothing," Joe said, with an even wider grin.

"I'm flattered that you thought of telling us first," I said, with no hint of emotion in my voice.

"Their names are Matthew Cantrell and Butch Roeder, both aged 18 from Westin."

Joe's smile had not diminished as he continued, "The break came from an anonymous caller," he paused, then said, "Roeder gave a confession implicating himself and Cantrell."

According to Joe, the anonymous caller was a woman who would only give the names of those involved in the murder and where they lived. Joe pressed for additional information but she would not give it. When he told her that she could perhaps be entitled to a reward—which was not true—she hung up the phone. Joe admitted that the confession taken from Roeder was not the best in that it was short and lacked details. Roeder told him that there was only one motive and that was money. Joe felt that the suspect was holding back on key information, but he could not get him to divulge more. Joe's initial jubilation and smile started to wane—I suspect because he realized he still had minimal physical evidence and nothing on Cantrell, other than Roeder's sparse confession implicating his friend.

"Good job, Joe," I said, wondering if I sounded like I meant it.

He shook his head, looked down, then up at me. "Not me, and…"

"And what?" I interrupted.

"The kids are different."

"All kids are different, Joe," Cindy shouted the words out, her tan cheeks now looking as pink as her blouse. "What the hell are you guys talking about?"

A knock at the door interrupted our conversation.

"Come in," I said. It was the tribune reporter, Randy Denny. He wore his usual Cubs baseball cap pushed firmly down over shoulder length, hemp-colored hair. Plate glass thick lenses magnified blue eyes that matched the color of the cap.

"Have a seat, Randy," I said.

Randy touched the bill of his cap as a greeting to everyone. Joe nodded and Cindy smiled.

"Sit down, Randy," I said.

"Don't have much time, Nick," Randy replied.

"Sit down before I call Ron." Ron didn't like reporters talking to the prosecutors. He felt that they often did not quote us accurately, and if they wanted information they should attend the trial. Most of us talked to the reporters anyway. Randy gave me good publicity and I trusted him. If I told him not to write something or not to divulge who gave him the information, he would honor that. He knew that if he ever betrayed me in the papers, I would never feed him information again.

"Since Joe is here, I'm guessing you all know about the arrests?" Randy asked.

"Do you know anything else?" I asked.

"I think I have something."

"Speak!" I said, the command stunning him.

"I found out that Attorney Howard Rose will be representing Matt Cantrell and Anne Borsch will prosecute. Don't know who's representing the other kid." Attorney Howard Rose was a skilled trial lawyer who represented clients all over the country. He was particularly effective in the insanity defense. Joe got up and went to the window to stare out. He had his hands on his hips. When he turned around I could see the rigidity in his face and prominent blood vessels on his forehead and temples. With the smile gone, this was not the time to mess with Joe. He stomped out of my office.

"I better go," Randy said.

I nodded goodbye.

"Why would Ron appoint Anne?" Cindy asked.

"Maybe she asked to prosecute the case," I said.

"Like you used to do when you were a young prosecutor?"

"Spider has some experience but this case is out of her league, especially with the Rose legal empire defending. I can understand Joe being upset."

A week later in the evening, while I was in my study talking to my oldest son Nick Jr., on the phone, a knock at the door halted the conversation.

"Hold on son, I'll get rid of this person." Whoever it was had bad timing. Hopefully, it wasn't Randy or anyone from the prosecutors' office.

A man in a suit with an unbuttoned camel overcoat and beige cashmere scarf was standing outside the door. He stood erect and carried an extra large leather portfolio in his left hand and what looked like a Blackberry in his right hand.

"Mr. Papais?"

"One and the same and I'm not interested in any products, services or religious talk." His attire though made it clear he wasn't here to discuss the afterlife or the origin of man.

"I have nothing to sell, Mr. Papais, and I do not believe in religion. It's you I want. My name is Eilert Kurtz, Jr. Now, you're probably wishing I had a sales pitch or was a man of faith," he said.

"Indeed, those were my thoughts. Come in, Mr. Kurtz." We shook hands and I motioned him to the couch near the window overlooking the lake. "I'll be with you after I hang up a phone."

By the time I had returned, Mr. Kurtz had removed his coat and placed the portfolio to his left side. "I'm sorry for your loss, Mr. Kurtz. How did you know where I live? I keep my address and phone number pretty secure for obvious reasons."

"I have ample resources," he said straight-faced.

"As I recall, you're an architect?"

"A long time ago. I own a company that employs many architects." Damn Joe, he never told me that.

"I'm not going to waste your time, Mr. Papais. I know quite a bit about you and your office." His small, sunken eyes never left my face. His eyelids must have been wired open because he never blinked. He continued. "For almost thirty years, you have been the best prosecutor not only in this county, but perhaps the state. Anne Borsch, or Spider as she is referred to by some, is a few light years away from trying a case like this, especially with the best defense team in the Midwest. I know of your retirement plans, but there is still plenty of time to prosecute this case and retire within your time horizon," he paused, "you look perplexed."

"Mr. Kurtz, some evidence suggests mental illness in the Cantrell family, which coupled with the hiring of a firm that specializes in the insanity defense leads me to believe that the defendant may be mentally ill. I'm not condoning nor excusing the brutality of the murder, but rather offering an explanation for the murder. I'm aware that explanations are of little comfort to victims' families. Having prosecuted many murder cases, as you seem to know, I don't want to go off on a tangent, but..."

"If I may interrupt, Mr. Papais, neither you nor I are mental health professionals. You are a prosecutor. Your career has been spent putting violent people in prison or on death row. Let us leave explanations of insanity to those in the behavioral science field. Let us leave any changes in the insanity law to the legislature. I know about your public interest in mental health, abuse and neglect cases. Prosecute the case and let the jury decide his mental state. Your job is to see that justice is done. Maybe justice in this case is a not guilty or not guilty by reason of insanity. My family, what little is left of it, does not need any explanation for the murder..."

"And now if I may interrupt, the chief has already assigned this case to another prosecutor."

His lips curled into a smile. "She'd back down if you agreed to take the case."

"I don't think so, Mr. Kurtz. She evidently asked for the case."
"In the past, Mr. Papais, she has agreed to step down and assist
you in the trial." I didn't want to ask him how he knew that.
Somehow, I was beginning to think that the man was well
informed and accustomed to getting what he wanted.

"Why should I do it, Mr. Kurtz?" I asked.

"Why? Because you're the best, and you don't want a shrewd
defense lawyer dominating a judge, an inexperienced prosecutor
and intimidating a jury. If the defense is insanity, you have done
well with insanity cases. I've had a couple of experienced trial
lawyers look at this case. Quite frankly, they say it's not a strong
prosecution case and the defense doesn't need to use the insanity
defense. The one boy, Cantrell, is exceptionally brilliant, an IQ of
180 and can speak several languages. To date, there are no
fingerprints, no DNA, no weapons, no motive, nothing, except
perhaps robbery. I'm told Roeder's confession is weak and has the
appearance of being coerced by what's his name, Joe, Detective
Joe Matanovich. If it can be won, you're the one to win it. If I
may, Mr. Papais, being a prosecutor is not just what you do and
what you have done, it's who you are."

"I will need to look at the complete file," stunned and
dumbfounded, I didn't know what else to say. His eyes never left
mine and they never blinked. What did Joe say about the son?
That he was assertive, bold, and not mournful.

He pulled back the sleeve of his shirt and suit coat to look at
what I knew to be a Rolex.

"The file should be here by special courier in about ten minutes,
Mr. Prosecutor. My family thanks you. Have a good evening."

CHAPTER 3

Snow had begun to fall the night before and continued to fall with no sign of ceasing. It cloaked everything in white. The weight of the snow bent the branches of large oaks and hickories. With no wind to push it, the snow fell straight down, accumulating in an even depth that could be measured with a ruler. Had I been younger I might have appreciated its beauty. Instead, I had left my condo and was seated at a chair by a window adjacent to the biography section of Barnes & Noble. I had been coming here every Sunday morning for the past six months. I needed a weekly break from sitting in the study of my condo and excessive nostalgic thoughts.

"Excuse me. It's Mr. Papais, correct?"

"One and the same. And you are?" I asked, looking up.

"Angela."

She didn't give a last name. Angela had authoritative facial features, porcelain skin and wore minimal makeup. Her scarlet hair, wet with melting snow, sparkled in the overhead lighting. She wore black jeans and a black sweater. Her narrow, copper toned, green eyes appeared more Asian than Caucasian. In her hands were two books on forensic science and one on criminal profiling.

"How do you know me, Angela?"

"I don't. I had a question about a book on criminal profiling and one of the cashiers directed me to you. She said you teach criminal law and criminology."

"In your hand is a good book on profiling. Chapter eight is intriguing. Have you tried Google or other search engines?"

"Sure, but the opinion of someone who has taught and worked in this area means a lot." She spoke with a gentleness that contrasted her authoritative appearance. I motioned with my left hand for her to take a seat. I learned Angela had a degree in psychology but worked as a private investigator and paralegal. She had thought about a career in psychology but felt she could make more money in criminal investigating and criminal defense trial work. Besides, psychology wasn't as interesting as she had once believed.

She had been in the area for two years after having left South Dakota following the death of her husband in a hunting accident. He had been pheasant hunting when his partner tripped, discharging his shotgun and mortally wounding him. We talked, or rather she talked, and I listened. She had the appearance of someone relaxed, someone in no hurry to leave. We ordered coffee and continued to talk. Angela liked big game hunting. She and her late husband had hunted in the United States, Canada and Africa. I told her I had just started hunting small game a few years ago. Angela had grown up in a small town in Idaho near where Hemingway had lived and learned to hunt from her father. Not surprisingly, she enjoyed everything about Hemingway. She talked about his travels and could quote extensively from his novels. I told her I had done a lot of traveling, but enjoyed places with coastal settings rather than inland.

"Did you always want to teach?" she asked.

"I teach part time. I'm a lawyer, specifically a prosecutor."

"Really? How long have you been a prosecutor?"

I paused a little before replying, took a sip of my coffee and said, "A long time."

"Too long, right?"

"Probably."

"Did you always want to be a lawyer?"

"No. Many professions interested me. I wanted to be an astronaut until I got my first pair of glasses at age thirteen." We both laughed at that. "Then I became interested in architecture and meteorology."

"Why meteorology?"

"The violent forces of nature fascinated me. You know, dark skies, interesting cloud formations, tornadoes, the like."

"Instead of nature's violence, you deal with man's violence?"

"Very good, yes, I suppose you're right," I said, wondering why the analogy had never occurred to me.

"Did any other occupations interest you?"

"My favorite occupation has always been marine biology," I said without hesitation.

"Of course, that invites a follow up question. Why aren't you a marine biologist?"

"My parents didn't have the money to send me to colleges on the east and west coats such as the University of Miami. Lack of money confined me to Midwestern state schools, landlocked schools with no oceans to facilitate hands-on study, no significant marine biology programs."

"Finally, why law, Mr. Papais?" she asked, looking interested.

"Nick, please. I didn't excel in math or science, but I could read, and the Perry Mason television series fascinated me."

"But," raising her right index finger, "didn't the prosecutor always lose?"

"He did, but we've changed that. The prosecutor now wins, well, more often than not."

"What did your parents think of your career choice?" she smiled wryly.

"My dad thought law was dry and boring. He discouraged it."

"Was he right?"

"Some of law is boring, but not criminal law." Enjoying our talk and feeling comfortable, I wanted to ask her over to my place.

"You have any plans for the rest of the year?" I joked. She beamed. We both laughed. I told her I was prone to occasional frivolous and stupid remarks, a luxury I felt getting older bestowed upon me, a feeling of being less concerned about what others thought of me or their reactions to what I had to say.

"I can't imagine you're like this in your trials?" she asked, amused.

"Why don't you come and see? Although I should mention that you will have only one more opportunity since my next trial will be the last. I'm retiring."

"Retiring? Why?"

"I don't need to practice law anymore to be happy. Many trial lawyers have done one too many trials. One day it occurs to them that most of their lives are gone and no interests having been cultivated during their working years. I don't want that."

"When does your last trial begin?"

"In about three months. It's a brutal, murder case involving two teenagers, one of them may plead insanity."

"Three months—a long time."

"It's been my experience that I can always use another week. It's strange, but I often feel not ready for a trial. There's always some witness whose testimony needs work, some lab that needs to be prodded to do an analysis." We looked at each other for maybe thirty seconds. I felt a little awkward since I wasn't used to talking to a fairly attractive single woman. Cindy's attractive, but married and untouchable. It had been awhile since Mary and I divorced.

Angela broke the silence. "I think I know the case," she said with an expression I had trouble interpreting. "Some newspapers are indicating that one of the boys may have severe mental illness?" It was a question, not a statement.

"What papers?"

"Is it true, Mr. Papais, Nick, I mean?" She didn't answer my question.

"I'm not a psychiatrist, but I have spent years studying mental illness. I have had to for two reasons, one is my job. Mental illness is not necessarily equal to legal insanity."

"Yes, I know, but there must be some criteria, some standard, some line that is crossed when it just isn't right to prosecute someone severely mentally ill, especially a child."

I'd heard her argument many times from others throughout the years. Thinking of her as one of my students, I replied, "The statutes and laws are fairly clear on competency to stand trial and the meaning of insanity. We try to do the best we can, but we do not have the luxury of working with a precise science. It's the grand jury that decides to indict a person and a jury that decides guilt or innocence. I just present the evidence to the jury in a light that is, what shall we say, most unfavorable to the defendant," I explained.

"But, grand juries indict whoever the prosecutor wants indicted," she pressed. Though correct, I chose not to respond.

"How do you feel about his history of mental illness?"

"Who says he has mental illness?"

"As I mentioned it's in the papers, local and national."

"Oh, of course, the press. Why do we need a legal system?" This conversation was reminding me of the one I had with Eilert Kurtz, Jr., at my home a few weeks ago. For some reason I wanted to challenge her, to fight her. Instead, I stared into my empty cup of coffee.

"Are my questions irritating you, Mr. Papais? Do we need sarcasm? What if I was one of your students asking these same questions?"

"If I may Angela, do you have this same interest in all cases of mental illness and alleged insanity, or is it this particular case that ignites some special interest," I countered, "also, I should mention that I don't mind talking law or trials in general, but I'm not going to get into specifics on any particular case. It would not be proper. And, quite frankly at this point, I still do not know that much about the mental makeup of the one defendant at the time of the crime, or any other time."

She looked outside then back at me. No longer finding her attractive, I started to gather my coat and gloves.

"It's time for me to go. If I may, you're not as informed as you may think. Please put the book back because I don't think you'll find it helpful."

"I'm sorry. I had no business talking like that. You mentioned a second reason why you have studied mental illness?"

I quickly got up to leave without answering her and without looking at her face, which I'm sure must have shown shock or malice, or both. Walking towards the door I could still hear her yelling out.

"You look like a sensitive, conscientious type…" Her voice started to fade away, but I think I heard her say something like, "or does a conscience dissipate after many years of prosecuting."

Joe called me a few days later to tell me that arrangements had been made to search the Cantrell home for additional evidence that may have been overlooked during the first search.

We arrived early in the morning and were let into the house by Matthew Cantrell's brother, Lennie, who looked at us with curiosity. I had never seen Matthew, only pictures of him, but he and Lennie had no physical characteristics in common. Could one have been adopted, I wondered.

The house had an odor but I couldn't identify the source, whether food, animal, human or environmental. This place needed to have its windows opened and a strong gale rip through it. I decided to breathe through my mouth in the hope that my nose would suffer less insult.

Joe went right to the basement. I proceeded to Matt and Lenny's room with Lenny shadowing me. The ceiling fixture didn't work, so I turned on a lamp, the only one in the room, but it had low wattage. I pulled the curtains open, but that didn't help either. With my flashlight, I began a thorough scouring of the room and found what I expected: nothing. But, there was more than just nothing. The walls had no pictures, posters, model airplanes, anything to indicate that two young men lived here. Isolation cells in prisons had more personality.   The master bedroom was just that—for the master, Clinton Cantrell, principal of Westin High School, assistant pastor of the county's largest Lutheran church. Above the headboard was the biggest crucifix I had ever seen. Three photographs on a chest revealed pictures of Mr. Cantrell and Eilert Kurtz in outdoor settings near a lake, probably Kurtz's property. But, it was the last two photos that fixed my gaze and caused the hair on my body to perk up. I looked at Lenny, but not for an explanation, since I could see his face and neck start to quiver, Adam's apple moving up and down. He shifted his weight and turned his head away from me. He started to wring his hands. Lenny could not talk. The one photograph showed a young Clinton Cantrell in a tuxedo, and a woman in a wedding dress, but the face and head were crudely ripped out from the photograph. The other photograph appeared to be a few years old and depicted a picture of Clinton Cantrell with two male figures in pants, and a woman in a blouse and slacks. As in the other photograph, the heads of all except Mr. Cantrell had been torn out of the picture. I wondered whether these photographs had been displayed during the first search.

I didn't expect to find anything in Bonnie Cantrell's room. The previous search had found nothing worth tagging as evidence. The walls were painted a smoky gray like the other two rooms. She had two sets of casement windows, one with the curtain drawn. It looked out onto a back yard which had a blue spruce, a sassafras tree, and a swing set which should have been discarded years ago. Finches and Grackles flew quickly over the yard finding nothing to attract them to the Cantrell property.

Mrs. Cantrell had an armoire with clothing in it that had been tossed around and laid in a heap. On the bottom shelf were several small boxes containing photographs, most of them taken in the past. A recent photograph showed her with an attractive woman, a little older than herself and appearing vaguely familiar. In another box were some newspapers and magazine articles with pictures, more than vaguely familiar—they were articles and pictures about me. Why hadn't Joe told me about this, or did they even look in her armoire. True, the articles were not evidence, and the police rightfully left them, assuming they even saw them, but I didn't sense that Mrs. Cantrell was a member of the Nick Papais fan club. My head started to ache as I attempted to figure the relevance of these articles in her armoire. I turned around and Lennie was gone. She had a small mahogany jewelry box lined in felt but no jewelry in it. I put it back and started to leave the room, but something about the felt in the lid of the box brought me back. I pulled the felt loose and found a black and white photograph of whom I believed to be Matthew Cantrell tied to what looked like a support pole, like those commonly found in basements to support an overhead beam. I bolted for the basement to look at the support poles, knowing they would reveal nothing, and that is what I felt I knew about this case. After prosecuting over 300 murder cases in thirty years, I knew this trial would not follow a typical sequence or script. It would be as bizarre as the killing, as unusual as this house, as unusual as its occupants.

Joe emerged from a crawl space. I expected it to be a little colder down here, but I was wrong; it was freezing. The basement had not felt heat this winter. Joe's jeans were covered in dirt and his shoes so foul looking and smelling that they would need to be scrubbed with an industrial solvent and hosed down. At the edge of the crawl space there were bankers' boxes full of books.

Trying to catch his breath, Joe said, "Nick, I think you might be interested in a few of these books I found tucked away in a dark corner of the crawl space."

Perhaps at a later date I might find some delight in Joe's discovery, but currently the house and its residents are what consumed my thoughts. I don't know if love had ever found occupancy in this house; but, if it did, it was of short duration and left with no reminders and no forwarding address.

CHAPTER 4

Rarely was I glad to see or talk to anyone about the case and upcoming trial, but today I welcomed Randy's visit. Perhaps, it took my mind away from thinking about the Cantrell home. I could never tire of Randy's appearance, his country boy, John Denver type of look, with Cubs hat proudly seated on his head, bending the tops of his ears outward, a little more than usual this time.

"What do you want, Randy?"

"Your case is getting a lot of attention."

"I don't care."

"National attention, Nick."

"Randy, I don't care if the wire services on Mars are writing about it."

"I'm going to miss your jokes and humor, Nick."

"Let me ask you something, Randy. Have I become cold, heartless about prosecuting?"

He thought before answering. Every word had to be correct with Randy. "No," he said.

"I was going to ask you to limit your response to a couple of minutes. As a journalist, is that the best you can do?"

"I'm sure you know the legal community thinks you're fair and conscientious."

I shook my head and said, "That's original and thoughtful, Randy."

"Give me time to come up with something more unique."

"Your time is up. Get out and find some news," I said half jokingly. He ignored my command.

"Nick, why did you ask about the cold, heartless stuff?"

"I met this woman in the bookstore and she said something about losing my sense of fairness or conscience due to many years of prosecuting."

Touching the bill of his cap as if that would help him formulate an answer he asked, "Was she attractive, Nick?"

"What does that have to do with anything, Randy," shaking my head, "you're getting to be as useless as Joe."

Chuckling, he turned to walk towards the door, stopped and said, "I almost forgot. What do you think about the plea agreement?" My look and silence must have indicated ignorance. "Oh, Nick, you evidently don't know." He paused as if to wonder if he should be disclosing this information. "Jim, the assistant chief, gave a plea agreement to his friend the Pink Penguin for his client Butch Roeder to testify against Matt Cantrell." The Pink Penguin, or Tim Rogers, was a well known defense lawyer who dressed in solid, colorful suits and had the body of the marine bird. He was representing Butch Roeder.

"That bastard. Nice chatting with you, but I've got to get to the office." I quickly grabbed my jacket and sped for the office, leaving Randy trailing me.

After arriving and saying nothing to anyone, I bolted to Ron's office. I knocked on his door and entered without waiting for a response. That seemed to be the protocol around here. Ron and Jim were having a lively chat. Jim gave me his usual greeting of just saying my first name and I returned the same, but this time I added a little more.

"You low life bastard, how dare you give a plea agreement to Roeder for a reduced sentence without my consent."

With his eyes and mouth wide opened, Jim yelled to Ron, "Are you going to let him talk like that to me? We don't need that insubordination from anyone in this office."

Ron's left eye started to twitch and he began loosening his tie. He told Jim to go to his office right away. Jim left, slamming the door behind him.

"Ron, did either of you think about asking me for my opinion on whether we needed to offer a deal to one of these murderers?" Without giving him the opportunity to answer, I fired off another question to him. "I assume this plea was made without the knowledge of the Kurtz family?" He didn't have to nod or say anything because I knew the answer. I wanted to scream and knot his tie so as to choke him. Ron started to shift in his chair.

"What the hell were you and Jim thinking? Kurtz's son will no doubt be pissed." I had the file with me and placed it on the lower right corner of Ron's desk. I could have placed the file anywhere since the desk had nothing on it other than desk accessories. The placement was symbolic. When Ron assigned us a case, he always placed it at the lower right corner of our desks. "Find someone else, Ron."

Moments later I heard knocking at my office door. Cindy walked in.

"Nick, I'm concerned about you. Didn't you hear my knocking?"

"Sorry, what do you need?"

"Nothing. Ian is in trouble upstairs picking a jury. He asked for a recess and the judge reluctantly granted him ten minutes."

I bolted out of my chair and ran up the stairs that led to the courtrooms. Unfortunately, I forgot to ask which courtroom. Looking down the stairs towards the prosecutors' office I could see Cindy holding up two fingers. I nodded in appreciation and knew I was going to miss her. Ian was in the attorney conference room of courtroom number two.

"Quickly," I demanded. I felt for Ian. He was one of our new prosecutors and was unlikely to make it as a trial lawyer because he lacked aggression, quickness and the ability to adequately prepare. Extreme quickness is not absolutely necessary, but being slow and low-talking lulls a jury into lapses of concentration or worse, sleeping. I preferred the jury to be lethargic when the defense talked and not the prosecution. Ian informed me that it was a rape case, black on black, meaning black defendant and black victim. Ten jurors had already been selected. He briefly described the ten.

"Doesn't sound too bad. That's not why you called me up here?" I asked.

"I only have one more challenge."

"What does the rest of the panel look like?"

"Several middle-aged whites, one old and one young Hispanic, one old black and I think two young blacks."

Charging into the room, the bailiff said, "Let's go."

I pulled Ian aside in the hallway and asked him to repeat my two usual trial preparation questions.

He slowly replied, "Are you prepared for the case?"

I nodded and asked, "And number two?"

"Are you prepared enough not to lose?" He removed the glasses he was wearing, wiped the lenses and resettled them on his sweating, taut face.

"Did you study the law and procedure on challenges for cause?" I asked. Without waiting for a response I asked a second question, "Did you prepare sample questions for typical challenges for cause?" I looked to him for an answer.

"Not exactly."

"That's why you have a possible problem here. We don't have time to educate you on this subject. Just try to remember to show that the juror you want out cannot be fair and impartial, that he will not follow instructions. Continue to question him until you get

him to admit what you want. Who do you think should be
excluded from sitting on this jury?"

It took a while before he answered. I couldn't imagine Ian and
Joe together on a timed response quiz show. "Young men."

"More specifically, Ian."

"Young blacks and Hispanics. What if I can't get rid of them?"

"It's pretty simple. You will lose or get a hung jury. For a
prosecutor a hung jury is a defeat," I stated flatly.

He pursed his lips, shook his head and said, "Thanks, Mr.
Papais."

Cindy was waiting for me back in my office, her reddish gold
hair needing some attention.

"Something wrong with my hair, Nick?" Cindy asked, running
her fingers through it.

"What?"

"You glanced at my hair and made a disapproving look."

"No, it looks fine," I lied. "Nice new blouse," I quickly said.
"Is it new?"

With a look that indicated dissatisfaction with my responses,
she said, "No, I just don't wear it much for some reason."

"Cindy, I gave the case back to Ron."

"I know, Nick. In fact, everyone in the entire government
complex knows. Your name is on a list beginning with the letter
'S,' and it doesn't mean special, either."

Ignoring her comment, I quickly said, "It's unfortunate when
you have prosecutors who don't actively prosecute and don't
understand the implications of giving a plea agreement to a
codefendant. Attorney Rose will make Cantrell look sympathetic.
He will convince the jury of the unfairness of giving an equally
culpable defendant lesser punishment. Juries don't like unfairness,
or two equally guilty individuals being treated differently.
Where's the justice, Rose will ask? Is it fair that a sick kid gets the

maximum penalty while the other gets a break for who knows what reason?"

"What did Ron say when you gave the file back, Nick?"

"What?"

"You're not here are you, Nick? Don't tune me out because I count on my husband to do that. I'm assuming you didn't give Ron a chance to say anything did you? Nick, I'm not a prosecutor, but I believe Roeder would be helpful. And, he is less guilty so to speak than Cantrell." Looking away, then back at me she said, "Look, this case begs for more evidence and an exceptionally skilled prosecutor."

My head started to ache and my mind started to wander. "Sorry Cindy, a lot on my mind." I looked away, then said to her, "I thought you didn't want me involved in this case because you believe Cantrell to be dangerous, evil."

"Oh, I still believe that, but I don't feel comfortable knowing that he could be out on the street if he's not convicted. Nick, this kid may only be eighteen, but he's sharp, cunning. He's one of the most brilliant defendants you and I have ever encountered. Too, Nick, I'm a little concerned for my own safety. After all, I'm the one he called on the phone. He knows who I am. I have no doubt he knows where I live and where you live. So, what I'm saying is, I feel like the victim's son, Eilert Kurtz, Jr., in that if there's anyone who can convict him, it's you." She got up to leave.

"Please stay, Cindy. I...I'm going to miss you and our conversations," I said, my voice trailing.

"You know I will too. I've shared things with you that I haven't even told my girlfriends or my husband. I expect you to call me and to..."

"And to what?" I asked, but she quickly turned to leave.

The following evening as I was looking across the lake from my deck at the sky, I could see geese flying in formation, a sight that never tired me. I hadn't gone to work but Cindy called to tell me

about an unannounced visit Mr. Kurtz made to Ron. She said
Randy had written a fair summary of it in the day's paper. I
grabbed the paper. It read in part:

> **FEUD IN PROSECUTOR'S OFFICE OVER
> STORE OWNER KILLING**
>
> The county prosecutors' office is without
> a prosecutor in the brutal killing of
> wealthy, retired store owner, Eilert
> Kurtz. Originally Anne Borsch was
> assigned the case when veteran prosecutor
> Nick Papais chose not to take it due to
> his imminent retirement. Papais took the
> case only after an emotional plea from
> the victim's family.
>
> In another reversal, Papais gave the case
> back to his boss, Ron Benjamin, when he
> learned that assistant chief prosecutor
> Jim Gant negotiated a plea agreement with
> one of the defendants without Papais's
> knowledge or consent. Eilert Kurtz, Jr.,
> the son of the victim, is also reported
> to be outraged at the secret deal.
>
> Papais could not be reached for comment.
> Chicago Attorney Howard Rose would not
> comment on the dilemma of the
> prosecutors' office other than to say it
> didn't matter who prosecuted the case
> since his client was innocent.

Ron's going to have chest pains after this article from Randy.
No doubt he'll banish him from the office for awhile, I thought.
And, Randy never solicited a comment from me. He'll pay for
that. Though relieved to be rid of the Cantrell file, I knew Anne or

whoever prosecuted the case would seek my opinion on numerous issues from now until the end of the trial.

Three days later at dinner, my oldest son, Nick, Jr., and I were eating lamb, stuffed grape leaves and feta cheese when the doorbell rang. It took me a few seconds to realize who was at the door.

"Sorry for the intrusion. You were right, chapter eight was good," she smiled charmingly.

Not wanting to talk to her and with my hand still on the door knob I asked, "How did you find me? It seems lately people have no problem finding my residence."

"Remember, I've done some private investigating work. It looks like you're busy. I just wanted to give you my card and thank you for the book recommendation. Maybe we can go out sometime," she said as she pushed the card into my hand.

"Unlikely," I said, still perturbed with her from our encounter at the bookstore. Studying her as she walked away, I knew resisting her would be difficult. Her gliding, confident walk exuded intrigue and excitement. Angela's outfit did the rest. She wore tight camouflage pants and boots with a black constricting sweater. She must have purposely left her coat in the car—better to reveal the clothing on her fit body. It was a hunter or trapper's outfit, but the game was not animal—it was man. Yet, it was something else, something not physical, but rather a perception, an uncomfortable feeling that she knew me or about me.

"Maybe," I yelled out. She turned around and her face seemed to say, if you're not interested fine, but rest assured some other man will be. Then there was Cindy—the Cindy who was still married. Do I even have the time for this or the desire I asked myself. I've already messed up one woman's life. I tore the card up—then I put the pieces into my pocket.

CHAPTER 5

On Labor Day eighteen years ago, Bonnie Cantrell had delivered her second son, Matthew Loyola Cantrell. Her labor nearly broke the hospital's record of thirty-three hours. It was as if Matthew had fought to avoid coming into the world, but once in the world he had done well, at least academically, until recently. The primary school years were uneventful, but his grades were outstanding and he graduated second in his class. His English teacher believed he could have graduated first, but he had developed a crush on a basketball cheerleader, his rival grade competitor. He failed to turn in a project and received a B in the course. The cheerleader got an A and in the process bumped Matthew out of the valedictorian spot. At the graduation ceremony some in attendance believed he gave up the A, and hence the top spot, because of his crush on the cheerleader.

Matt hadn't played any sports in grade school or during the summers. Like the rest of the family, he helped Eilert Kurtz maintain his property by mowing, trimming trees, tending to the lakes, placing rock or gravel on small interior access roads, painting, chopping wood and other projects. Too, Eilert Kurtz always wanted the place to look like it was occupied, since he vacationed a couple of months out of the year and didn't want trespassers to think his home, and the two little cabins on the property were not occupied. Though the Cantrell family enjoyed the benefits of picnics, fishing, hunting and all that the property had to offer, the relationship with Kurtz was not solely symbiotic. Kurtz was a businessman and understood money, but one needn't have a degree in business or finance to know that teachers didn't make much money. Clinton Cantrell had not yet become a high school principal until a few years ago. So, in addition to enjoying what the property had to offer, Kurtz would periodically give each of the Cantrell's varying amounts of money, more specifically cash in envelopes, envelopes from his store, of course.

In high school, Matt enjoyed reading, languages, speech and drama and played the lead role in two plays. On a standardized national test, he scored in the top one percent of the country in math and science, but had no interest in either subject. In study hall, he studied but not school subjects, preferring instead books and materials of his own choosing.

Matt crashed in his senior year. It was as if that year's summer vacation had precipitated something alien. Matt's homeroom teacher hadn't thought it was possible for a student to undergo such a change. She likened it to an alien force snatching his brain and personality, something reminiscent she said from the movie, *The Invasion of the Body Snatchers.* Matt withdrew totally. He stared a lot, missed school, no longer studied and didn't turn in assignments. His appearance became that of a drifter and he began to lose weight. He moved like a zombie, prompting students to joke about his trance-like state. In Matt's favor was his brilliance and the fact that his father was the principal. The school set up a meeting to be attended by a social worker, school district psychologist, special services department and Matthew's mother. Psychological testing had been ordered but Matt never attended, saying there was nothing wrong with him. At his mother's urging he agreed to see their family doctor. The doctor had been uncertain of a diagnosis, but called it an affective mood disorder or depression, since the rest of the family other than Clinton had similar diagnoses.

I rubbed my eyes and looked away from the file, distracted by the rain pummeling my study window, but the warm weather was a pleasant welcome. Following another visit and plea from Eilert Kurtz, Jr., who appeared less stoic than his initial unannounced visit months ago, the case or file was once again mine, where I let it sit in my desk drawer for almost a month. Too thick for the standard folder and fastener, Cindy had placed it in two separate brown expandable document containers.

A lack of motivation made it difficult for me to make any progress on the case. Since I couldn't very well admit that to anyone, I relied on my standard response that I didn't want to burn out or peak too early. I have often felt that preparing for trial is analogous to getting ready for some kind of competition or athletic event, and though a trial is a mental event, it's still similar to physical competition or events, both demanding peak performance and leaving one exhausted or spent at its conclusion.

I sat in my study where I did most of my work because the office was too distracting and governmentally plain. My only use for the office in this case would be to interview witnesses. Ron knew better than to complain about my chronic absenteeism because he had gotten what he wanted: I took the case back.

Another distraction, albeit a more pleasant one, was Angela. About a week after she dropped off her card, I had called her and we had dinner in Chicago. We had seen each other a few times since. I appreciated her interest in the case, though she believed that Matt Cantrell should not be prosecuted because of the severity of his mental illness. She knew as much about the case as Joe and Cindy—perhaps too much. Though we had become intimate, we seldom stayed overnight at each other's place, preferring our own beds for sleep. We shared an interest in reading and physical activity to stay fit. She missed hunting big game out west but joined a gun collectors club where she could skeet shoot and use their firing ranges. We had seen a couple of movies and attended a few programs at the Chicago Symphony. One of our greatest pleasures was eating at ethnic restaurants. Being a big game hunter, I imagined her food preference to be meat or land animals, so it had come as a surprise to me when she enjoyed seafood and shellfish. For exercise, we hiked and swam.

I broke out of my reverie and went back to reading the file. A psychiatrist hired by defense attorney Rose disclosed that Matt suffered from schizophrenia. His lengthy report concluded that Matt was mentally ill at the time of the crime and was a danger to himself and others. The defense also hired a psychologist who likewise concluded that Matt suffered from a psychotic condition.

Notes in the file indicated that Matt kept to himself and had one friend, Butch Roeder, the high school's premier bad boy. If there had been a poll taken among the students as to who would most likely end up on death row, Roeder could have claimed easy victory. School officials believed Roeder to be a bad influence on Matt and had suspected both boys of using drugs. The Roeders lived a couple of miles from the Cantrell's, though Clinton Cantrell often wished the distance had been greater. Mr. Roeder never worked much. In fact, he had never earned three consecutive paychecks, relying instead on his wife's income as a nurse's aide. He was abusive, an alcoholic, and had an iron clad claim to being the area's most renowned ne'er-do-well. Not much was known about Mrs. Roeder other than she was often tired because of her physically demanding work and appeared older than her stated age.

A few relatives and friends liked to believe that Bonnie, Matt's mother, had never fully recovered from the exhaustion and stress of Matt's delivery. Gradually she had begun to be plagued by insomnia and a lack of interest in activities she previously enjoyed. Her demeanor, never effusive, evolved into one of irritability and occasional mood changes. Mr. Cantrell assumed her illness was stress related because of their limited finances. When her condition worsened, their family doctor suspected a thyroid condition. He prescribed some medicine that didn't help. Bonnie continued to experience symptoms of ill health, including occasional shortness of breath, crying episodes and chest pain. Relatives and friends believed she had an uncharacteristic closeness to Matt. The doctor never thought to refer her to a mental health professional, choosing instead to do nothing or to prescribe an anti-depressant that lessened some symptoms and did nothing for others.

Though Matt received plenty of attention from his mother, the oldest son, Leonard, received little. The same could be said for her husband, but that was understandable since frequent school functions, church activities and faculty meetings required him to be away from home.

Bonnie gradually grew worse and the family doctor recognizing that her condition was beyond his expertise, referred her to a psychiatrist, who after his examination of her promptly called an ambulance to have her committed to the local hospital's inpatient psychiatric facility. Her treating doctor recorded a diagnosis of depression, chronic and severe. By Matt's seventeenth birthday, she had been hospitalized twice for severe depression and was being seen regularly by a treating psychiatrist. During her second hospital stay she had been given electroconvulsive therapy, ECT or "shock therapy," as it is commonly known. Leonard also suffered from mental illness. He too had been hospitalized for a suicide attempt after high school and placed on various drugs until his condition stabilized. Nothing in the file indicated any psychological abnormality with the father, but neither had he ever been examined by a mental health professional.

The doorbell rang. Randy stood there with a cup of iced coffee and his trademark Cubs hat pressed tightly on his head, clothes soaked, and smelling of warm rain.

"Couldn't be reached for comment?" I queried, partially opening the door and wondering whether to let him in.

"Sorry about that, Nick. It slipped in the final copy."

"Yeah right," I doubtfully said. "What do you want?"

"Hope I'm not interrupting anything."

"You've interrupted me for thirty years," I said half jokingly and half truthfully.

"You only interrupt the ones you love."

"A new line for journalists."

"It's original."

I directed him to the dining room table and said, "I didn't think you guys had anything original." He said nothing and set his coffee down.

"Nick, how do you feel about this case? The trial is near and I know your style is usually one of early preparation."

"Usually, is correct. I'm concerned."

"Your face and eyes show concern, but you've been telling me that about every major case you ever tried. Randy put his hand to his chin, shook his head slightly and asked, "Nick do you recall your first trial?"

Without hesitating, I said, "Yes, an auto theft and kidnapping."

"Do you remember your greatest fear?"

"Well, the case was before a difficult Judge."

"No, that's not it. You were concerned that you might freeze, that no words would come out of your mouth. 'What if I can't talk,' you asked?"

I chuckled and nodded. He gave me an introspective look, shook his head again and said, "I was in the front row of the courtroom with a couple of veteran prosecutors who were observing your trial. You uttered your first word… and haven't stopped talking since."

"Many would agree with you," I reluctantly conceded.

"Why the concern? How is this any different from any other brutal insanity murder case?"

"I can't be quoted on this."

"You have my word." I knew I could count on that despite his recent screw-up.

"I'm concerned about Cantrell's mental state. There's mental illness in the family and I suspect he has at least moderate to severe mental illness. He had a strict, cold upbringing. I was in his house Randy, and I can tell you it scared me. It was cold, literally and figuratively."

"Nick, the public should know about this."

"It'll come out at trial. Randy, if you look back at my insanity cases, and I know you will after leaving here, you'll find I never lost for several reasons. The most important of which is that none of the accused had any documented history of severe mental illness or even family members with extensive mental illness. I might qualify that by saying that at least the defense never presented a convincing history of mental illness with the defendant or in the family," I explained.

Randy didn't need me to explain that most defendants pleading insanity did not have a longitudinal history of mental illness. In the mental health profession, longitudinal meant long term, as opposed to short term, brief or episodic. Instead, their defense is concocted to show insanity at the time of the crime or that they could not appreciate the consequences of their acts at the time of the crime. Randy held onto his iced coffee, but didn't drink any of it. Ice still floated in it.

"Nick, I can tell there's something else on your mind about this case."

"Well, Randy, I want you to figure it out. Tell me what you would do if you were the defense lawyer in this case. You've reported on hundreds of cases. What's the problem here besides the mental aspect?" He hesitated and shook his head.

"Sorry, Nick, I don't know. Are you going to tell me?" He leaned forward with his face begging me tell him.

"Not yet. It won't take you long to figure it out."

The door bell rang and it was Angela. Randy said he should be going and I didn't discourage his departure. He left after acknowledging Angela.

"Come in."

"I was in the area and thought I would drop over."

"Sure, Randy too. Looks like everyone is in the area," I said tiredly.

"Would you prefer that I leave?" she asked, eyes narrowed, face tense.

"Sorry. I've been busy going over the file and then Randy was here for awhile. Besides, dressed as you are, you're safer in my place than in public." She wore a thin, white tee shirt tucked into short, tight fitting, camouflage cargo shorts.

"With only shorts on you're more than half naked. Isn't there something about not trusting a naked lawyer?" she asked teasingly.

I smiled back and jokingly said, "That refers to civil lawyers. You can trust naked criminal lawyers."

"Have you been able to do any work on the case?" she asked, her face expressionless, the previous hint of humor gone.

"What do you mean?"

"Well, working here at home in your study."

"The study's a lot better than the distractions at the office."

"But, what about taxpayer or public money and you working at home?"

"I don't know where you're going with this," I quickly said, "but I've been giving taxpayers excellent results for thirty years." I took a seat on the couch and stared out at the rain not caring if she stayed or left.

"I don't know why I said that, Nick. I'm sorry." I said nothing. She cuddled up next to me on the couch, a smile on her face and quiet, inquisitive eyes replacing the focused glare of a minute ago. She pressed her face against my chest.

"I can hear your heart beating," she whispered. Her fragrance made my mouth water.

"What is that perfume?"

"Most men would know by now."

"You know, I'm not most men, nor do I want to be. I try hard to be different. If I knew the perfume, I might buy you some."

"The only thing you buy me is lingerie that appeals to your prurient interest. As regards to being different, Nick, my guess is you achieved that status shortly after birth. I think 'strikingly odd' would be a more apt description." Her smile was so wide I could see all of her teeth.

I removed my glasses, closed my eyes and touched my head with the right earpiece a few times as if contemplating the future and said, "I have a vision, a vision of good things happening."

"For you or me?"

"Let me close my eyes again and think. Well, there's me…wait, yes, you too!"

"What about you and Cindy?" she asked slyly.

"We've had a special friendship. I have never been able to talk to anyone so candidly, so uninhibited, not even with my wife."

"Have you two ever…?"

"No."

"Have you ever wanted…?"

I paused.

"Obviously, you have," she stated flatly and drew away from me.

"Where are we going here? What does it matter? Have I scrutinized your life? I know nothing about you—your past in South Dakota and elsewhere," I protested.

"Nick, no one has a past in South Dakota. A future perhaps, but no past. I don't like her."

"So I've heard."

"I'm not sure what you find interesting in her other than her looks. She's married and has no education or interests," she said, malice conspicuous in her tone and words.

"Angela, enough. Enough!" I shouted angrily.

"What do you envision for the outcome of this case?"

"What?" I heard and understood the question, but I was so taken aback by how quickly and matter-of-factly she asked the question—as if the Cindy inquisition had never happened.

"I don't know."

"You look so serious, Nick. I'm worried about you," she pressed.

"I don't know how to explain it. Something is missing in the case—more than one thing, actually."

"What could be missing?" she asked. "You have a codefendant and well, some physical evidence."

"Reality is this. Roeder's confession is not good. It's short, sterile and appears contrived. The confession sheds no light on Cantrell's state of mind and believe me, prosecutors have lost cases with confessions and co-defendants testifying against their conspirators."

She looked at me over the top of her glasses which were perched midway down her nose. I didn't know Angela's age and she never disclosed it. Perhaps I'm dating an octogenarian, I thought.

What did it matter? Why am I concerned now? What's wrong with me? Was it her attack on Cindy? I got up, started to walk back and forth and began sweating.

"Could you stop pacing, Nick? You're sweating, honey. What's wrong?"

"I don't know. I pace because I think better that way."

"I suppose you've thought about who you want on the jury?" she asked, no doubt to get my mind off whatever was bothering me.

"Oh, probably about ten times a day. Question is who must be kept off."

"And?"

"Well, think in terms of categories like age, sex, race, occupation, domicile and so on."

"What about religion, politics?" she asked.

"Those questions or issues won't be on any juror questionnaire form, but that kind of thing may come out indirectly, though. Any thoughts, psychology major?"

She paused. "No drug counselors, mental health professionals."

"Go on."

"No social workers."

"Right, no one in behavioral sciences. Good job, Ang. We probably don't want any young jurors, especially males, perhaps not even most mothers of teenage boys. What about twelve wealthy storeowners? Or maybe six, or one, or how about one poor storeowner?

"I like it when you joke around. Something else trouble you about the case?"

"Oh, about three hundred things." We both laughed and then I said, "It's odd that there are no family photographs in the Cantrell house. Every family photograph that has a picture of Bonnie Cantrell or the boys has been crudely torn out."

"What do you mean?" she asked with disbelief.

"Just what I said. There are only pictures of Clinton Cantrell, his family or friends, but not one photograph of the principal with Mrs. Cantrell or the boys."

"Why would that bastard do that?" she asked, quickly getting up. I don't know if she expected an answer, but I didn't have one. Ethically, I was getting concerned about discussing much of the case with her, but she seemed to know a lot about it anyway.

"These photos," she paused, collecting her words, "you personally saw them?"

"Yes."

"Anything unusual about the arrest?"

"From what Joe told me, both Matt and his father appeared comfortable and at ease, like two friends."

"And what did Bonnie do during the arrest?"

"Bonnie? You say her name as if you know her."

"As you've said, Nick, I'm pretty familiar with the case. We've discussed it many times, the people seem real to me," she explained.

"Bonnie was crying at the time of the arrest. Excuse me, but I need to tell Joe something." I called him on his cell phone.

"What do you want?" Joe answered rudely.

"I want a daily diary of what Matt does in his cell. Next, I want to know who his visitors are. Next."

"Hey, I'm not on duty. I'm trying to have some fun here," he protested. He asked if Angela was with me.

"Yes," I replied.

He whispered softly, "Angela carries heat. Be cautious."

Looking away from her but smiling, I asked, "How do you know?"

"I know."

"Thanks for the heads up. Now I have some advice for you. Limit yourself." Joe didn't like to be told how much to drink. He hung up and then I realized I forgot to ask him one more thing to do. I saw curiosity in Angela's expression.

"Did Joe say something about me?" she asked.

"He told me tell you 'hi'," I said simply.

"I don't believe you. Joe's like Cindy. The only greeting he would extend to me is 'go to hell.' What did he say, Nick?"

"Ang, it's not important. You know, man talk." Her face was skeptical. I needed to refocus her on the trial. So what if she carried a gun. After all, she did do private investigative work.

"Why do you want that stuff about Matt?" She was back on the trail again. I breathed a sigh of relief.

"I'm troubled by a few things that don't make sense. Also, I'm disturbed about the motive," I said.

"Robbery isn't good enough?"

"Unfortunately, robbery wasn't the motive." Her face looked puzzled and confused.

"Please explain."

"I will when I learn more," I said thoughtfully.

"Why don't you get some of these answers from your main witness, Butch?" She was asking some good questions.

"I want to get some independent proof before I find out if he corroborates some things. That way, I know if he's telling me the truth." She nodded.

"Why didn't they kill Matt's father?"

"Good question and I don't know the answer. He may have been a future target, but I think that killing one's best friend inflicts more long term harm and suffering"

"Elaborate, honey."

"If I kill you right now, your worries, your pain, whatever, is over with. But, if I kill your best friend, the pain and sorrow of that loss are going to stay with you for a long time. I also want to know what they did immediately after the killing."

"Wasn't that answered in Roeder's confession?"

"Unfortunately, not. I also want to know questions like whether they told anyone about the killing. Also, did they buy drugs? And, who was the anonymous caller?"

"I assume Mr. Cantrell will testify for the defense." It was a statement and not a question; nevertheless, I answered it as if it were a question.

"Undoubtedly. If I was attorney Rose, I would call him as my last witness. Mr. Cantrell has a degree in theology, supposedly is a strong believer in God, frequently quotes scriptures, and often serves as a lay minister in his church. Who has more credibility than a man of God?"

CHAPTER 6

With the trial only a few weeks away, it was time to move at an accelerated pace. I had to meet my star witness, Butch Roeder. The Morton County jail was in the attached building to the left of the courts building, where my office was located. The two story limestone building sat in the southern part of the county at least three miles from any residential area. Though some might think the structure still attractive after thirty-five years, it lacked the beauty of old courthouses one sees in many Midwestern counties. Minimal landscaping adorned the south or front end of the structure. An open area between the jail and court building held a granite memorial dedicated to policemen and firemen killed in the line of duty. A mix of daffodils, tulips, forsythia and Magnolia trees encased the site.

I preferred interviewing witnesses in a non-custodial setting like the comfort of my office, but that is not possible with incarcerated inmates. With them I had no choice but to see them in the jail in a small conference room painted blue, the same color as the inmates clothing. In thirty years I have seen very little of the entire jail since my purpose was always limited to interviewing an inmate witness or offering an accomplice a deal to testify for the state. Thus, the blue room was always my destination.

My arrival was expected; and, of course, after thirty years I was well known to the jail staff and guards. I had seen many of them retire or pass away. Few ever left for other jobs since the county jail was located in a high crime county and it offered secure employment. As I was being escorted to Roeder, I got to thinking about leaving the prosecutor's office. How does one know when it's time to retire? In my profession it might be when you are no longer bothered to go to the jail and talk to a killer. After all, he's just a witness—assuming he testifies—like any other witness in a murder trial. It's routine. Yet, I pondered how talking to such a person could become routine? Had I become cold, insensitive as Angela had said when we first met at the bookstore months ago? Was that normal? Had I perhaps crossed some kind of mental line or barrier? Did emotion leave me some time ago? Was it a gradual process? Would I be able to summon the necessary strength and emotion for one more trial? Had Matthew Cantrell, Roeder or even Bonnie Cantrell crossed some kind of mental line or barrier? It might seem odd to some, but I had never asked other prosecutors how they felt about visiting a murderer. Their reaction might be something like it's part of the job of prosecuting violent crimes, and if you can't do it, either do misdemeanor traffic cases or civil practice. I never wanted to display too much emotion in court, just enough to infuriate the jury, enough to send them into the jury room remembering the horror of the crime, enough to make them want to punish, enough to think that this victim could have been their husband, father, family member or close friend. If I could get the jurors to imagine that, or worse—that they themselves could have been the victim—my job was more than half done. That was my goal. I needed to gear up for such a battle but could I? And, it is a battle which leaves the combatants tired, exhausted and yet, somehow relieved afterword.

I entered the interview room. I doubt if Alzheimer's could ever erase my memory of Roeder. His appearance became indelibly stamped on my brain as if minted on a coin. He had a shaved, bald head somewhat like myself, though mine was cut short, rather than shaved. I had a few inch height advantage. We were both dressed in blue, mine a suit and his a standard dark blue jail clothing, but he had discarded the blue shirt and wore only a tee shirt for his upper body, no doubt to enhance his physical features and present an intimidating appearance. I didn't need special vision glasses to appreciate his defined upper body. The tee shirt could barely contain him. The file referred to his weight lifting and muscular body, but I wasn't expecting to see the Incredible Hulk. I couldn't help but make a discreet backward glance at the guard. He nodded slightly, as if appreciating my apprehension and acknowledging that he was there for me. Roeder could have killed Kurtz or most men for that matter with his hands. Kurtz had no chance. I hadn't seen Cantrell except from photographs, but he couldn't look like this, I thought.

I took a seat opposite him and let my mind wander and think about his role in the killing of Kurtz, but something brought my attention back to Roeder. I could feel his defiant glare.

"Butch, I'm Nick Papais and I've been assigned to prosecute Matt Cantrell."

"Good for you. When am I getting out of here?" His unpleasant directness surprised and irritated me.

"What's the rush? This confinement counts towards your ultimate sentence," I said in an equally unpleasant manner.

"I don't like it here and I don't like Matt nearby." He crossed his meaty arms over his chest.

"You see him often?"

"Around...we don't talk."

"Butch, I'm not staying long. I just wanted to introduce myself, meet you and tell you something."

"Speak man."

"Butch, your deal calls for you to cooperate and testify against your friend Matt Cantrell. Can you do that?"

"I think so. I thought the deal was already done."

"Oh, and you don't have to do anything else? Butch, do you think we are that stupid?" Uncertain of the answer myself in view of the unnecessary plea agreement given to Butch, I suppressed a chuckle.

"Butch, let me tell it to you this way and I want you to look into my eyes." That was probably unnecessary since his eyes never left mine. "Have you heard of me Butch?"

He said nothing but nodded.

"What have you heard big guy?"

"My lawyer says you seldom lose."

"Remember this, Butch. If you go cold on me at trial, refuse to talk, jack-me-around or lie, I will ask for a recess, stop the trial, and I will rip up your plea agreement. The trial will be rescheduled. You will be found guilty of murder and get life in the fucking joint. Any part of that you do not understand or wish me to repeat?" He remained very still, head and eyes not moving. Now that I knew that I had shocked him, it was time to leave. I preferred not to swear but it was my experience that vulgarity, especially when first meeting most violent inmates seemed to work best for getting their attention and for a lasting impression. Also, I find it helps to speak their language and to appear strong. If you appear weak, they will try to control you, to manipulate you and most significantly, not disclose everything you need to know. There are many important things about a trial, but one is you never want to be surprised by any witness's testimony, especially your own witness. I thanked the guard and left the jail.

In my office at my desk Joe sat comfortably looking out the window.

"Get out of my chair," I said. He mumbled something, grabbed his papers and took a seat opposite my desk.

"What do you think of Roeder?" he asked.

"It will be difficult getting information out of him. This case doesn't make sense, Joe. There's gaps and question marks.

"Gaps?"

"Chasms, Joe."

"You've never lost a murder insanity case, and there will not be any gaps when the trial starts. The case is going to get stronger," Joe said with a confidant smile.

Stronger, I wondered? Does a case become stronger. It's either a good case, weak case or in between, but it doesn't change strength.

"How are you and Ang getting along?"

"Fine."

"She and Cindy don't like each other."

"And you, Joe?"

"Does it matter?"

"Yes, it matters."

"I wonder if she has your best interest in mind?" There he goes with questions. Why do I bother to solicit his opinions?

"If I had time I'd dig up her past," he continued, looking at me closely.

"Joe, you need to be working on this case rather than worrying about whether Angela had a traffic violation a few years ago in South Dakota." I then quickly asked, "Do you have the information I requested about Matt's interests, his activities, and the books he reads in addition to what you found in the crawl space?"

"Working on it." He barely looked at me and that meant he had done nothing on the requests, but I knew he would get to it. I also reminded him to have guards unobtrusively monitor Matt's behavior and actions in and out of his cell.

"Joe, back to gaps and chasms. I want physical evidence. Where is the vehicle that they arrived in at Kurtz's place? Where's DNA? Where are their clothes? I want the hammer, pipe, whatever they used to kill Kurtz. I want prints, blood analysis, etc. I want motives, as in plural. I'm not going to have them beat us. They don't even need an insanity defense. Right now, all Rose has to do is sit back in his chair in the court room, play with his Phi

Beta Kappa key and watch us look embarrassed trying to convince a jury that his client was even involved in the case."

"Nick, of course, we have Roeder."

"What have I taught you over the years regarding so called star witnesses?"

"That you need physical evidence and cannot rely solely on an accomplice to make your case."

"How did you know she carried a gun?" I asked abruptly.

"She was granted a permit to carry one and I saw the gun in her purse one time," he replied cautiously.

Looking at him with doubtful eyes, I asked, "Does the fourth amendment right to privacy mean anything to you?"

"I felt threatened," he quickly said without looking at me. Before I could respond to his inadequate legal defense, I recognized Anne's light tap at the door.

"Come in, Anne."

"Isn't your daughter getting married soon, Joe?" I asked.

"In a few weeks and we expect your attendance along with a large check."

I laughed. "Sure, I'll see if it's possible to borrow against a few future pension checks. Take a seat, Anne."

"I'd like to, but I don't have time."

"Everyone in my office sits except me, the pacer," I said sternly.

Anne was of small stature, a little wide at the hips with long, dull brown hair and matching eyes, which she covered with equally plain glasses. Spider never wore make-up and dressed in pant suits with black shoes and no heels. It's unlikely anyone ever accused Anne of sartorial splendor.

"I only have a few minutes before I have to go back to court. I've got a problem, too."

I handed Anne a partially duplicate file of the Cantrell case and said, "I had Cindy make this file for you. After your trial you'll only be working with me, Joe and Cindy on the Cantrell case. Any problem with that?"

"No. I've always wanted to learn from you."

"I may have you do a lot, Anne."

"I want to learn from the best." Anne had always been willing to learn, unfortunately lack of ability and toughness intervened.

"Nick, as I said, I have a problem with my case."

"I heard you the first time. Did you prepare?"

"Yes."

"Do you want to win?"

"Yes."

"So, what's the problem?"

"My witness has gone cold, she's scared and refuses to talk."

"When you prepared for the case did you see this as a possibility?"

"Yes."

"So, you're not totally surprised by this development?"

"No." I threw up my hands and made a facial expression as if to ask, what's the problem then?

"Are you this way with all prosecutors?" She looked at me, not sure whether to be angry or cry.

Joe volunteered, "Believe me sweetheart he is."

Anne quickly shouted, "With all due respect Joe, I don't want to be called sweetheart, honey, young lady or other similar words. Anne or Mrs. Borsche will be fine."

This was a side of Anne that I had not seen before. Why couldn't she respond decisively and quickly in court, I wondered? I made a slight facial gesture and head nod to Joe to refrain from making any further similar comment.

Joe turned his head slightly away which was good, because I knew if he looked at her he would say something like, "Bitch, be thankful I don't call you something worse."

Anne said, "I know the case law about impeaching your own witness and the foundation that must be laid."

"You want to know practically how to do it?"

"Yes."

"When does the trial resume?"

"Five minutes."

"Why does everyone come to me with five minutes until court time?" I said to no one in particular.

"Sorry."

"Penguin's the lawyer?"

"Yes."

"Who is the Judge?"

"Wilkins."

"Ouch, not a good combination. The jury probably knows that she's scared, but you must bring that fact out anyway. Even if she refuses to answer that she's scared, still ask her. Try to personalize her by using her first name and acting maternal. Go up to the witness stand and stay there throughout. Take her statement with you, and if she refuses to testify, ask the court to declare her a hostile witness so you can ask leading questions and get her statement read to the jury. Of course, ask if she recalls giving the statement. Are you scared, Anne?"

"I think I'm more scared than she is." Her eyes were huge and wet. I didn't have any other answer for her. Any prosecutor who has prosecuted violent crimes for years will encounter witnesses who are scared and do not want to testify.

"As you question her, look back and forth between her and the jury."

Placing her right hand on her stomach and slightly bending over, she said, "Nick, I don't know if I'm cut out for this," she protested, looking nauseous.

"We'll talk about your abdominal issues at a later date. Right now get up to court and do what I said." I went into the cheerleader mode. "I want you to stick that indictment in the Penguin's, well, you know what. You're a good prosecutor. We need you. The trial will be over soon and it will be a memory. In a close case like yours, it's my belief that the deciding factor for the jury is the credibility of the attorneys. Don't be offended, but I figure the jury will believe a nondescript, diminutive individual over a flashy, pushy, snake oil salesman masquerading as an attorney. Try not to get too bothered in closing argument when he mentions his usual stuff about, 'before I was a lawyer I was a policeman and I value justice.'"

"Aren't those…"

"Yes, they're not evidence, but as you know there's always a certain amount of what I call 'detritus' that goes into a closing argument. Just smile and jam him in your final closing."

"Detritus?"

"You ever have an aquarium?"

"No," she answered, looking puzzled.

"Detritus is garbage, waste and debris that settles at the bottom of the tank."

She nodded, tried to smile and no doubt wondered about whether I deserved the reputation I had.

"And, look and talk decisively. Don't show you're scared, particularly with an ignorant judge and intimidating attorney. Stand up to them. You may be vertically challenged," I smiled, trying to put her at ease, "but you're big enough to try a case like this; after all, I recommended you for the case." She looked at me as if to say, please no more favors and abruptly left. I knew she was too scared to do any more talking or to say thanks.

Joe hunched forward, shook his head and said, "I can't imagine you're sitting at the same table with her throughout the trial. She's unattractive, too short, dresses in pants and is not thankful or appreciative. She's married right? What could her husband see in her?"

"Someday I'll tell you."

"As if you know," he grunted. I didn't know, but I pretended to just to stop his attack on Anne.

Joe left, leaving me to think about tomorrow's pre-trial conference with Judge Conlon, but my mind drifted to Cantrell's attorney. It's important to know your opponent because the legal system is mostly adversarial. As I used to tell my wife Mary, an operating room nurse, everyone in the medical field is there for the health and recovery of the patient. In a courtroom no one cares about your health or wishes to aid you in any manner. On the contrary, some opposing lawyers may secretly wish you ill will and want you to lose.

As a veteran prosecuting attorney, knowing my opponent was usually not an issue or something I thought about too often, since I had gone against many of the same lawyers more than once and knew their style, technique and tactics. The Cantrell case concerned me because about ten years ago Rose decided to limit his practice to specializing in the insanity defense and he became good at it. So successful was he and his legal team that many criminal defense lawyers throughout the country hired him and his firm to represent their clients where competency of a client to stand trial was an issue, or the client truly had a significant mental impairment, or an insanity defense was the only remaining defense or hope for a client. He was even used by civil law firms in probate cases, especially large estates where the heirs would challenge the competency of the person making a will or revising a will, or the need to appoint a guardian of a person or the person's estate.

Rose had been destined for success before he began his criminal defense specialty. After graduating first in his class from an Ivy League law school, he started work as a plaintiff's attorney doing personal injury work with a large firm in Chicago. He did well and made money for the firm's partners, but he wasn't satisfied. When a son of one of the partner's was charged with a residential burglary, the firm was prepared to hire a well known criminal defense lawyer to represent the son. The defense lawyer suggested that the boy take a plea agreement and serve a couple of years in prison. At a meeting of the firm's partners, Rose thought the case was weak and worth defending it in court. Rose was right and the boy was found not guilty. A criminal defense firm hired Rose and they never regretted it. He did well and eventually left the firm to go into private criminal defense practice for himself.

Rose's memberships included The Order of the Coif, a scholarly legal society with limited membership, a lifetime achievement award from the state's Trial Lawyers Association, and frequent reference in legal articles as one of the best criminal defense lawyers in the country.

I hadn't tried a case against Rose in awhile, but I remember him as being comfortable in court with a perpetual smile, always prepared and charming to the jury. I didn't have his accomplishments, but I was smart enough to know he would be prepared for trial and would not make any mistakes. If the above weren't enough, he had large resources to help him in trial preparation, research and assistance. By assistance, I meant a scholarly legal team; yes, a team of lawyers and paralegals.

Thinking of my "team"—Anne, Cindy, and detective Matanovich—provoked a brief, nervous chuckle. Joe may have had one or two years of college. He was thorough but slow, and had to be frequently reminded of what needed to be done. Anne was a rookie prosecutor. Cindy, though skilled as a paralegal, was often overwhelmed with other tasks in the office because of our shortage of paralegals due to budget cuts. My heart started to beat faster and when that happens I get up and start pacing the room.

And, of course, I knew Roeder's confession was inadequate, even Eilert Kurtz, Jr., when he made his unannounced visit to my place, referred to the confession as "weak." It smelled of deception and lacked full disclosure. I knew I was going to have to work Butch over to get him to tell me more.

But, there was something else—the question I had posed to the reporter, Randy, who despite his years of experience was not able to figure it out. What if for some reason Roeder was not able to testify?

CHAPTER 7

I sat in my office looking outside at people arriving to the court building and moving at a quick pace to avoid the early morning heat. Over the past few days, many were already complaining that the weather had been too hot, evidently forgetting their comments made during the past brutally cold winter that they would never complain again about oppressive summer heat.

Judge Conlon had set today for a pre-trial conference to discuss the trial, its duration, number of witnesses, motions, sequestering of the jury and change of venue request because of enormous publicity that the case had drawn.

Prior to going into court I always listened to rock music to get myself psyched up along with strong coffee. This morning I chose music from the Stones along with two cups of Greek coffee.

Joe walked in with a slight nod and seated himself.

"Ready?" I asked.

"Are you?"

Choosing to ignore him, I gathered my papers and headed out the door with him behind me. We walked up the stairs to the second floor and before reaching the top, Joe complained about the smell of sewer gas, a comment he often made when the Pink Penguin or Tim Rogers was near, a reference to the copious amounts of cologne he allegedly doused himself with every morning. A bold dresser, the Penguin could wear a yellow, pink or purple suit and feel comfortable in it, along with the conspicuous display of a plethora of jewelry. He got the nickname not only from his colorful attire but his body shape, which resembled the sea animal. Rogers had black, curly, shoulder length hair. He represented Butch Roeder. By the time we got to the top of the stairs Joe wasn't complaining about anything because he was out of breath.

Randy Denny and others from different newspapers stood outside courtroom number four. He didn't have his usual smile as he handed me a note saying, "Read it later…not now."

I didn't say anything to the other reporters. After thirty years, some of them still couldn't spell my last name, which contained only six letters. I didn't dare to think how most of them would have spelled my name had my Greek grandfather not dropped seven letters at Ellis Island in 1914. They wanted to talk to me, but I told them to come inside and listen to the proceedings, but a few didn't want to take the time to do that. Like many trial lawyers, I also did not like to talk much prior to hearings or trials, preferring instead to be focused on the upcoming court procedure.

Joe and I walked into a packed courtroom filled with press, family, friends and the public. All the criminal courts on this floor looked the same. Two huge, brown doors opened the way to the interior of the courtroom. Attorney and client conference rooms are to the immediate right and left. In front of these rooms are rows of padded chairs for the public. A four foot high semicircular mahogany rail separated the public from the interior of the courtroom. This rail connected the width of the courtroom wall to wall. In the middle of this rail was a swinging door through which witnesses and attorneys passed through. A lectern stood a few feet in front of the swinging door. To the right and left of the lectern were large tables for the defense and prosecution. Left of the defense table and by the left wall was the section for the jurors. Photographs of past judges decorated the courtroom walls. The Judge occupied an elevated bench to the center and back of the courtroom. The court reporter's station was to the right of the judge and to the left was the chief bailiff's station.

I took my seat at the prosecution table. Anne had a doctor's appointment and couldn't make this hearing. Rose sat in the middle of the other table with Cantrell to his left and a lawyer to his right. At trial I figured there would be additional lawyers and paralegals. Rose wore his trademark smile.

This is the first time I had seen Cantrell. He sat quietly in his dark blue jail attire, looking straight ahead. At trial he would have short hair and be wearing a conservative suit. Defense lawyers always have clients looking their best for the jury. His affect appeared flat, a term mental health professionals use to describe a client or patient's expression or emotion. Having done many insanity trials, I knew a flat affect meant lacking an appropriate emotion or expression. As if sensing my gaze, he turned his head towards me. Our eyes locked but his expression didn't change. We continued to stare at each other until I blinked, a default or victory he must have been waiting for since his lips curled upwards into a little smile.

Attorney Rose had a permanent smile that did not leave even while he talked. It was a worthwhile trait for jury trials and a feature I didn't have. Instead, court observers said I had a serious demeanor, despite my penchant for witty humor.

Either Rose's white shirt was too long or his suit coat sleeves too short because his white cuffs extended at least two inches beyond the coat sleeves. He whispered something to Cantrell, got up and came towards me, with an even wider grin.

"Good to see you again, Nick."

"Really?"

"I would have preferred any prosecuting attorney in the state but you," he whispered, no doubt not wanting Cantrell to hear the compliment. We made some small talk and he returned to his seat next to his client. I knew Rose would not offend the jury or make any slip ups. My advantage, or so I believed, was thirty years of criminal trial experience.

Just as knowledgeable was the Hon. Melvin Conlon, a rare judge because of his intelligence and expertise in criminal law. He might appear to some as occasionally dozing off during a proceeding but such was not the case. He had droopy eyelids that almost covered his eyes, making color identification impossible. Sometimes during a hearing he would raise one eyebrow without raising the other, sort of a questioning glance or stare. If it was directed at you, it caused you to be concerned, because he appeared to be questioning or raising doubts about what you were doing. All lawyers knew that Conlon knew what he was doing. Thus, if he knew what he was doing, the person in error had to be you.

Randy's note, printed in green ink concerned me, so I had to read it. I couldn't wait.

> Nick, I researched your insanity cases back thirty years. You were almost right, but you did lose an insanity case twenty-six years ago. A teenager charged with murder was found not guilty by reason of insanity. He was released after a few months in a mental health facility. All family members with a history of mental illness. Defendant noted to be exceptionally brilliant. Father, a public figure, task master at home. Nick, as you probably know, an article about this case was found in the box of materials Joe retrieved from the Cantrell crawlspace.

"Is the defense ready?"

"Yes, your honor."

"Is the state ready?"

"Yes, your honor," I said, knowing that I was a long way from being ready to prosecute this case. Fortunately, today's hearing was not the beginning of the trial. The note shocked me and caused me to lose my concentration. Rose was talking and I didn't even realize it. Now I knew why Randy had not wanted me to read the note until after the proceeding. Seated three rows behind my table I glanced in his direction. The expression on his face said, "I warned you."

The note shocked me because of the factual similarity to the Cantrell case. Second, I really thought I had never lost a murder insanity case. Third, if jury precedent was any indicator of like cases being decided in like manner, then this case is lost. *Get a hold of yourself,* I thought. There is no such thing as jury precedent. *Am I losing it? The public deserves better,* I thought.

"Your honor," Rose said with his permanent smile affixed and circling his right index finger and thumb around his Phi Beta Kappa key to make sure it was still attached to his suit vest, "the defense withdraws its motion for change of venue from the county because of pre-trial publicity. As the court and prosecutor are aware, we have previously filed notice of an insanity defense, though we sincerely do not believe the state can show a prima facie case on the evidence it has."

Questioning glances, furrowed brows and murmurs from many of those in the courtroom reflected the surprise they had of Rose's withdrawal of the change of venue motion. Many, including the press had been led to believe that Rose would want the case tried in a distant county because of the extensive publicity the case had attracted. I'm sure very few understood Rose's comment with regards to the prosecution proving a prima facie case. This simply meant that a judge had to find that there was at least some evidence on each and every element of the charged offenses after the state rested its case. If not, then the judge had the duty to dismiss the case without the defense even having to present any evidence. Defense lawyers almost routinely make the motion to dismiss the state's case in almost every trial. Much of what goes on in a trial is done to protect the record should the defendant be found guilty and the defense appeals the case. As a general rule, a defense lawyer cannot object or complain about something on appeal that he did not object to at the trial level.

I had no need to say anything in response to what Rose said. After telling the court about how long we expected the trial to last and the number of witnesses each of us had planned to call, the pre-trial hearing was over.

I took one last look at Cantrell until probably the trial. Again, he slowly turned his head to the right and our eyes locked. Was that a look of confidence on his face? As well, it should be. Right now, all we had was Roeder, and that wasn't much. I knew the trial would be different and unorthodox. It would be unlike any I had ever tried. I sensed considerable drama, a foreboding feeling of uncertainty, a lack of control, of someone else choreographing the case, the trial and verdict.

I didn't feel like talking to anyone, so I exited through the Judge's back door and went to my office, leaving Joe by himself. I sat there maybe twenty minutes, just staring out the window. I called Cindy into my office. We didn't talk too much to each other these days. I wanted to talk, but she didn't. She came in and took a seat without any greeting or smile. When I wasn't thinking about the trial, I would think about both Angela and Cindy and how they were similar or dissimilar.

I enjoyed Angela's boldness, her excitement, her intuitive understanding of my case, but she lacked something I couldn't identify. What was it? How were the two different? Cindy was warmer, more responsive, less witty and more compassionate—the girl next door. Angela? She was a man's temporary pleasure. In reality, she was a man. She didn't need preliminary pleasures, no tactile stimulation, minimal cuddling. Like a trained marksman all she needed was to lock and load and fire when ready.

"Cindy, I want you or Joe to get me updated information about Dr. Glowacki, the defense's psychiatrist and the psychologist. Specifically, find out what type of patients or clients they have been seeing. How often do they testify and for whom do they testify? How many times have they testified that someone was sane?"

Cindy's look outside said she could care less about what I wanted.

"Nick, I believe you've questioned them before. And don't you mean insane rather than sane?" she said this while still not looking at me.

"No, sane. And, yes, I am somewhat familiar with them, but I want updated information about them to see if there's been any change in how they testify and what they say and do. Please look at me because I've got to go to talk to Roeder about Cantrell."

"Oh, I won't stop you, Nick. See whoever you want, Angela, Roeder, I could care less," she said derisively, then continued, "but you need to understand something."

"Please, tell me?" I asked.

"You've got to break away from Angela. I think I can understand your interest in her. She's sensual and provocative. But, Nick, she's got her own agenda; it's short and doesn't include you. I think she's using you for some reason. Don't you think it's odd how you both met? Did a cashier or book clerk at Barnes & Noble really know who you were? I know a lot of people know who you are, but in view of the ending conversation you had with her, it all seems a little strange, contrived if you will. And, then she appeared at your condo with a card wanting to go out with you? Then, of course, her strong interest in your case and not wanting you to prosecute Cantrell."

I said nothing because I didn't know what to say.

"Well, if you have nothing to say, I'm out of here." She walked out without looking at me.

I sat opposite Roeder in the blue conference room. He then stood up, walked a few paces, and resumed his seat. Butch didn't seem to walk normally because his muscular legs and thighs seemed to compete against each other for space. Likewise, his arms never seemed to rest parallel to the side of his body. They seemed to extend outward about twenty to thirty degrees. Butch Roeder looked more like the son of Clinton Cantrell than did Matt. It was a body crafted by years in a weight room, except Butch seldom ever lifted weights. His physique was natural, scary.

"Hey, Butch."

"Speak."

"I want to know everything about Matt."

"That's not part of the deal."

I promptly left and returned two hours later with the Pink Penguin and the plea agreement. We were back in the same room.

"You wanted me to speak? I'll speak and I'm only going to say this once or I'll tear this agreement up. I want to know everything about Matt from the day he was born until today."

"I thought I just had to tell you about the day of the crime," Butch said, looking more concerned than two hours ago.

Tim Rogers, also known as the pink penguin spoke, "Butch, I haven't got time for this. You tell him every damn thing he wants to know. I don't care how unimportant it may seem. If you don't he'll tear the agreement up and you'll have to find another attorney, because I can't do any better for you than what I have already worked out with the prosecutor's office. Got it? Answer me, damn it." Again, profanity seems to work best with many criminal defendants.

"Yeah, I got it." Butch's attorney left with the plea agreement in hand.

"How long have you known Matt?"

"How come you don't ask anything about me or the day of the crime?"

"Later."

"I've known him since about third grade."

"How have you gotten along with him?"

"He's my, or was my best friend."

"Have you always been close—up to now?"

"Yeah."

"What do you like about him?"

"You know, he's cool in a different way. He has helped me a lot with school work, stuff like that."

"Does he have any other friends?"

"No."

"Why?"

"He's different."

"When did you first start to plan to kill the store owner?"

"Last summer."

"Who got the PVC pipe and from where?"

"Matt got it from some hardware store out of the area."

"And the wood?"

"Same answer."

"I assume the hole for the PVC pipe was dug out sometime in the summer when the ground was soft?"

"Yeah."

"Why kill him?"

"For money and because Matt wanted his dad to feel some pain."

"What did you use to kill him?"

"Matt used a pipe and struck him many times in the head and face."

"Did you guys have any guns in your possession? If so, why not shoot him?"

"Yes, we had shotguns but that would make too much noise."

"Why not kill him in the house?"

"That wasn't Matt's plan."

"Had you ever been in the Kurtz home?"

"No."

"You must have had blood on your clothes after the killing. What did you guys do with the pipe and your clothes?"

"Matt got rid of everything, but first he power washed the stuff."

"What about your truck?"

"Matt sold it and got rid of it."

"To whom?"

"I don't know."

"Why didn't you go in Kurtz's house?"

"No need to—we already got the money, and it was taking a long time to do all this. We figured we needed to get back home," Butch's gaze wandered. He was getting restless.

"Where did you go after leaving Kurtz's?"

"Matt drove to Doc's and bought some LSD and crack."

"Who is 'Doc'?"

"Hey man, I don't know much about him and I don't want to. He's a scary dude, supposedly mob ties or something, you know what I mean?"

"Butch, I don't imagine too many people scare you."

"Yeah."

"Where's Doc's place?"

"About five miles from Matt's house. It's a big, red brick house in the country."

"Did you or Matt ever tell anyone about the killing?"

"No."

"Supposedly a woman, an anonymous caller told the police you guys did it," I said looking to him for an answer or explanation but not getting any.

"Slow down, give me time to think," Butch said, shifting a little in the chair and glaring at me.

I wanted to keep the fast pace so that he wouldn't have the opportunity to think, to try to conjure up answers, spontaneous responses—that's what I wanted.

"Tell me about his father, Butch."

"He has no soul."

"But, he's the principal of a high school and an assistant pastor."

"I don't care what his titles are, the man is a nut job."

"To everyone?"

"I think mainly to his family. He used to tie Matt to a pole downstairs and beat him."

Of course, I recalled the photo in Bonnie Cantrell's box in her amoire of a picture showing Matt tied to a pole in the basement. I was making some progress with Butch and believing that he was mostly credible. "Why would he do that," I asked.

"Don't know, man."

"What about Lenny?"

"I don't know much about him. He's a little older and we have never really done much together, and Matt never really talks about him."

"What about Matt's mother, Bonnie?" He looked away from me, then at the walls as if the answer may have been written on them.

"Mrs. C is a quiet, good woman, but not home much and..."

"And, what?"

"You know, not home much, tries to avoid the reverend, like everyone."

"I'm about done, Butch, just a couple of more questions. What's the relationship between Lenny and the reverend?"

"As I said, I don't know much about Lenny, but from what I've seen, the reverend gets along better with him than either Matt or Mrs. C."

"What about your family and the Cantrell family, ever any interaction?"

"My mom works a lot and doesn't like to be around the reverend because of his loud, abusive voice. As for my dad, he's drunk most of the time and doesn't have any close friends."

"I understand that the Cantrell's worked a lot for Mr. Kurtz, or used to on his property. Were you ever involved in any work at his place?"

"No."

"You knew him, of course, because he would allow you and Matt to hunt on his property, right?"

"Yeah."

"How often would you hunt there and for what kind of game?"

"Deer, rabbits, and we fished, too."

"Butch, I need to ask you something. The reverend is a big strong man with a booming voice, right?"

He nodded.

"I know you're strong too, Butch, and I have no doubt, one on one, you could take him out, but are you scared of him?"

"Mr., what's your name?"

"Papais, Nick Papais."

"Well whatever, anyway, everyone is scared of the reverend."

"What about Mr. Kurtz?" I asked, "Do you know if he was ever scared of the reverend?"

"Mr. Papais," the guard came in and told me that I needed to see Cindy right away.

While on my way back to the office I thought about our conversation. It didn't bother me too much at this time, but I knew Butch was holding back on some particulars. What was he hiding? I could understand the concern and fear. And, I knew about Doc. Our office had prosecuted him years ago for possession of drug paraphernalia, extortion and later for aggravated battery. As I recall, he beat one or two of the charges, but was found guilty of one and served a couple of years in the joint. Of course, he wasn't a doctor. He didn't even have a driver's license. His real name was Angelo DeVechio—and he had mob ties. Ruthless best described his character.

Cindy was waiting for me in my office.

"How did the visit with Roeder go?" she asked.

"I'll tell you later. I have an unpleasant feeling you have something to tell me that I need to know and that I'm not going to like, correct?"

"Yes."

"Please."

"I personally talked to or questioned everyone at Barnes & Noble the day you met Angela."

"Continue, Cindy."

"If you recall, she told you that she asked one of the cashiers or assistants about a book and they referred her to you who happened to be in the bookstore at that time."

"That's correct."

"Nick, no employee, no worker, absolutely no one that day, that Sunday, or any Sunday ever directed Angela or any woman to you."

CHAPTER 8

I couldn't sleep last night thinking of Cindy's disclosure about Angela at the bookstore. There had to be an explanation—perhaps an employee who no longer worked for the book store, or an employee who had been transferred to another store. Of course, Randy's note to me outside the courtroom about losing a murder insanity case similar to the Cantrell case likewise caused me to toss and turn in bed. How could I have not remembered the Murdock case, but more disturbing was that an article about the case had been found in the Cantrell crawl space.

I had begun to lose track of time, even whether it was morning or afternoon. My focus was only on the trial, as if I had blinders on that narrowed my vision to that event. Retirement no longer preoccupied me. Yet, I still needed some diversion and distraction from the case. I felt fortunate to be blessed with some great friends, even though we were all separated by hundreds of miles. As if sensing my unrest and discomfort, the phone rang and it was Roger Reason, an Indianapolis attorney. Rog and I were roommates in college and have stayed in touch ever since. I could always count on Rog and Tom, a childhood friend from Lake County, Indiana to both lift my spirits when I was down. Unfortunately, someone was knocking at the door, so we terminated our talk with a pledge to talk later. I hoped it was Tom, as in Tom Collins because I wanted a drink, but it was Randy.

"I'm tired, Randy. What do you want?"

"You ever go to the office anymore?"

"This is my office. State the nature of your business please."
My no nonsense talk halted his entry into my place, but reluctantly
I let him in.

"A little formal aren't you, Nick? You look tired."

I nodded.

"Nick, sorry to have shocked you with that note about the
Murdock trial that you lost years ago."

"When I think about it, I'm more disturbed about an article
about the case in the Cantrell home."

"If I may Nick, you know there are mental health organizations
from throughout the country following this case. At some point
they would like to talk to you."

"No," I said simply, but went a little further, "what do they
expect me to do? Dismiss the case? Yes, between you and me,
Cantrell's childhood and upbringing were horrible, but I'm sure
most of the country would rather see him hang than be treated for
mental illness."

"Well, Nick, I guess some wonder because you have been an
advocate for better mental health treatment," he said.

I decided to answer his comment in a different fashion. "You
know, Randy, there are many facets to justice. Justice is not
always about guilt or innocence. It's not always about the death
penalty versus life in prison, treatment or no treatment,
incarceration or parole or probation. It's also about compassion
for the victim's family. They have to have justice, too. Justice for
them is a trial, even though they may quarrel with the verdict. But,
are we to foreclose their right to a trial, even though technically it's
the defendant's right to have a trial?" I paused for a few seconds.
We looked at each other.

"Good point, Nick. I can tell there's something else you want
to say"

"Yes. I don't know if you covered the case or not, I suspect
you didn't, but I remember prosecuting a murder case of an

African American female who had only one distant relative show up for trial. I felt like I and the police were the only people who cared and could give justice for this woman. There wasn't even much press coverage of the trial. Your office must have figured it was only the killing of a poor African American woman with no family, thus not worth the effort. Why spend much time reporting that kind of case, right?" Randy looked down at his note pad as if to find a response to what I had said, and no doubt ashamed of what I was telling him. I paused then continued, "If I recall correctly, the person who did show up was used by me to identify a ring found on the deceased's finger. It was a horrible crime. She had been burned to death to cover up the actual method of killing, which I believe was a gun shot to the head. Her ring was the only method of identifying her. I don't recall dental records or other means of identification. I managed to get a conviction. She got justice, Randy. Even victims with little or no family are entitled to justice. I remember it as the ring case. I will remember it not for its brutality, but for no one being interested in it."

He nodded somberly. "Nick, it's your last trial, a big one. What if there's a not guilty verdict or not guilty by reason of insanity or guilty but mentally ill?"

"Who wants to lose any case? I don't want to lose my last case, just as an athlete about to retire does not want to lose his or her last athletic event. Sometimes, we are remembered by the last thing we did. I don't want that memory of me to be the loss of a big case. Yet, does it really matter? I have lived by the jury system for over thirty years. I must also live by it when the verdict is not what I want. As defense lawyers like to point out, a prosecutor's job is not necessarily to prosecute but to make sure that justice is done. Justice could very well be a verdict for Cantrell."

Shortly thereafter, Randy left to follow up a lead on a story.

It couldn't have been twenty minutes later and Joe arrived looking upset. His clothes were soiled. I could smell scotch on his breath and he was breathing heavily.

"You okay?" I asked.

"Yeah, that Viagra crap doesn't work."

"Picking up women in bars again? I don't know much about Viagra and that stuff, but are you supposed to take it with a fifth of scotch?"

"Go to hell, Greek."

"Now, that's the Joe I know. Have you been up all night?"

"I got some sleep."

"Did you ever get the information about the surveillance of Matt in jail?"

Joe pulled out five sheets of paper and handed them to me. There were date and time entries made by different guards. Matt had been removed to a cell as far away from the other inmates as possible because of complaints about his nightmares and screaming. One entry read, "…saw him standing in the corner of his cell for hours, head down, arms behind his back, wearing only shorts…" Another, "…sits and stares for hours…" Another, "…he seems content." Another guard noticed, "…relaxed appearance when writing, which he does often…occasionally, smiles." One guard observed that he "…seems pleased by confinement…doesn't bother anyone." As regards visits, one guard noted, "…has visitors…mother, brother and father a lot, and defense mental health experts."

I read it all and looked up at Joe whose eyes were closed.

"Thanks, Joe," I said. Why don't you sleep here?"

"No, thanks, I'd rather go to my Martha's place." Martha was his ex-wife. "Besides," he added, "I had enough of your closeness when we were together in the big war," referring to our time together in Nam.

"Before you leave, anything significant about Angelo DeVecchio that I don't already know?"

"Doc, aka Big Fella?" AKA meant also known as—or simply, an alias.

"Is that another alias?"

"Right."

"Nothing that you don't already know. He used to bust some knees for the mob, but they kind of stopped using him because of his frequent arrests."

Rubbing my chin and shaking my head, I looked at Joe for more information.

"What," Joe asked, "let me guess, you want me to find some evidence that doesn't exist, or to have someone do surveillance?"

"Could there be more to him?" I asked, not completely satisfied. "I'm not so much concerned about involvement prior to the killing, but afterwards, you know, maybe getting rid of a pipe, clothes, truck, etc."

I gave him my unyielding, business look.

"Okay," Joe said disgustedly, "I'll have surveillance on him. You know, Nick, you need to get out in this beautiful June weather to fish, golf, whatever. "

"Let's go fishing in a few days," I said, "I want to get some more things done before I relax a little."

"What else is on your mind, Nick?"

"I don't know if I asked this before or not, but how did they know Kurtz would be home?"

"I think you did ask and I assumed they figured he'd be home. I mean it's near Christmas time, where else would he be? Further, I assume they drove by the front of the house to see if it looked occupied."

"Christmas time, you say? Well, he could just as well have been visiting his son in Ontario," I said.

"Enough of this, Nick, I'm tired. I'll see you in a few days to go fishing."

No one could have crafted or designed a better June. Farmers may have wanted more rain, but other than them, no one complained and everyone felt we deserved a good late spring and summer after successive, harsh and vindictive winters. The weather was ideal for any outdoor activities.

Joe and I were fishing on the lake behind my condo. Neither of us was saying much. We sat at the edge of the pier. It had rained a little during the night, one of those late spring warm showers that left the air heavy and the lake cloudy. We weren't having any luck catching any fish, but it was enjoyable looking at the motionless, cloudy lake, which normally had a pea green color. Joe held his rod in his left hand, while his right jingled change in the right pocket of his black, nylon stretch pants.

"We ought to give this up and buy ourselves some real fish, a good lake perch sandwich at Bronko's." He looked at me and asked, "How can you just sit there on the edge of the pier, catch nothing and think this is fun?"

Ignoring his question, I said, "When I was young, I enjoyed fishing with my dad. It's one of my best childhood memories, along with going to the beach, movies and Kroch & Brentano's bookstore on South Wabash Street in Chicago."

"Did you and the old Greek ever catch anything?"

"We did all right—mostly crappie, bluegill and lake perch."

"Got one, Nick."

"I think you got a branch." He pulled the rod and line sharply upwards causing the line to snap. He shook his head and cursed.

"Haha!"

"Amusing?" Joe asked.

"Yeah, sort of."

"We should have gone to the firing range. I still need to renew my pistol certification with the dick bureau. Besides, I bumped into Angela and she says she's always willing to go to a firing range. I'd like to see what kind of a shot she is, Nick."

"According to her, she's good," I said with minimal interest.

"You don't sound too interested." He looked over at me, waiting for a response.

"Maybe it's the retirement and how I'll miss seeing Cindy." I didn't tell him about the information Cindy obtained from Barnes & Noble.

"I don't think she's happy with her husband, Todd," he said. I said nothing because he had told me similar information many times.

"Let's go to Bronko's for lunch. Oh, one more thing, Joe."

"What is it now?" he grunted.

"Of course, find out everything you can about the principal?"

"I suppose from time in the womb until present?"

"That should do—or from time of conception."

"Nothing else, I hope."

"One final thing," I said pleadingly.

"Nick, there are no final things from you—nothing but a continuous chain of requests. You know, just because you're bigger than me, doesn't mean I can't take your glasses off and beat you severely about the head and shoulder area."

"Amazing, Joe. That's exactly what I want."

"What the hell are you talking about?" he asked, understandably puzzled and curious.

"You've got a lot of junk in your garage or rather your ex-wife's garage. I want a chain, about three feet long, not too thick and not too heavy."

"You're going to have to tell me the reason for this one."

"You'll see the reason."

CHAPTER 9

A ferocious early summer wind swept through the area raising dirt, debris and everything not securely attached. I was in my office looking out the window at people with their heads down, clutching briefcases and holding onto dresses and hats. Some ran unsteadily from their cars to the courthouse trying to resist the gale.

It was late June and jury selection was scheduled to begin two weeks from Monday, with the trial to begin immediately thereafter. I was waiting for Spider. She showed up attired as usual in a pant suit and minimal makeup.

"Anne, there's something I want you to do." Her face showed concern and she leaned forward, looking attentive.

"What do you need, Nick?"

"Many years ago, I prosecuted a case uncannily similar to our case. I lost it. I need to know why."

"I thought you never lost a murder insanity case?" she asked with a surprised look.

"Yes, I thought so, too. Somehow, I must have blocked the case out of my mind. I have no recollection of it. Cindy will get you the file and a transcript of the proceedings."

"Nick, what if I can't tell why you lost? Maybe it was just a bad jury."

I shook my head. "There's a reason why that jury thought he was insane. We need to know that reason."

"I appreciate the trust you put in me, Nick. I hope you don't get disappointed."

She left and closed the door behind her. I yelled for her to come back.

"Anne, one more thing," I said apologetically because I knew it was asking a lot.

"I guess I didn't get out of here quickly enough. Joe says you always have one more thing to request." She ran her fingers through her thick, disheveled hair, marginally improving its appearance.

"Joe, what does he know?" I asked jokingly. "Sorry, Anne, I know it's been many years since the trial, but if possible try to contact the jury foreman or defense attorney, or anyone who might be able to tell us why they thought Murdock was insane."

She looked puzzled and stared at me as if I was the one who was insane. She opened her mouth to say something, but no words came out.

"Thanks, Anne." She left my office with her head down.

A couple of hours later, I met Angela and Joe at the county police firing range. I went along because Angela wanted me to, and Joe always wanted someone with him when he fired his weapon, that someone was usually me. I think the real reason for my presence was that Joe liked for me to see how good he was with his weapon. I wasn't interested in shooting, so I just watched them fire their pistols at targets seven, fifteen and thirty yards away. Angela was dressed in loose fitting blue jeans and a blue denim shirt. Today she wore little makeup, though lately she had been wearing more. I watched the smooth and deft handling and loading of her weapon. She looked as comfortable firing her weapon as someone effortlessly driving an automobile. She glanced my way and made a slow, seductive wink while loading the gun. She then assumed a shooter's posture and fired at the targets without hesitation. She quickly took out the magazine, put another one in and fired again. There was something enticing about her stance, her professionalism and the smooth manipulation of the weapon. She fired with flawless execution. It was all business to her. She was a hunter—a killer. The place was hot or maybe it was me.

"You're sweating, Nick," she said matter of factly and with a contrasting cool appearance.

"It's a little warm in here," I said.

"Really?" she asked doubtfully.

Twenty minutes later and they were all done. Joe and Angela congratulated each other with high fives on their superb scores. This was the first time I had seen Joe happy around Angela.

A half hour later, I returned to the office. There was a note on my desk from Cindy to see jail guard Reiner right away. I knew most of the guards, including Reiner. He had been a guard for about five years. I went to the jail to find out what he wanted. He told me he had been served a subpoena to testify for Rose. He wanted me to know that he felt odd testifying for the defense and didn't want to. Like most jail guards, Reiner was pro prosecution. I told him not to worry about it and to testify truthfully. He assumed he was being subpoenaed because of his observations of Cantrell while on duty at different times. I told him that is what I figured, but I didn't want to engage him in a conversation without talking to Rose first. There are many legal rules and procedures about how to find out what a witness will testify to. I figured I would get all I needed to know by talking to Rose. If for some reason he refused to tell me about Reiner's anticipated testimony or was going to play hard-ball, then I would have the court order him to disclose the nature of his testimony or take Reiner's deposition. A deposition is a legal proceeding to find out in detail what someone knows about something. It is taken under oath with attorneys for both sides present and a court reporter who records everything said during the proceeding. Whatever Reiner's expected testimony, more than likely it wouldn't be favorable to the state, otherwise he would not be called as a witness by the defense. I called Rose but he wasn't in. A few minutes later he called.

"Rose here. What do you need, Nick?" I wondered if he still wore a smile when there was no one around him—like alone in his office.

I got right to it. "Nature of Reiner's testimony?"

"He will testify that my client has been talking strangely and almost in a different language."

"Oh, sounds like most of my friends," I said. He roared with laughter.

"Anything else, Nick?" he asked, still laughing.

"No. See you and your team in a few weeks." I couldn't help but give him a jab for all the legal assistance he would have available to him at trial.

"Team? I may have a team, but you have the vast resources of the state at your disposal."

"How come I've never been able to find those resources?"

"I hope it stays that way, Nick—at least until our trial is over."

"Thanks for returning the call, Howard."

"See you, Nick."

I sat and thought about what I needed to do, but it bothered me that I hadn't even talked to my sons lately or my brother, Tony in Indiana. Cindy knocked and came into my office.

"The court psychiatric exam reports are here. You need to read them, Nick."

"Talk to me, Cindy."

"Why don't you talk to Angela?" she asked, while turning towards the door.

"I have."

"Her conversations aren't satisfying you?" I ignored the remark, but told her I would like her to stay.

"You ever play the game, charades?" I asked.

"Yes."

"Did you enjoy it?"

"Yes," she said, her summer blue eyes searching my face for some clue as to where I was going with this.

"What about a game where someone asks you to tell a story from just a few word lead-off?"

"Where are you going with this, Nick?" she asked, starting for the door, then paused, turned and said, "I'm upset with you lately," she said, with an edge to her voice that I had seldom heard.

"I understand. Quite frankly, I'm not feeling too good about myself either, or anything for that matter."

Shaking her head and with a look of no doubt wondering whether she should participate in this game or line of questioning, she said, "Let me guess, Nick. You want me to tell you a story from a few words that you are going to give me?"

"Yes."

"Give me a few sentences or twenty."

"Gladly," I said. "Assume, a middle-aged, successful prosecutor, good looking of course, with exceptional ability, and a paralegal of comparable beauty..."

She started to frown and I knew why.

"Right, I'm sorry, of incomparable beauty, and who has often been mistaken as a sister of her daughter." I was glad to see her frown and displeasure with me replaced by what looked like a slight smile, perhaps a look of some forgiveness.

"You forgot intellect, Nick?"

"Sorry, an oversight." She looked at me anxiously waiting for the revision.

I paused, and continued, "A woman of such intelligence that many who had met her believed she possessed advanced degrees from the world's finer institutions of higher learning.

Unfortunately, a bird flu pandemic wipes out the country, but somehow they survive—sole survivors, if you will. Story please?"

She paused briefly, looked down and then glared into my eyes.

"She kills him right away, proclaims women superior, and lives in joyful solitude the rest of her life." I quickly sprinted towards the door which had been partly left open.

"Come back, Nick."

"What for?" I demanded. Now, it was my turn to be upset.

"Sorry, Nick," she looked pleadingly at me, "I want to tell you a story that you will never forget. It will be one of the best stories you've ever heard." Instinctively, we both walked towards each other until there was no space separating us. A sheet of paper placed between us would not have fallen to the floor. I looked down at her and she looked up at me. Our arms hung anxiously at our sides, as if fearing to use them to touch each other. She had to have heard my heart beating. We said nothing for what seemed like minutes, but it was the most enjoyable time I had spent doing nothing in a long while. We slowly scanned each other's faces and bodies making sounds rather than words. Our faces lightly touched, and our lips waited for the command to engage. I started to raise my arms and hands to hold her, but she slowly turned her head downward to the side and started to pull away.

"Before I tell you the story, Nick, you have to do something."

"I'll do anything," my heart said, though my brain was disengaged.

"I'm not sure you will, Nick." I started to grab for her and she stepped back further. I raised my arms and hands looking for an explanation for her retreat.

At that moment, Angela herself suddenly appeared. I cursed myself for not having closed the door. Cindy and I had been on display and anyone could have heard our conversation, though we didn't talk loudly.

"Did I interrupt a private moment?" Angela asked, with a snarling glare at Cindy. I wondered how much she had seen and heard.

Cindy made for the door without acknowledging Angela, saying she had work to do. She reminded me again to read the reports from the court appointed psychiatrists.

"I suppose you have work to do, too?" Angela asked. She stood tall with her arms crossed in front and eyes narrowed—a look that demanded an explanation.

"You know I have a lot to do in this case. I need to get more information from Butch. Why are you here?" I asked with an edge to my voice.

She ignored my question and said, "You might get more done by spending less time with her."

I looked at her sharply and said, "She's a great person. I'm sorry you can't see that. Now, I've got to see Butch. Have a good day." She blocked my exit and closed the door.

"Step aside," I said. "We'll talk later."

I apologized to Butch for being late.

"Yeah, man, I got tired of waiting for you. I thought about leaving," he giggled, and I laughed a few seconds later after realizing what he had said.

"Little slow today, Mr. Prosecutor?"

"What's the Doc's real name?" I got into my fast questioning routine with him.

"Heck, if I know."

"I know all about Doc and who he is, Butch."

"Why ask me, then?" he asked, looking disappointed.

"I've been asking questions for over thirty years. When I ask a question I try to look at a person's face, eyes, hands and body movement, change of speech. I'm trying to judge his or her credibility." He seemed to understand what credibility meant. I wanted him to know that I still might suspect what he had to tell me.

"Did Matt see the Doc often?"

"A few times."

"Alone?"

"Yes."

"When was the last time?"

"Not sure."

"Did they get along?"

"I don't know if you would call it getting along, since Doc doesn't want any friends or close ties. I heard you wanted out of this case?" Butch asked, his face showing a pleased look.

"That's right," I nodded. "Butch how long did you have the wood for the cross?"

"A few months."

"Who notched out the wood so that the two pieces would intersect?"

"I did."

"Where was the wood kept?"

"In our garage behind some wallboard so no one would notice it."

"What did Matt want to become in life," you know, "what were his goals?"

"Matt had a lot of goals, such as a lawyer, psychiatrist, teacher of languages."

"What did your folks say or do Butch when you got arrested?"

"Mom cried, and dad said, 'what took you so long to end up in jail'? My dad is useless and served time years ago."

"Did Lenny have any part in any of this, Butch?"

"I don't know."

"You have seen the doc too, haven't you, Butch?"

"Yes, I think I've told you that before."

"Butch, did the reverend have any part in the killing of Eilert Kurtz?"

"What the hell you talking about? They were friends!"

"Are you sure?"

CHAPTER 10

It was misting and had rained hard during the night. Looking across the lake from my deck in the early morning, dense, charcoal clouds hugged the horizon. As they reached upwards their tops grew thinner, resembling wisps of cotton candy, as if they were being pulled apart from above. Contrasting this was a strata of velvety, purple clouds higher in the horizon. The Master had painted another eye-catching vista.

I decided to go inside and resume looking at trial photographs. The time until trial was short. I sat cross-legged in the middle of the living room floor with photos of the Kurtz case spread out around me. The door bell rang and I hoped it wasn't Angela, but there she stood in white shorts and a light pink shirt.

"You might not want to see these," I cautioned her. "Have a seat on the deck and enjoy the cloud formation. I'll be with you in a minute." She ignored me and came over to look at the photos with what looked like detached interest. Most people shrieked in horror when seeing 8x12 photos of murder victims, especially victims whose faces and bodies resembled chunks of meat in a slaughter house. Not Angela. She knelt beside me and looked at the photos with studied concentration and curiosity.

"I can see why defense lawyers object to these types of photos. Why are they displayed like this?"

"I've got to decide which ones to try to admit into evidence. There are seventeen photos of Kurtz. The Judge will only allow a few in, unless I can show the relevance of admitting more." I explained to her that the main requirement for admitting photographs into evidence is that they be relevant. With mutilated bodies the Judge must also consider the additional factor of whether the photos are too inflammatory or unnecessarily gruesome. In reality, photos of savagely beaten victims are inflammatory, and their introduction into evidence is meant by the prosecutor to infuriate the jury.

"We haven't been together much lately," Angela said.

"Look at all this stuff." I waved my hand at the file, papers and photos by way of an explanation for my not seeing her. In truth, I felt less excitement around her.

"You haven't been seeing Cindy, have you, Nick?" Her eyes searched mine as she took out a small mirror from her purse and looked at herself in the mirror. She had been wearing more makeup lately, especially a deep shade of crimson lipstick. Her eyes were also rimmed with black eyeliner and thick mascara.

"The only people I've seen have somehow been involved in this case. I haven't even seen much of my boys nor talked to my friends, Rog and Tom from Indiana. Nick, Jr. and I have golfed only a couple of times this year. Now, the press—they call often. They're starting to annoy me."

"What press?"

"Mostly from out of the area."

"What do they want to know?"

"Well, their questions have to do with mental illness and my views on famous trials with the insanity defense, and any thoughts I had on those cases."

"What do you say?"

"I think I shock them when I tell them that quite frankly I think some defendants have in fact been severely mentally ill and should not have been found guilty."

"Well, sweetheart, I'm proud of you," she said with a slight smile and eyes wide open. "What cases, Nick"

"I don't want to get into this much Angela because I'm tired of talking about it, but there have been a number of cases in the last several years where there's no doubt in my mind that the defendants could not have appreciated the wrongfulness of their activities, and should not have been found guilty."

"Certainly, Nick, they must be asking you how you distinguish those cases from Matt Cantrell's case?"

"Of course," I replied tersely, in a tone wanting to end this conversation.

"Nick, what…"

Before she could ask another question, I changed the subject matter to telling her about a reporter who asked me what I thought about Cantrell's father asking his church to raise money for Matt's defense. She said nothing other than she was pleased to know that I felt some defendants should not be found guilty

"Does that make me more human?" I asked. "As we say in law, each case should be decided on its own merits. Some cases of postpartum depression or psychosis have been so severe that women have committed suicide. Maybe they know right from wrong, but the desire for self destruction or killing is irresistible. Admittedly, perhaps they aren't truly insane, but of a reasonable, rational mind, or to appreciate the consequences of their actions? Angela, I've got to go to the office and interview some witnesses."

"I understand, but let's get together soon."

"I'll call you." I said, but not really believing that I ever would. "Later."

I arrived at the office in the early afternoon. I had already started interviewing witnesses for the trial. About a fourth of the witnesses were law enforcement and expert witnesses who had testified on other occasions. I would spend some time prepping them for trial, but not much since they had testified many times before and knew the routine. My main detective was Joe and he knew what I wanted.

Besides going over their testimony, a trial lawyer also tells his witnesses the standard admonitions: If you don't know the answer to a question, say so. If you don't understand a question, have the lawyer rephrase it. Don't argue with the lawyer. Don't rush into an answer. Don't worry about your responses or bad answers, because it will be my job to try to rehabilitate you on redirect examination or put a positive "spin" on it in closing argument.

About the only witness I never talk to unless it's crucial to an issue in the case is the pathologist. The pathologist testifies as to cause of death. The prosecutor must prove that the victim did not die a natural death. Nevertheless, I wanted the pathologist to graphically detail Kurtz's death to horrify the jury. Unfortunately, most of our forensic pathologists do not speak English well, making it difficult for jurors to understand them. Many of them are not from this country. Most doctors prefer one on one patient care, but that requires an adequate ability to communicate with a patient. Forensic pathologists do not need extensive communication skills with people. Therefore, I make it a point to follow up my questioning of pathologists with questions that contain their previous answer.

The most time is spent with eyewitnesses, if there are any. I had an eyewitness who was also a participant or killer. Defense lawyers attack participants or co-defendants who testify against their client. They have no choice. In most instances, if the jury believes the co-defendant, then the defendant will be found guilty. Here, the murder was not disputed, well, that's not entirely true, either. I was still troubled by the fact that without Roeder how would we prove that Cantrell killed Kurtz? Where's the forensic evidence? Where's the DNA, the fingerprints, other physical evidence such as clothing, tire prints, weapons, etc?

The psychiatrists? As in politics, they are often partisan. Defense psychiatrists testify that the defendant could not appreciate the difference between right and wrong, or that he was suffering from a mental disease or defect. The state or prosecution usually does not have any independent psychiatrist or psychologist. Instead, they rely on the Judge to appoint two psychiatrists to examine the defendant. These psychiatrists or psychologists usually find that the defendant was sane at the time of the crime. Thus, he could distinguish right from wrong and appreciate the consequences of his acts. In some instances, juries dismiss psychiatric testimony when the psychiatrists contradict each other because the jurors cannot reconcile the inconsistencies.

Many insanity trials are decided by the testimony of lay witnesses—not psychiatrists or psychologists. The law basically allows anyone to comment on someone's mental health, hence the importance of the testimony of anyone who had known or observed Matt. Obviously, this list of people can be quite extensive. Often, it includes going back to a murderer's childhood and teachers, neighbors, and anyone who had any significant opportunity to observe the defendant's behavior.

Butch said Matt's father had no soul. How would he testify? Would he testify? Would he lie? Would the defense set me up to attack a person who was an assistant pastor of a church? Would they somehow attack the principal to show that he was responsible for his son's insanity? The rules of evidence preclude a lawyer from attacking his own witness. This rule has a rational basis. When a lawyer calls a witness to the stand he or she is vouching for that witness's credibility. One need not graduate from law school to appreciate that attacking your own witness tends to discredit that witness. And a lawyer cannot argue with a witness, especially his own witness. Argument is reserved for the end of the trial when all evidence has been presented.

The principal was listed as a witness, but would the defense really use him? Was the defense trying to get me to waste a lot of preparation time on someone they did not plan on calling? A witness listed to testify does not mean that he will necessarily testify. From what I had read about the principal, evidently he appeared quite normal to those he worked with and to his congregation. What I had seen in the Cantrell house led me to believe that there was significant evidence of a very dysfunctional family. The fact that Mr. Cantrell was an assistant pastor cloaked him with credibility. I had had clergy on the witness stand before, but never one who was so critical to a case. The principal was a big man with a booming voice who was used to having a captive audience—a man who had spent years convincing people that the scriptures and gospel are not suggestions, as a stop sign is a command to stop and not a suggestion. He was a man who had convinced people that papers two thousand years old had meaning. Mr. Cantrell would be at ease in the witness chair. He would look at the jury and talk to them, as if personally or one on one. They would lean forward in their chairs. That would not be good. He would speak to the entire courtroom and they would believe him.

I would be the only person trying to get him to say what he did not want to say. I needed to be slow and cautious. As I knew from past experiences, it doesn't take much to lose a case. A wrong word, a wrong approach, an offensive remark are enough to have the jury find against you.

Questioning an important witness requires a plan or goal. What does the examiner wish to achieve or want the jury to believe? Does it make sense? How does the objective or goal fit in with the overall case? Grabbing a legal pad, I wrote down my goals for the cross examination of the principal should he testify:

1) Show respect, but lessen his stature.

2) Show that he really did not know much about Matt.

3) That he abandoned Matt and the rest of his family.

4) That he stole Matt's—

Joe walked in out of breath with Cindy right next to him.

"And, what brings you to the real office?" Joe asked.

"I've been interviewing witnesses and preparing questions for the principal."

"That reminds me," Joe said, as he reached into the inside of his crumpled herringbone sports coat and retrieved some papers, "here's some additional paperwork you wanted on Mr. Cantrell, DeVecchio, and others." I read the whole thing while they sat there looking at me.

"Joe, I don't know what to say. This is good but what about lab work, DNA, etc?"

"I didn't prepare the report and we are still trying to get physical evidence, but Cantrell must know a lot about how to leave a crime scene clean."

"What about not preparing this material?"

"Angela's boss, the private dick, prepared it."

"Couldn't you have done this?"

"Not under your time constraints. Angela figured you could use it." I tried to make an unobtrusive look towards Cindy to see her reaction at Angela's name. I didn't do a good job because our eyes locked and her face showed disappointment.

"Well, I've got to go," Joe said, making for the door. "Got to write out a few checks for Aleisha's wedding." Looking at me, he said, "You can be thankful you don't have any daughters."

"Yes, Mary has often said that. See you, partner."

With his hand on the door knob, he asked, "How's Mary doing?"

"I haven't seen much of the family lately, but I think she's planning a short trip with her boyfriend, and I believe she's going to want me to watch the dog. Why not? I don't have much to do. You know, just working on the biggest case in the country right now. Speaking of not seeing someone much, where's Anne?" I asked.

"I think she's trying to avoid you," Cindy said. "Something about a tough assignment you gave her."

"I'm out of here." Joe left.

"Me, too," Cindy said.

"Can you stay?" I asked.

"What for?"

"Let's have a drink?"

"You have alcohol in a government work place?"

"I didn't know it was a work place."

"I want to know what's going on with you and Angela, Nick,"

"Cindy, I don't want to see her anymore."

"Are you sure?"

"Yes."

"What do you have to drink?"

"What would you like?"

"You mean, you have more than one type of booze?"

"Just tell me what you want?"

"Something colorful."

"Well, let me check the supply for something colorful," as I opened the bottom right drawer of my desk. "Ah, yes, right here." I filled two coffee cups with premixed margaritas, regretting that I hadn't cleaned the cups earlier. "Here, 'opa', as we say in Greek."

"Are these cups clean, Nick?"

"Of course; well, if not, the tequila in this is quite strong and will clean anything."

"What other booze do you have in the drawer?"

"Nothing else."

"Nick, I have no idea why I have ever had any interest in you."

"Nor can I understand why you do," I said, "and generally I have no interest in anyone that would find me interesting."

She roared back with laughter and said, "I must have some bizarre fascination with troubled, tormented people."

"I like that and hope I can live up to your assessment of me."

"Nick, it's four in the afternoon. This office closes at 4:30. I remind you of that since you haven't been here much lately and probably have forgotten about normal work hours."

"Very funny," I said.

"More, she commanded." I filled up our cups again. "Do you like the drink, Nick?" she asked.

I looked at her and said, "Not particularly, but I'd drink Clorox to be with you." Her chest heaved. She looked like she was trying to decide whether to smile, cry or go into shock. Maybe five minutes elapsed or longer. She got up and walked to the window and then resumed her seat. We drank more and didn't talk for awhile. I put my feet up on the desk and she did likewise. Eventually we talked at length about our work here and people who had left or retired. The setting sun and darkness in the office cast a dark bronze glow on her legs which matched the short skirt she wore.

"You ever dream about me, Nick?"

"No," I lied. She turned her head in disbelief. "In over thirty years, you've never dreamed about me?"

"Of course, I've dreamed about you." We drank more, a lot more. The sun had disappeared and darkness and quiet were our only company.

"How are things with Todd?" I asked. For some reason I never could bring myself to ask her much about him.

"Fine, no problems."

"Good. Feel free to you leave whenever you want."

"Is that what you want?"

"I don't ever want you to leave," I said without hesitation. She poured more margarita into her cup.

"Where are you—what are you going to do when you retire?" Her thinking and speaking started to get unclear.

"First, I have to decide what I want to be when I grow up. Next, well, many people have asked me to write a book about my murder trials."

"Do you—what did you say?" The alcohol was getting to her and I know it was affecting me, also.

"You look blurry, Nick. Can you see me?"

"Loud and clear." We both laughed when we realized what I had said.

"Your watch alarm is going off, Nick."

"That means it's late and time for you to go home to your family. There are two uniforms in the parking lot to make sure you get home. One will drive your car and the other will drive you home."

"Maybe I want to stay with you."

"No. It's already been arranged for you to go home."

"How are you going to get home?"

"Maybe I don't want to go home."

"Nick, I'm sorry for not having seen it before. Your divorce has affected you, hasn't it? And, I need to tell you something. I lied to you. Todd and I are, uh—."

She looked like a figure from an impressionist painting, but from a considerable distance. Her lips were moving. She was saying something, but I couldn't hear the words. What would impressionist words be like, I wondered? I couldn't think. Garbled? Yes, inaudible. She was getting further away or maybe I needed a new prescription for my glasses. I didn't want to wake up. I wanted to be with—

"Nick, wake up. I can't believe you spent the night here on

your office floor." I looked up and saw Cindy.

"Close the door."

"It's closed. You think I'd let anyone see you like this? You look like something waste management wasn't able to properly dispose of. Here's some strong coffee. Unfortunately, Spider needs to see you. She says it's important."

I drank all the coffee without pausing. There was knocking at the door, but it went unanswered. Cindy looked at my face as if searching for something familiar, but not finding it.

"You look awful."

"Young lady, I've worked hard to achieve this look."

"Nick, get off the floor and into your chair. You need to talk to Anne. She's anxious."

"I'm not thinking too clearly. Would you mind staying? Before answering that question why didn't you stay last night?"

"Because there were uniforms outside that you evidently had arranged for in advance to take me home. Recall?"

"Vaguely."

"Nick, I'll stay for your talk with Anne. Afterwards, I want you to go home and clean up. Hopefully, you can leave without attracting too much attention." She grabbed my phone and dialed Anne's extension. Anne came a few minutes later. She looked puzzled at Cindy's presence and then said, "You don't look too good, Nick."

"So I've been told." I looked at Cindy, who briefly looked away from my gaze.

"What do you have for me, Anne?" She opened up her laptop and proceeded to tell us in detail about the insanity trial I lost many years ago. Occasionally, she would look up at me as if for approval or comment. I said nothing. Her slow, boring narration caused my tired, hung-over mind to wander. She summarized the witness testimony and arguments with nothing significant, so far. Then, she started to speak faster and her voice reflected concern after she started to tell us about the testimony of the mental health professionals. The defense had utilized a psychiatrist and a psychologist, both of whom testified the defendant suffered from schizophrenia and met the legal criteria for insanity. Testifying for the judge or court were two board certified psychiatrists. The first one testified that the defendant was psychotic and could not appreciate the wrongfulness of his conduct. The second psychiatrist likewise concluded that the defendant had a mental disease or defect which met the state's criteria for insanity. Thus, all four expert witnesses testified the defendant was insane. Anne had located three jurors. In view of the unanimous psychiatric testimony, they felt they had no choice but to find the defendant not guilty by reason of insanity.

"Good job, Anne. Well, I think we're in good shape and I can see why I lost that trial. Tough to win with all four psychiatrists, both defense and court-appointed testifying that someone was not of sound mind at the time of the crime." Cindy was staring at me incredulously. *What's her problem*, I wondered. "Again thanks, Anne. You can go."

Anne looked at me with surprise and bewilderment, and quickly left.

"Nick!" Cindy got up, put her hands on her hips and said,

"Didn't you read the reports from the court appointed psychiatrists I gave you a short while ago?" she demanded to know.

"Not yet," I said, slowly realizing what she was about to tell me.

"Obviously. They said Matt was insane at the time of the crime. So, the defense psychiatrists and court appointed psychiatrists all agree the boy was insane—same as in the case you lost over twenty years ago!"

CHAPTER 11

The phone rang and it was Cindy, who rarely called.

"Are you okay?"

"Nick, my dog is dead," she said. I didn't know much about her dog, and quite frankly my concern was a lot less than it might normally be. In a few days, I would be starting the most difficult trial of my life and one of the most publicized cases that I had ever prosecuted. There would be reporters from throughout the country storming the courthouse property every day of the trial, and mental health professionals demanding a reform in the criminal justice system to prevent an individual from standing trial when all expert witnesses have concluded that the defendant is of unsound mind or insane at the time of the crime.

"Nick!"

"Sorry, I guess I'm shocked and don't know what to say." What was she telling me for? Did I look like a vet? It was one of those rare small dogs. "Had she been ill?" I asked.

"He, Nick, a male dog!" she screamed at me.

"Maybe she—I mean he—ate some bad stuff outside."

"He wasn't an outside dog, Nick. You're not much help," she sobbed and hung up.

Didn't she realize I had a slight problem now? An understatement to be sure. I was still confused and disappointed about the court appointed psychiatric conclusions. I had promptly read the reports while Cindy sat in my office. After reading them I crumpled them in disgust and threw them against the window. I knew Drs. Catlin and Rice. Catlin had once described Hitler as only having a personality disorder with inappropriate behavior. Neither ever believed anyone to be insane. Why would they start now? What in Matthew Cantrell had caused them to believe that he was insane at the time of the crime? The next morning I called Mr. Kurtz and told him about the reports. He let loose with a barrage of profanity and proclaimed that the psychiatrists had to be incompetent. I couldn't help but wonder whether with his resources and determination he would try to come up with something to assist in our prosecution. Dragging my mind back to the present, I knew I had to call Cindy back right away and ask for more details about her dog.

"Where was the dog yesterday and the day before?" I asked.

"Here."

"Who was home?"

"No one."

"Anything else out of place or unusual in or about your house?"

"No." I could hear her crying and breathing shallowly.

"Are you interested in taking the dog to a vet and having an autopsy performed?"

"I can't think now, Nick, goodbye."

I asked for a few more details, expressed my sorrow again and told her to take the day off.

I arrived at the office late in the morning. Cindy was gone and evidently had taken my advice to take the day off. I dialed Anne who promptly arrived.

"First, I meant to tell you a little while ago, congratulations on winning that murder trial against the Penguin. I knew you could do it." She looked as uncomfortable as a deer being chased by a pack of wolves. Anne may have been apprehensive, thinking that I had another research assignment for her. If she thought that, she was correct.

"Your advice helped," she said.

I liked to think it did. I had a few simple, worthless theories about winning and losing trials. These theories assumed as usual, that the evidence favors the state more than the defense. I then assigned to the three participants, judge, defense lawyer and prosecutor different degrees of intelligence or experience. If all three are experienced or intelligent, prosecution wins more often than not. If all three are inexperienced, the prosecution usually loses. Where there is an experienced defense lawyer and inexperienced judge and prosecutor, defense wins. Ian's trial had been in this last category. With an experienced prosecutor, but an inexperienced defense lawyer and judge, prosecution usually wins. Lastly, where there is an experienced defense lawyer and an average, credible prosecutor, but an inexperienced or incompetent judge, the prosecution wins more often than not. Anne's trial typified the last scenario.

"Anne, we need to find out about supreme court insanity cases in this state where all expert witnesses were unanimous in finding the defendant insane at the time of the crime." She looked away and then back to me.

"Sure, Nick," she said obligingly.

"There shouldn't be much more research, Anne. I appreciate it."

"I'll get on it, Nick."

"If I may Anne, how's married life?" I asked, trying to get to know her a little better and take her mind off the trial.

"Fine."

"I bet he thinks you're working too much and that I'm asking you to do a lot."

With her eyes barely opened, Anne looked like she could use about fifteen hours of sleep. She didn't have to answer me. I knew what I said was true because I had gone through it, and Mary had had a tough time adjusting.

"He doesn't understand, Nick."

"Maybe he does and the problem is just us and this type of work we've chosen. Well, you better go, Anne." She nodded and attempted a smile but failed and left.

I needed to go back to the jail to discuss a few things with Butch. Forty five minutes later we were face to face.

"Hey, big guy," I said.

"Yeah."

"I know this isn't pleasant."

"You know?" he looked at me doubtfully. "When did you last spend time in the joint?" I chose not to get into that kind of discussion with him and took out a copy of his confession to Joe.

"Butch, I like my witnesses prepared not for just what I'm going to ask them, but more importantly, for what the defense lawyer is going to ask them. I want to go over some significant points with you. If any of these are not true, let me know:

  1) Matt planned the robbery and killing.
  2) Matt drove to the property.
  3) Matt brought Kurtz out to the crater area.
  4) Matt struck the blows that killed Kurtz.
  5) Matt was high but he knew what he was doing."
I looked closely at his eyes, lips, hands and head movement in an effort to gauge his credibility.

"That last one," Butch said, hesitating a little and crinkling his face, "Matt was pretty screwed up."

"But he knew what he was doing, didn't he? He was able to talk and walk. He planned the digging of the post hole in the crater area during the previous summer when the ground was soft. He had the idea about driving to a very distant hardware store to buy fasteners and the wood to make the cross to place into the PVC pipe. It was he who planned to beat Kurtz to death with a pipe, right? It was he who power washed the pipe, clothes, truck and got rid of all that stuff, right?" I wasn't giving him a chance to answer, but I was getting a little concerned because Butch's face looked ashen and wet from sweating, and an appearance unlike any of my previous visits with him. I was leading him, but I wanted to emphasize certain points that were important to the case.

"Yes."

"Yes, what?"

"Yes, to everything you asked and said."

"Butch, I've got to tell you that Attorney Rose is going to hammer you about the plea agreement."

Butch's mouth opened, his eyes widened, and he tilted back in his chair, shaking his head. Shock and disappointment etched his face. "My lawyer says he can't do a damn thing about that agreement."

"Well, he can do nothing and yet a lot." Butch's raised eyebrows and questioning eyes begged for some explanation.

"What the hell you saying?"

"True, he can't do anything about the plea agreement. What I'm saying is that he can try to make you look like you would say anything—even lie—to get a good deal. You're my witness so I will bring all that out when I'm questioning you. This way we steal some of the thunder away from him and make it look like we're not hiding anything. I just wanted to tell you to expect considerable grilling about the plea. He will want to show the jury how unfair it is that you got a good deal and Cantrell didn't. That's my problem and I'll handle that." I didn't want to tell Butch that I wasn't quite sure how I was going to handle it.

"Another troublesome area will be the motive for the killing. Why don't you tell me about the real reason Kurtz was killed?"

"Money, what else?"

"I wasn't there and you were." I kept pressing him. "Butch, I think I know why the store owner or farmer as he liked to be called was killed. Rose is going to rip into you on this one."

"Hey, people rob and kill all the time."

"Not when they already have money."

"What money?"

"You guys already had some money, albeit not much, but enough for occasional booze and drugs. The point is this. It plays into his defense. It's not normal to kill somebody for nothing. That will be one of his arguments." He nodded and I assumed he understood what I was saying. I then told him that both Rose and I would question him a lot about Matt's mental situation, particularly factors indicative of insanity or severe mental illness. There would be questions like, how did Matt usually appear? What irrational stuff would he say on occasion? What if anything unusual did he say or do? How did he interact with people? Any bizarre or unusual behavior? How was his concentration, memory? Did he make appropriate responses when asked something? How was he acting immediately before and after the killing? I was getting ready to leave.

"You left something out, Butch. Want to tell me about it?" He looked away from me and remained silent. I waited and a minute or two passed. After drawing a long breath he finally asked, "When are you coming back?"

"The day before you testify." He nodded. I left wondering how much more I could get out of him. I didn't know for sure he had left something out, but I suspected he was hiding something important. In any event, I often tell important witnesses that I believe they're leaving something out, but it was only a tactic to try to get them to disclose something I may not know. The witness stand was not the place for surprises.

I returned to my office to find a note that Angela had called. I had already emailed her to tell her boss thanks for the report about Mr. Cantrell's background, DeVechio and other information. I chose email because I didn't want to see her or talk to her, but it looked like I was going to have to call her.

"I was just getting ready to call you," I said, hoping I sounded truthful.

"Sure you were," she said doubtfully.

"Really. What's up?"

"There's something I need to tell you, and I'm making one of your favorite dishes, linguini with calamari. Can you come over tonight at six?"

"I should mention that I don't feel like talking too much," I said, which was true because I'd been talking a lot every day to witnesses and a few press people. My voice needed a break. I didn't know how to tell her, but I needed a break from her—a long break, a permanent break. Other than the trial, my thoughts were about Cindy.

"See you at six," she said, but now sounding a little less cheerful. Perhaps my disclosure about not wanting to talk much bothered her. While I was talking to Angela, a voice mail had arrived. It was from Joe telling me to stay in the office because he was coming right over. A few minutes later the jingling of coins announced his closeness. I yelled out to him to come in. He walked in, chest heaving, mouth open searching for air, face white and showing concern.

"Stop jingling the change, Joe." The repetitive movement of his right hand in the right pocket made it look like he had some kind of tremor, neurological disease or Parkinson's. He took a seat and wasted no time in talking.

"Angela's husband was killed in a hunting accident a couple of years ago in South Dakota," he said quickly.

"So you couldn't resist trying to find out something about her past? Don't you have enough to do with this trial and your daughter getting married? I already know about the death of her husband from a hunting accident, Joe. She told me that when we first met."

He shook his head. "But did she tell you she was the one who killed him?"

CHAPTER 12

I called Angela to tell her I would be a little late for dinner. Joe's disclosure halted my breath, but I felt there had to be an explanation. If she killed her husband why was she not in custody in South Dakota? It had to have been an accident or something; yet, if so, why didn't she tell me. Needing more information than Joe gave me and wanting it fast, I placed a call to South Dakota and to Randy.

After making a stop at a liquor store that claimed to have many foreign wines, I bought a bottle of retsina or Greek wine for dinner. At 6:45 p.m., I arrived at Angela's place. She opened the door with a big smile, tugging at a mint green blouse to make a last second adjustment.

"Busy working on the case?" she asked with an enthusiastic smile.

"I had to check up on something."

"Everything all right?"

"I'm not sure."

"You look serious. No smiles for me?" she asked.

I tried to muster a smile, but as many people have told me, I'm not good at disguising emotions—no doubt a surprise to many who believed veteran trial lawyers to be like actors.

"Well then, let's eat. I don't want the calamari to overcook. There's a salad with feta cheese, cucumbers, tomatoes and kalamata olives—a Greek salad made special for you," she said simply without expression, her tone having lost its excitement. I told her I had hoped she didn't go to too much trouble preparing the dinner. Three candles provided the only light in the dining room. From somewhere in her condo I could hear a piano concerto. We ate and didn't talk much during dinner. The calamari was excellent—not overcooked, but for what was on my mind, I might as well have been eating bologna. I knew I couldn't wait any longer to broach the subject.

"Angela, you remember once you said no one had a past in South Dakota?" Her eyes darted back and forth, uncertain about where this conversation was heading. She pushed her plate towards the center of the table, got up, blew out the candles and turned on the overhead kitchen light. My question had extinguished the romantic atmosphere as quickly as one turning off a light switch. It took awhile for her to respond, as if weighing her answer carefully. She folded her hands and placed them in her lap.

"Do you realize you hardly ever use any words of endearment when addressing me? It's either Angela or Ang," she said, staring into my eyes.

"I hadn't realized."

"And you can use leading questions with me, Nick. I'm not one of your witnesses. Yes, I have a past. I don't like to talk about it. Are you sure it's that important to know?" Her eyes, wet and about to overflow, hadn't left mine.

"Tell me a little bit about it." I'm sure she knew what I was talking about, but I couldn't bring myself to confront her with it. If she disclosed that she killed her husband, should I then act surprised, as if not expecting that answer? Maybe I was just asking a general question about her past to find out more about her. I didn't have to decide how to inquire about it. She took a long gulp of the retsina and spoke.

"Yes, I killed my husband—it was an accident while hunting. What am I supposed to say when I meet someone, 'I killed my husband—it was an accident?' That initial approach would cause suspicion and turn someone away." She looked away as if disappointed in me. Then with a piercing glare she raised her glass in a mock toast and said, "To our relationship. We all have a past, don't we Nick." It was not a question. Her lips curled into a slight, wicked smile—an informed smile. Her eyes grew large and her face darkened. Despite the overhead lighting the room grew colder. An almost sinister atmosphere enveloped the room. How much did she know or how much did her boss know? Like Eilert Kurtz, Jr., she seemed to know a lot or have the resources to find out a lot. After a few uncomfortable minutes with neither of us saying or asking anything else, I told her I was sorry and left.

I knew the killing of her husband was suspicious. It didn't make sense. She was good with weapons and hunting accidents are seldom referred to the prosecutor for serious investigation or grand jury consideration—hers was. I had called the prosecutor's office in Sioux Falls, South Dakota and was briefly told what happened in her case. A grand jury had chosen not to indict her. It is well known that grand juries generally do what the prosecutor wants them to do. Thus, if the prosecutor wants an indictment, he will present enough evidence and argument for them to indict. Angela knows how a grand jury works. When we first met she said something about grand juries being a rubber stamp for the prosecutor. An indictment is a piece of paper charging someone with a felony or misdemeanor. The only difference between a felony and misdemeanor is that in most states a felony is punishable by imprisonment for a period of time exceeding 365 days. Angela had not been indicted by the grand jury, but it helps when the accused is having an affair with the prosecutor—an affair which caused the prosecutor to be removed from office for "…inappropriate contact with an alleged defendant and conduct unbecoming an officer of the court…" In the short time preceding dinner, Randy was able to find out a lot of information for me from a newspaper in Sioux Falls. The new prosecutor had secured an indictment charging Angela with the murder of her husband. A trial followed but after four days of deliberating the jury could not reach a verdict. The judge declared a hung jury and the prosecutor chose not to retry Angela. At trial she took the witness stand and claimed the killing was accidental. It is difficult to prove intent to kill in a hunting environment. In Angela's case the prosecutor relied heavily on an insurance policy that Angela had taken out on her husband seven months before the killing in the amount of $500,000.00. At first the insurance company had refused to pay the insured amount, but after the trial and the prosecutor's statement that she would not be retried, they had no choice but to release the money to Angela.

I wanted to lash out at Joe for starting this mess, but I knew he had my best interests in mind, and I guess his detective curiosity about her past got the best of him. Then too, thoughts of what Angela knew tormented me. Was there knowledge behind that devilish smile? Could her facial expression have been benign? After all, she looked tearful. Could she be using me for some reason, as Cindy had proffered? Then too, shouldn't I accord Angela the presumption of innocence which she was entitled to— the system of justice which I had lived by for thirty years? After all, she had not been found guilty of anything. Of course, I knew that just because there was a hung jury and she was not retried, did not mean she didn't intend to kill her husband.

Was I any better than her? I had a past that only my family and a few people knew about. I'd lived a lie for years. Most people believed my time during the Viet Nam war was in the Marine Corps Judge Advocate Generals Office in Okinawa. That was true, but only after I had requested a transfer from being a sniper with the 5th Marine Regiment Sniper Platoon in Viet Nam, where I had killed more men than Angela. One day it hadn't been a man. I had killed a boy, undoubtedly a teenager. I didn't know the exact age. He was at least four hundred yards away with a rifle in his hands. According to military rules of engagement, he was fair game. I had purposely fired one shot near his feet, hoping he would seek cover near his hut or home. He had been tending some crops but had a rifle slung over his back. Instead of seeking shelter, he started to fire his rifle in a couple of different directions, unsure of my location. If I had fired more shots to get him to leave the area, it would have disclosed my location, jeopardizing my life and the life of my spotter, Joe. A spotter assists a sniper in locating targets, estimating distance, confirming kills and also shoots at the enemy. He also scans the area looking for enemy who are looking for us. I had the kid in my sights. I hesitated for a long time. Joe said to take him out quickly. He reasoned that the kid could have been responsible directly or indirectly for the deaths of other Marines killed in the area. I knew all I had to do was squeeze the trigger and he would die. I took my finger off the trigger—then I put it back on. I could hear my heart beating fast and feel sweat rolling down my face and body. My hands and trigger finger were wet. I took my eye off the scope. Joe nudged me hard in the ribs. I focused again on the kid and squeezed the trigger. He collapsed immediately. From nearby, a woman ran out to him, clutched his lifeless body and stared crying into the sky. I assumed it was his mother. That image is still indelibly stamped on my brain.

I had liked to think that somehow the boy survived the shot, but it was "recorded" as a confirmed kill. When Angela looked intently at me and said we all had a past, was that what she was referring to? Could she or her boss be that good in trying to uncover such remote, obscure information? Would they have had a reason to look into my past?

I also liked to think I'd paid the price with PTSD or post traumatic stress disorder. After that incident I didn't want to be a sniper anymore and had requested transfer to another MOS or military occupational specialty. I was a college graduate and wanted to go to law school, that along with knowing the commanding officer who I had had the privilege many times to play chess with, was enough to get me transferred to the JAG office, 3rd. Marine Division, Okinawa, where I served out the remainder of my enlistment.

Strangely, I had never been gung-ho in the Marine Corps. I wasn't as big and strong like many Marines, but I had the ability to fire a rifle better than anyone. After a couple of weeks at the firing range in Marine Corps boot camp at Paris Island, South Carolina, I knew I would be headed for Viet Nam as a sniper. In wartime the Marine Corps would never have one of its expert shooters sitting behind a desk.

Several days had elapsed since that night with Angela. We hadn't talked since. Now, in the courtroom, I had to focus my attention on choosing a jury. Choosing jurors is a scary process. One wrong choice could screw up weeks or months of work. Jury selection is so important that many lawyers hire jury consultants to help select the "right" jury. The right jury is not necessarily fair or impartial. It is a jury that is partial to your case. Fairness and equity are issues for law professors and courts of appeal. In real life, you want a jury that will side with you or can be persuaded to side with your case.

I sat at the prosecution table with Anne on my left and Joe behind us in the first row of the gallery section on the right. At the defense table sat Rose with three lawyers assisting and Matthew Cantrell. Matt sat to Rose's immediate right and wore a powder blue blazer and hair cut shorter than the last time I had seen him. He seemed to sense my gaze. We looked at each other. No smile this time. The three lawyers had books and laptops in front of them. All were dressed in dark suits, white shirts and short hair. They reminded me of J. Edgar Hoover's image of how FBI agents should look. There had probably been fewer lawyers and equipment in *Roe v. Wade*, the famous abortion case. Anne and I were armed with one computer and three notepads—at least they were legal size.

"Both sides ready?" The judge asked.

"The state is ready, your honor."

"Defense is ready."

The obligatory thing to say is "you're ready" when asked by the judge whether you are prepared to proceed or not. Readiness is a relative term. No matter how much I prepared for a trial, I always felt as if I needed one more day to prepare. Yet, I knew one more day would not help either the weakness of this case or with my personal life. Intrusive thoughts of Angela and Cindy kept bombarding my brain in a blitzkrieg like fashion that denied me complete focus or attention to the case. I told myself that I had had so much experience that I should be able to do this trial despite distractions—not necessarily win, but to make a good showing.

It occurred to me that this was my first big trial while not with Mary. When we were together I didn't feel distracted with trial work. I could focus totally on the trial—but that was in the past. How could we be apart after almost thirty years together? We had gone out to dinner twice a week and had more communication I believed than most couples. She also liked the fact that I remembered important dates and occasions. Additionally, despite all the trials, I had spent considerable time with the children because of the flexibility that my job allowed, which Mary didn't have as a nurse in surgery. I did a lot of the child care when the boys were young because we had difficulty getting babysitters. I even took them to work a lot with me and sort of "hid" them in my office while the boss looked the other way. Joe had often entertained them in my office with hand tricks, card games and handcuffs.

I was going to try a different approach with the news media for this trial. I had agreed to meet with them early this morning, but after today they would have to get their information from Randy, who would be kept informed about the case and would act as a liaison. I had never seen so much press as today. A few times in the past for big trials I arrived at the back of the court building in an unmarked police vehicle so I could exit and get to my office without attention. Even though I agreed today to meet with the press at 7:00 a.m., they still attacked me like a school of piranha.

We had been outside the main entrance to the prosecutor's office. One bushy haired reporter with long side burns had asked, "Mr. Papais, you've been quoted in the past as believing in some nationally publicized insanity cases that the defendants were insane or suffered from severe mental illness at the time of the crime. Some court observers have said the same thing about Matthew Cantrell. Any comment on that?"

"No." I turned quickly away from him because that was one question I did not want to get into an extensive discussion about. I had had enough of that issue being raised by Randy and Angela.

Another one asked, "Isn't it true, Mr. Papais, that you lost a similar case to this one over twenty years ago?"

I shook my head and said, "I have no recollection of that."

Another question. "Mr. Papais, why did you give a plea agreement to Butch Roeder?"

"Listen to the testimony at trial and find out why," I said.

From the back one asked, "Mr. Prosecutor, some say you're the best this state has ever had?"

"If that's true then I apologize to the people of this state. They deserve better." Some chuckles and laughter followed.

Another asked. "How do you plan to prove that Matthew Cantrell was not insane?"

In return, I asked, "Does that assume at some point that he was insane?"

"Mr. Papais, you're known for surprises at trial," asked a reporter with an outstretched hand holding a microphone. "Can we expect any at this trial?"

"I don't believe in surprises at trial; it's all planned." A number of other questions followed and I answered them with a few half-truths. Randy stood towards the back of the mostly out of state press group. He joined me afterwards as I headed up to the courtroom. He wore the biggest grin I had ever seen.

"What are you smiling about, Randy?"

"Nick, I've never known you to be so dishonest, evasive and short with your answers."

"You know, Randy, it felt good."

"More interviews then with the press?"

"Not a chance."

I stopped my reverie and gazed at the standing room only gallery. Angela sat in the front row, center on the right side. Opposite her, but on the left side, sat Cindy. She would be in that same seat for much of the trial. I wanted her nearby during big trials for help on various issues.

The state doesn't have money for jury consultants or prefers not to spend the money. In this case the defense did not have any jury consultants. Good. I didn't want them to have any more advantage than I had. Ultimately, the choice of a juror is determined by the lawyer's experience and gut reaction. An attorney is given a limited time to decide whether to reject or retain a juror. Judges want a jury picked as quickly as possible so they can get the trial started. I looked at not only my choice of a juror, but also to prevent the defense lawyer from influencing, "prepping" or "conditioning" a prospective juror. It is, however, proper to educate jurors about issues in the case and to question them individually about whether they can be fair and impartial. In all criminal prosecutions there are general issues to be addressed such as the duty to follow the law or the instructions given by the judge. Other general issues include what is meant by proof beyond a reasonable doubt, the elements of the crime, and whether a juror could impose a penalty of life imprisonment. In this case there would be specific and lengthy instruction on what constitutes insanity.

On both the defense and prosecution tables were juror questionnaire forms. These forms indicated the juror's name, address, occupation, whether they had ever been the victim of a crime, whether they were related to any law enforcement people, and a few other items of general information. This information gave the attorneys a little background information about a juror and possible reasons why that juror should be retained or excluded.

Anne and I looked the forms over while the judge talked to the jury pool about what they were to experience, their civic duty and the nature of the case. For each juror, Anne and I would cast a vote—"Y" for yes and "N" for no. I would make the ultimate decision.

Non-verbal communication was also important. Did a juror smile at the prosecution table or the defense table? How did the juror respond to questioning by the defense attorney or by me? I'm not necessarily talking about their answers but clues as to their true beliefs. Unfortunately, this is even less reliable than a lie detector test, but an attorney doesn't have much else to go on. It's a highly subjective process. Nothing scientific. Where they grew up is important. What kind of neighborhood—high crime or little if any crime? I looked for small details, body language—anything that might show partiality to one side or the other. In this case I would be looking for any religious artifacts worn by any jurors because of the expected testimony by the part time pastor, Mr. Cantrell.

Equally significant is the sociability of the prospective juror. Is he or she a dominant person? Timid or persuasive? Gullible, extrovert or independent? I'm looking for who might be the jury foreman or foreperson. Who might try to control this group. Someone will be the foreman and persuasive. I want that person on my side.

The jury selection process began in the usual fashion. I started out by telling the panel some basic statements of law and soliciting some answers from them. Rose's questioning of the prospective jurors followed standard protocol. He asked them whether they had heard of the case. To no one's surprise, every single juror had heard of the case. Fine, he would reply, but he followed up with asking whether they believed everything they read in the papers. Could they keep an open mind and not form a conclusion about guilt or innocence until the end of the trial? Could they give his client the fair trial that he was entitled to?

He also asked each juror whether they had heard of me. About one-half said they had. That was followed up with a question about whether any had heard of him—to that, most replied they hadn't. His smile was even wider now. He asked whether they would hold that fact against his client, to which a few chuckled.

He then proceeded with statements and questions regarding insanity. He explained that state law allowed a defendant to plead insanity. I listened closely because I did not want him misstating the law. He told them that despite the insanity defense, I still had to prove the elements of murder and murder during the perpetration of a robbery. Further, he told them that I had to prove that his client knowingly committed this crime.

After a few other inquiries, he finished by asking each of them whether they would hold it against his client the amount of legal representation at the defense table. He told them that they should not look at this as a family's attempt to buy a favorable verdict. Of course, he got wide smiles and the assurances he sought from them.

For each of the jurors he questioned, I followed up with asking that they please not have any bias against our case because some of them had heard of me. After all, what they had heard may not have been good. Also, I asked each juror if they had any problems with the fact that I had only one lawyer at my table—I hoped that would neutralize some of the "points" he scored.

Now for the more difficult inquiries. I had to make sure each juror had no difficulty finding a teenager guilty of murder if we proved our case beyond a reasonable doubt; further, we were talking about not only a young man, but one who is alleged to have had mental illness. I inquired of each of them if they had any problem with the penalty in this case if the defendant was found guilty—that penalty being life imprisonment. As to insanity, I wanted them to understand that the burden of proof for insanity is on the defense, that I need not disprove insanity. I doubt most of them understood this, but I was gauging their respective reactions, knowing that I would have additional opportunities to make sure they understood these concepts.

I told them that I would be using an accomplice or co-defendant to testify against Matthew Cantrell. I asked them if they had any strong feelings about a co-defendant who was equally involved in the murder testifying against the defendant, but receiving a lesser sentence in exchange for his testimony. It was best to tell them about Roeder now rather than being surprised at trial when Rose hammered him about the light punishment.

We had eight jurors impaneled in three hours, among them a male steelworker fifty years of age, an unemployed middle aged construction worker, a female licensed practical nurse working at a local hospital, and an elderly, retired, female professor of Russian government in college. The other four were a female factory worker aged thirty-five with no children, a housewife with an older son still living at home, a retired male postal worker and a speech therapist. Next up was a woman in her sixties whose husband was a store owner. I asked no questions of her and neither did Rose, but obviously he would use one of his peremptory challenges to get rid of her. The next prospective juror was a forty-five year old divorced maintenance man for an apartment complex. I wasn't sure about him. Anne wrote a Y. I didn't know what to do. I wish I knew more about him, but my gut reaction was to strike him and that's what I did. We still had only eight jurors and I could see the Judge getting a little irritated. Next was a female barber who couldn't stop talking. Y for us but the defense removed her. According to my calculations, the defense had two challenges left. Next, a male lawyer, fifty, three children and married to a doctor. He was a stay at home dad who didn't need to practice law. I could see him being a foreman. I could also see him leaving the courtroom after the defense struck him.

One challenge left for the defense—good. I hope they get stuck with a bad juror. Next, a male photographer, widower, fifty-five. Retained. Nine impaneled. The next juror was a plumber, married, two children, age forty-seven. Retained. Ten impaneled. Next, a young unemployed man with past employment as a male rehab counselor. I didn't need to know more. He was history. We had two challenges left. The next juror asked a question about how much time is served with a life sentence and the difference between mental illness and insanity. Smart man. He disclosed his occupation as a greeter at Sam's and a retired owner of a Burger King franchise. The judge answered him. I could see the defense striking him. We voted unanimously to keep him. Surprisingly, the defense did not remove him. Eleven now seated. The next juror asked to be excused because she had a sick mother to take care of. We allowed her to go. The next juror had experience as a carpenter for the park department. Information disclosed a single, fifty-seven year old man. A lot of discussion went on at the defense table about this possible juror. To get rid of him would leave them with no more challenges. They would then have to resort to challenges for cause which are not easy to get a judge to accept. He was retained and we had twelve jurors seated. We then picked three alternate jurors in quick fashion. The judge declared an end to the day with opening statements to begin tomorrow at 8:00 a.m.

In the gallery sat Eilert Kurtz, Jr. I pulled him aside and took him into one of the attorney conference rooms. I told him that before every trial I gathered the family together to tell them that I would not be talking much to them during the course of the trial. I explained that a trial is stressful and I couldn't talk about every little thing that developed in the trial or how the case was progressing. What little time I had during a trial is needed for thinking, conferring with witnesses, colleagues, research and rest. I told him I felt good about the jury, but the case was weak because of all the expert witnesses who would testify that Cantrell was insane at the time of the crime, plus minimal physical evidence.

Later in the office in the early evening, Joe and I discussed the jury.

"Any ideas about the foreman?" Joe asked.

"None."

"Sure you do. Why do you play this game with me?" he asked, rapidly jingling coins in his right pocket.

"Who do you think will be the foreman, Joe?"

"The Sam's greeter," Joe said and looked to me for confirmation.

"He's personable and seems smart, but I don't think it will be him."

"Who then? The photographer?"

"My bet is the retired Russian history teacher."

"How do you figure?" he asked, looking surprised.

"She will have the greatest recollection of the facts in the case. History teachers are used to retaining and recalling facts."

"Do we want that with the little evidence we have?"

"We want her not so much for the evidence but for her knowledge of Russian government, the courts and..."

"But, this is the U. S. of A, boss," he said, interrupting me with a puzzled look.

"The Russian government was not tolerant of dissidents, criminals and fair trials," I said.

"That's in the past and she's an American."

"True, but her life and career was spent teaching about Russian government and that government is still not tolerant of those who commit crimes against the state—and the state is the government. Most people would prefer the hard line that Russia took and still takes on crime, even after the breakup of the Soviet Union in 1991."

He shook his head, unconvinced of my explanation. I realized I had something else on my mind, but couldn't remember what, until now.

"Joe, my gun is missing."

CHAPTER 13

I've started every trial for the last five years wearing a black suit with light gray pin stripes and a flashy red tie of some kind. Today's tie was a spicy red one with wavy lines and different shades of red. The attire would be too conservative for Tim Rogers, the Pink Penguin, but more liberal than most attorneys would wear. Conventional wisdom dictated that an attorney should look professional, but not so flashy as to have the jury distracted. After all, an unmindful jury is not paying attention to your arguments or your evidence. I chose not to follow that advice.

To minimize my thinking in the morning, I would lay my clothes out the night before, along with my weekday breakfast of oatmeal and a measuring cup filled with the right amount of water for the microwave.

As I ate my breakfast, Joe played the piano. "Come and join me, Joe," I yelled out. When I was married I often bemoaned not having any privacy. It appeared that I still didn't have any as Joe had let himself into my place long before my alarm was set to go off. He stopped playing and joined me in the kitchen. Joe's wardrobe consisted of three sports coats, three pairs of pants and one pair of shoes. He had never owned a suit. Yesterday, he wore the herringbone sports coat and today a light blue sport coat. He never had to do anything with his hair since it was cut short, Marine Corps style.

"Where's my gun, Joe?"

"I don't know," he said, "but, I'll look into it."

"Thanks, and I don't really want to talk anymore while I eat my breakfast. I've got to save my voice for the jury."

"Just one thing—the history teacher?" Joe asked, ignoring my command, and as if our conversation from yesterday evening hadn't ended.

"It's just a hunch, Joe. She's educated, spoke unhesitatingly and didn't seem impressed by Rose. She probably has some familiarity with courts. I'm sure she reads the newspapers and formed an early opinion about the case. She lives in a fairly high crime area and is probably fed up with crime. My only concern is how she will value the psychiatric testimony."

"What about Roeder? She's sure not going to like him."

"No one is going to like him, but at least he will be credible." I looked away from him and started to eat my breakfast in the hope of signaling an end to the conversation. It worked. He grabbed the morning paper and began to work the crossword puzzle.

We left my place and Joe drove us to the back entrance of the courthouse. Though gray clouds blanketed the sky making it look almost like early evening, they did nothing to suppress the early July heat. I liked it hot, but not while I was dressed in a suit and in a vehicle with a malfunctioning air conditioner. Bothered by dry eyes for years, I kept my eyes closed because I knew they would take a beating with the bright, overhead lighting and air conditioning in the courtroom.

I situated myself at the left end of the prosecutor's table by the lectern with Anne on my right and Joe a few feet behind us in the first row of the gallery. I could see Kurtz seated in the row closest to the big courtroom entrance doors.

I glanced over to the defense table. From right to left nearest the lectern were Howard Rose, Matthew Cantrell, two lawyers and a paralegal. Rose always wore a three piece suit to enable his Phi Beta Kappa key to be looped through a vest button hole. His face displayed his charming persona and a reassuring demeanor that made people around him feel comfortable. Though I was comfortable in court after many years, knowing that a victim's family was just a few feet away observing me constantly had always made me conscious about how I appeared. A smiling demeanor or look was not what I believed they wanted to see in their prosecutor.

Cantrell wore a brown sports coat that looked as if it had been borrowed from a friend much bigger than himself. It gave him the appearance of having broad shoulders and short arms. He had a pen and notebook in front of him. I didn't expect him to say much, write much or do much. He looked like any other eighteen year old except that his attire was unlike youths of that age. His appearance gave no indication that he had masterfully and brutally murdered a man; however, in all my years of prosecuting, most murderers looked "innocent." On the national scene, even Jeffrey Dahmer, dressed up next to his attorney, looked as normal as anyone; yet, he was a serial killer, a cannibal. Ted Bundy? He certainly looked normal. Charles Manson was an exception. He looked evil and sinister with his appearance never changing.

It was time for opening statements. I didn't particularly care for them because they were risky and akin to political promises. If you win the election the voters remember what you promised them, especially if it's a tax increase. By analogy, you can't promise in the opening what you can't deliver; otherwise, the other side will remind the jury in closing argument that you did not produce this evidence or this witness.

The prosecution goes first, followed by the defense. I started out by telling the jury what the charges were and the elements that we had to prove. With only a brief outline in hand and looking from juror to juror, I started my presentation.

"...the defendant Matthew L. Cantrell is charged in a two count indictment with murder and murder during the perpetration of a robbery. The prosecution must prove that the defendant killed

Eilert Kurtz on or about…" I went on to explain that in any murder case the state must prove that the victim died an unnatural death—that he was killed by unnatural means. I told them that this would be proved by our first witness, pathologist Dr. Loh. Not much can be done to prepare a jury for the shock of gruesome photographs and frank testimony of witnesses about a horrible killing. They've read about true crime, heard about it, but they have never been held captive in a room with no way to escape the aural and visual effects of a slaughter. At home an individual can choose not to read a newspaper account of a murder or turn a different channel on the television. In the jury box there is no choice or election. You're fixed to the seat as if strapped down by restraints. Jurors will hear more than they want to hear. It is punitive. They will squirm in their seats and clench their teeth and jaws. They will glare at the defendant. Some will pray that the photographs and testimony be over with quickly, as if they were in a dentist chair praying that the drilling or root canal work be concluded with deliberate speed.

As I talked briefly about the killing, I would look at the jurors. I looked at them individually, but hopefully without them knowing that I was studying them. You never want to make them feel uncomfortable or a target. They feel more comfortable as a group than singled out for scrutiny. I study them a little to gauge their reaction and to see if they find me credible. I have always believed that the attorney is also a witness. His or her credibility is also being judged even though that attorney does not take an oath and is not subject to cross examination.

I'm a pacer, so I don't stay fixed at the podium as do most attorneys. This allows me to move about—hopefully not so much as to be distracting—and give the appearance of talking freely and thoughtfully about the crime rather than glued to a stand and reading from notes.

I explained to them that every crime has what are known as "elements," and that each of these elements must be proven beyond a reasonable doubt. The judge would explain to them what constitutes a "reasonable doubt." The killing must be proven to be intentional. Intent is an element, I told them. For the second count, I explained that not only must an intentional murder be proven, but that it occurred during the perpetration of a robbery, or what is known as felony murder. Rather than just murder alone as was one of the counts, the other count charged the defendant with killing while also robbing the victim. Thus, there is the murder plus a felony. Robbery is the taking of something of value from the victim. In this case it was the taking of $322.00. The felony doesn't have to be robbery. It can also be rape, burglary, whatever. Generally, the penalty is more severe for the conviction of a murder while committing another felony. The rationale behind the harsher punishment is that it is one thing to rob or rape a woman, but to also kill her deserves the state's greatest retribution. I could see Rose writing something on a pad. My guess was that it related to the robbery as a motive. Stillness enveloped the courtroom. Cantrell sat with his hands clasped together on his legal pad looking mostly in the direction of the judge.

"This killing was not done alone." I waited a few seconds and knew that I had their attention by their wide opened eyes and the forward posture of many of them.

"With the defendant was his best friend, Butch Roeder. The evidence will show that the defendant planned the killing. Roeder was also involved in the murder and our office chose to use Butch Roeder as a state's witness to make a good case even stronger." It was difficult to say that, knowing that the case was not particularly good, and without Roeder, we basically had nothing. I objected early in the case to giving Roeder a plea agreement, but with the advantage of 20/20 hindsight it proved necessary. Further, I had assumed that by the time of the trial, we would have gotten significant physical evidence linking the boys to the killing, but that didn't happen.

In my slow tour walking away from the lectern and speaking to the jury, I could see Eilert Kurtz, Jr. in the audience, seated next to his uncle, William Kurtz. Wearing a double-breasted black suit, Eilert Jr., had his hands in front of his face in a contemplative fashion.

Back at the lectern, I explained to the jury that the defense had chosen to interpose the defense of insanity. In other words, I told them, pleading not guilty by reason of insanity. Nevertheless, I said, the burden of proof for the insanity defense was on them and not the state.

"We must prove the murder, including the element of knowingly killing Mr. Kurtz. We do not need to disprove insanity. As you have heard and will learn more throughout the trial, a person is not guilty of an offense if he has a mental disease or defect, and as a result is unable to appreciate the wrongfulness of the conduct at the time of the offense."

Yesterday and today was a lot for them to absorb. I drew a deep breath and continued.

"You will hear testimony from what are called expert witnesses. An expert witness is one who can give an opinion about a matter to aid the jury in understanding something difficult. I believe the defense will call two expert witnesses from the mental health profession. We do not plan to call any expert psychiatric witnesses." I reasoned that we might as well let them know now so as not to speculate in the jury room. Prosecutors know it's best to bring out weak points in advance and not let the defense do it by surprising an unsuspecting jury.

I drank a little water and continued. "I should say there are basically two types of witnesses in a trial, lay and expert. Lay witnesses are not testifying as to any opinions or complicated matters. Interestingly, in this state and probably most states, a lay witness, that is you or I or Mr. Rose, can testify as to a person's sanity or mental health. That's right, as a general rule, you can testify as to your neighbor's mental health." I usually don't bring humor into trials or opening statements, but I sensed many in the courtroom to be a little tense, and the comments helped ease that tension by provoking a few limited, restrained laughs.

"Though we are not calling any expert psychiatric witnesses, we usually don't…"

"Objection your honor, that's improper, inappropriate and I move that be stricken from the record and counsel admonished to refrain from making such comments. Further, the defense moves for a mistrial." Rose got to his feet to make the objection. His glasses were half way down his nose as he peered over them at me.

"Your honor, I never got a chance to complete what I wanted to say."

Judge Conlon quickly replied, "motion for mistrial denied, comment stricken from the record, jury is to disregard the remark."

"What remark your honor? The objection was premature."

"Proceed, Mr. Papais." I think the jury knew I wanted to say that we never call expert psychiatric witnesses in insanity cases. On some rare occasions we have, but I didn't want the jury wondering why we weren't calling any such witnesses. I explained to them that the court had appointed two mental health professionals as required by law to examine the defendant. Calling up all the courage I could summon, I told them that the court appointed psychiatrist and psychologist would testify that the defendant was insane at the time of the crime. I didn't know whether any of them had done the math or not, but it would soon be obvious that with the two defense experts undoubtedly testifying as to insanity, and the court's witnesses testifying as to insanity, that all four expert witnesses would be unanimous in their conclusions of insanity. I tried to look as confidant and convincing as possible despite what I had just said—and despite what I would be asking them to do at the end of the trial.

I looked over at Anne to see any reaction as to how I was doing. No help there. She looked as stoic and expressionless as Cantrell. The jury seemed attentive and at this early stage that was what mattered. Though I tried to look at every juror, I concentrated a lot on who I believed would be the vocal ones, the possible foremen.

I briefly related the day of the killing and told them that they would hear more about it later. There would be a lot of testimony, I explained, from both sides as to the sanity and insanity of Matthew Cantrell.

"Members of the jury…" I leaned forward onto the podium and spoke in a softer, slower tone, "Listen carefully. Matthew Cantrell probably has some type or types of mental illness." I hesitated before continuing. "I will make Mr. Rose's job easier and concede that Matthew Cantrell had and still has some form or forms of mental illness, depression, perhaps anxiety or post traumatic stress disorder and a history of drug abuse. There will be witnesses who will say that he has mental illness. As I mentioned when we picked you as jurors, mental illness does not necessarily equate with insanity." I explained to them that I would not quarrel with any witness who says the defendant has mental illness, though I may question them extensively, but only as it relates to the legal definition of insanity in this state.

Speaking even a little slower, but more loudly, I said, "We must keep these two concepts separate: Mental illness and insanity at the time of the crime. Ladies and gentlemen of the jury, that sentence is the crux of this case." I backed away from the podium or lectern and walked back to the prosecution table behind Anne.

I told the jury that I knew they had an awesome responsibility, but I trusted that they had not left their common sense at the courtroom door.

"After all the evidence is presented, you will come to the conclusion that Matthew Cantrell knew what he was doing on that cold December day. He knowingly, let me repeat that, knowingly, brutally and savagely killed Eilert Kurtz, a retired store owner. A man who was deceived by the defendant to go out with him in the cold and help him start a truck which did not need to be fixed, a good samaritan if you will. That act of kindness cost him his life. Thank you." Anne nodded in agreement and managed to muster a smile. Joe looked at me and winked his left eye.

Judge Conlon nodded for Rose to begin his opening statement. Rose had trouble standing vertical. I suspected a back problem because he leaned or listed to the right about fifteen degrees or so. If he was a ship he would be taking on water. I didn't mind him fondling his vest key, but his glasses two thirds the way down his nose annoyed me. I felt like taking a wooden display pointer and pushing the glasses to the top of his nose. Perhaps I thought, I should not look into his eyes but at the middle or lower part of his nose.

With a smile fashioned by years of experience, Rose told the jury that yes, his client had mental illness, but that I had not gone far enough in explaining the severity of his illness. His client's illness was so severe he said that young Matthew was still a sick boy. He was ill and consumed with an uncontrollable, explosive rage. As a result of his illness, Rose said, with his left hand in his pocket and the right hand resting on top of the podium, he could not distinguish right from wrong or appreciate the wrongfulness of his actions.

"I'm now going to return the favor to the prosecutor. I will save him some time. How? Simple." He looked at me and gestured with his right hand as if bestowing a gift upon me. "We admit to the killing."

Big deal, I thought. I knew I could prove the killing despite any challenges or objections. He said that in part to look like a good guy in front of the jury, to let them see that he sought justice and did not care to waste their time. I had expected as much from him.

"Mr. Papais talked about the killing and robbery. I'm going to tell you something that he didn't." Like a masterful politician, he raised his right hand in a lightly clenched fist with the thumb raised upwards, and shaking the hand towards the jury, said, "Robbery wasn't the motive." I could sense the jury looking at me. In these situations, an opposing trial lawyer doesn't do much. I kept my head up and nonchalantly scanned the courtroom. Damage control would happen later. I knew at the end of the trial that I would have to address the motive issue. Did Roeder even know the motive? Had there been a motive?

Rose continued, "Oh, to be sure, money was taken, but Matthew and Roeder did not kill for money. Let Mr. Papais tell you why Kurtz was killed. Does the state know? I would hope so. After all, they're using their best prosecutor—a hatchet man used mainly for difficult or highly publicized cases—to put this sick boy in prison. Make no mistake, I have a lot of respect for Mr. Papais. In my opinion, he has been the best prosecutor this grateful state has ever had. It is a pleasure to be in the same courtroom with him."

Anne softly whispered, "Wow, I didn't know you were that good."

"I'm not. He could make a guilty, condemned man facing a firing squad feel good about himself. Rose was creating a rapport with the jury and doing it all with minimal effort."

He went on. "Yes, it was brutal. That's one thing Mr. Papais was correct about. My compassion and sympathy goes out to the Kurtz family." He nodded his head as if in understanding and turned around to look at Eilert Kurtz, Jr. and William Kurtz. Like former President Clinton, he might as well have said, "I feel your pain."

He continued. "Ladies and gentlemen of the jury, I'm really bothered by the absence of justice and fairness in this case. I believe all of you will be similarly troubled." He went on to say that Butch Roeder would only serve a brief time in prison and that he wasn't even sick or mentally ill. If the state had all that evidence, he asked, why did it need to offer a good deal to an accomplice?

"As Mr. Papais would say, let's keep in mind common sense." Rose went on to describe Matthew's childhood, school life, upbringing, illness and insanity. I knew he was about finished. A few minutes later he thanked the jury and took his seat.

Judge Conlon read to the jury what's called preliminary instructions. These are basic legal concepts for the jury to keep in mind throughout the trial. At the conclusion of the trial, he would then read to the jury their final instructions.

Judge Conlon declared a recess until 8: 30 a.m. the next day. Joe, Anne, and I went back to my office via the back exit of the courtroom. When we got to the office, Randy was already there with a small purple spiral notebook. A couple of minutes later Cindy joined us. In addition to her usual duties, I used Cindy as a coordinator and communications center between the office, witnesses and the courtroom throughout the trial. Occasionally, witnesses may be delayed or called to the witness stand earlier or later than planned. Additionally, she would act quickly on unforeseen developments that can occur during a lengthy trial. I stood by the window looking out with my back to everyone.

Randy asked me what I thought of Rose's opening statement and second about his complimentary comments about me. Turning back towards everyone, I could see his hair still showed a crease circling his head, revealing where his hat had been firmly pressed earlier in the day.

"His opening was good and what I expected. As regards his comment about me? Let's see what he says during closing argument. I strongly suspect it will not be as complimentary. And, Randy, continue to keep the press informed but away from me. Got it?"

"At some time you'll need to talk to them, Nick."

"When the trial is over…maybe."

I glanced towards Cindy and asked, "What did you find out about the death of your dog?"

"I didn't do anything. We buried him in the backyard."

It had been awhile since I had seen a smile or glow on Cindy's face. "Anne, what have you got for me with regards to your research on cases where all mental health professionals say the defendant was insane at the time of the crime?"

"I'll tell you later."

"There is no later, Anne." Anne worked hard, but she didn't appreciate the difficulty of prosecuting tough cases and the need for quick legal information. Her prior job with legal aid had not prepared her for the thoroughness of trial work. She probably would still have been working for legal aid had they not released her after nine months due to financial cutbacks. I think this was the first time I had noticed some gray in her dense brown hair—at least it was combed. Like Joe, Anne's wardrobe reflected a low budget priority and minimal consideration for fashion. Today was the first time, I believe, that Anne wore a skirt, a black one with thin gray pin stripes. It just occurred to me that we were both wearing similar colors. I knew the office had to be making comments about our uniform attire.

"There are only a few cases on this issue, Nick," Anne said, sounding a little timid. "Generally, the appellate courts have not overturned a jury's verdict disregarding unanimous psychiatric opinion. There have been dissents, though."

"I don't care about dissenting opinions from a minority of appellate court judges. Thanks, Anne. What about our witness list, Cindy?"

"Tomorrow's witnesses are already lined up, as you know. There's nothing out of the ordinary. I placed on both your and Anne's desks, a tentative list of witnesses for the whole trial."

"I think our case will go quickly," I said, "everyone know why?" Anne and Cindy nodded, while Joe had a blank stare and Randy was writing something in his little notebook.

"Obviously, Rose wants our case to go quickly," I said. "Admittedly, this is no profound statement since this is true of all opposing trial attorneys. His strategy will be little questioning of most witnesses, except Roeder. He will want the jury to quickly forget about my case. He will want the jury to see him as a pleasant guy who is not here to obstruct or delay things." I explained to everyone that Rose knows that I could get into evidence pretty much anything I wanted. Thus, there was no reason to be confrontational, except for half hearted objections for protection of the record on appeal should Cantrell be found guilty. Further, I said Rose knew that this case was going to be decided by six or seven witnesses and I only had one of them, Roeder. He had at least three of them: Cantrell's father, a psychiatrist and psychologist. The judge had the other two.

"Any questions?" No response. "Joe make sure your shoes are clean tomorrow. You may have to use a chisel to scrape some of that dirt off." He turned his head away from me, but I knew he would have them clean for tomorrow. "Anne, we will need to see Roeder soon." Randy had a puzzled look. "What's wrong with you, Randy?"

"Certainly there are other witnesses who have important testimony other than the six or so you mention?"

"True, school teachers, jail guards and the like, but every case, as you know, has its star witnesses. I have one star witness." Without looking at him, I could see Joe shift in his chair and disappointment etched on his face. "Of course, Joe is important for getting into evidence Cantrell's confession and his observations of Matt's sanity." I figured that should appease Joe.

We then briefly talked about each of our witnesses. Looking outside I could see that the gray clouds of this morning were darkening. Perhaps a storm coming or maybe it was later than I thought. A glance at my watch confirmed the latter. I had been standing and pacing for a few hours. I told everyone to go home, but asked Cindy to stay for a little.

"What's wrong, Nick?"

"Does it show that much?"

"Yes," she said, then started to laugh.

"What's so funny?"

"Some in the office are talking about you and Anne dressed in the same colors today."

"Yes, and to give you an idea how preoccupied I am with this case, I didn't even realize that until we got back here to the office. You don't think she knows that I wear the same suit at the beginning of each trial, do you? And what's with wearing a skirt, too?"

"All for you, Nick," she jokingly said.

"Oh, that's real funny," I paused, "and I want to say again how badly I feel about the death of your dog."

"Thanks, Nick. And, Joe tells me your gun is missing?"

"I've been so busy, I must have misplaced it somewhere."

"Nick, we may have another problem developing. One of the jail guards, I can't remember his name, but he says Roeder is starting to look ill.

CHAPTER 14

Like yesterday, Joe parked behind the courthouse to allow us to enter unmolested by the press. Unlike yesterday, the overnight rain caused it to be more humid. Though early in the morning, I knew today's temperature and humidity would exceed yesterday's by a few degrees and percent, respectively. At lunchtime yesterday, I had briefly walked out of the courthouse and could see the heat on the rooftops of homes and the asphalt roads in the form of an unfocused blurriness. This morning the heat and humidity altered the way people walked to the courthouse from the parking lot. They either walked slowly so as not to perspire or fast to seek the comfort of the building's central air conditioning. Many people pulled and tucked at their clothing to separate it from their wet skin. With no clouds in the sky, some had their heads down to avoid the sun's punitive glare and brightness.

We proceeded to the courtroom without first going to my office. My leather, zippered portfolio that my mother had bought me after I started work at the prosecutor's office contained all that I needed. Though it no longer zipped closed and its handles had withered, I still used it to carry my notes, legal pad, black and red pens.

It didn't take long for the courtroom to reach capacity. It would be standing room only for the remainder of the trial. Criminal trials are open to the public, so the courtroom held not only the relatives of the deceased and the defendant, but the press, friends, courthouse employees taking few minute breaks from their jobs, fellow prosecutors and the public. Though noisy now with people talking, standing and looking for seats, when the judge entered, quiet would follow like a conductor raising his baton to the orchestra. Joe took his seat up front in the gallery where he would remain for the rest of the trial, and I proceeded to my usual spot next to Anne who had arrived earlier. My gaze at trials usually focused on my table, the jury and the witness chair, seldom did I look left at those in attendance, but a cursory glance revealed Cindy, Randy, fellow prosecutors, members of the press and Angela. In an all gray double-breasted suit sat Eilert Jr., in the same seat that he occupied yesterday.

As the judge entered, we all rose. Anne sat next to me and whispered something that I couldn't understand. Her eyes fluttered rapidly and I sensed that she was nervous about something, perhaps the later visit to see Roeder in jail and my newest request that she do the questioning and prepping of him in jail. She had never been to the jail nor had she ever had to prepare an accomplice for trial. I wanted to touch her hand to soothe her, but I was afraid someone might see that and get a wrong impression. I caught Angela looking at me with a wide smile which contrasted Cindy's glum look. I had no doubt that Angela was the most puzzling, bewildering woman I had ever met. Her emotions and facial expressions could change in a second.

Shortly after the judge called the court to order, he told me to call my first witness.

"The state calls Dr. Loh, your honor." Many of our pathologists are not American born and do not speak English well. It is for that reason that I try to keep their testimony to a minimum; however, I wanted Dr. Loh to graphically detail Kurtz's autopsy findings to not only establish an element of the offense—that the victim did not die a natural death—but also to inflame the jury with the brutality of the killing, to stir in them a rage and desire for punishment. Unfortunately for prosecutors, most pathologists testify with as much enthusiasm as an urologist telling his male patient to assume the position for a prostate exam. Dr. Loh was no exception. He spoke matter of factly about the numerous broken bones to the face, skull and neck area. He could have been describing the furniture in the courtroom. Cause of death, he said, followed from extensive trauma to the brain and lacerations of numerous blood vessels. He could not identify what instrument or devices were used to inflict the trauma, but suggested a hammer, pipe and other metallic tools would not be inconsistent with such injuries. And not needing elaboration, but again to prove a homicide, the pathologist stated the injuries were not self inflicted. There was a third important reason for Dr. Loh's testimony, perhaps even more significant than the other two. His description of the injuries to the face, neck and head would corroborate Roeder's testimony of how Kurtz was killed.

I now sought to introduce into evidence photographs of Kurtz's body at the scene and on the autopsy table from the waist up. As expected, Rose objected to their introduction due to their unnecessary inflammatory nature, gruesomeness and irrelevancy. He argued with some conviction that their purpose was to prejudice the jury against his client—after all, though the state still had to prove that his client killed Mr. Kurtz, the main issue is the defendant's state of mind at the time of the killing. These objections are generally made by all defense attorneys and are usually overruled by judges, as Judge Conlon did. If photographs are unduly inflammatory, and without any relevance, the objections are sustained. It doesn't take much evidence for something to be relevant. Is it likely to prove or disprove an element in the case? Certainly the photos are likely to show that the cause of death was not natural, an element in the case. The photos would also corroborate other witnesses and evidence as to the method of the killing.

The next witness in a murder case is usually the person who identifies the body, usually a family member or close relative. This is the person who usually cries. Again, this is significant evidence for a prosecutor because it raises the ire of the jury. It provokes not only rage and punishment, but also sympathy and compassion for the family.

Obviously, all witnesses should be interviewed sometime before trial and briefed as to the questions which will be asked. My next witness demonstrated a failure to follow that simple routine. It had never happened to me before, but then I have never had a neighbor testify before as to body identification. Never. I have always had a family member or relative testify and usually there isn't much preparation work with them. Their spontaneous reaction is what the jury remembers. The problem arose because neither Kurtz's son nor brother wished to testify. Sometimes it is too emotional for some people to testify about the slaughter of a family member. So, we agreed on the store owner's next door neighbor, Mr. Schiller—not the best choice and not the best for emotional impact on a jury.

After some preliminary questions, I went up to Mr. Schiller with a photograph of his neighbor. It was one of the gruesome photos that had already been admitted into evidence through Dr. Loh.

"Mr. Schiller, I hand you what has been admitted into evidence as state's exhibit #3 and ask you to please look at this." He looked at it and then at me with no particular emotion. He and Dr. Loh could have been emotional brothers.

"Mr. Schiller, do you recognize what is marked as state's exhibit #3?"

He took a little time and said, "No."

I cursed myself for not having talked to him before the trial, but did he think I would be showing a photograph of some dead person other than his neighbor? I mean, wasn't the trial about the killing of his neighbor of many years? Of course, the face and head being so destroyed and unrecognizable, Mr. Schiller had testified truthfully. He didn't recognize his neighbor. I should have prepped him for identifying the photograph. And, of course, I made another mistake in not insisting that a family member testify.

I had no choice for what I was about to do, and I knew Rose would jump up with another objection.

"Mr. Schiller isn't that a photo of your neighbor, Mr. Kurtz?"

"Objection your honor; the prosecutor is leading the witness."

"Sustained. Next question, Mr. Papais." Hopefully, Mr. Schiller got the message now as to the identity of the person in the photo and what I needed him to say. Sometimes you have to lead a witness to get him or her to know what you want.

"Now, Mr. Schiller do you recognize state exhibit #3?"

"Yes. It is a photo of Eilert Kurtz." After only two short witnesses, I felt like I needed a break or maybe a retirement for the duration of my natural life. I hadn't smoked in more than twenty years, but I had an irresistible urge to inhale a strong cigarette or cigar, or anything that would burn.

I walked back to my table. Rose didn't need to ask any questions of Mr. Schiller. He got at least a tie out of a round with a witness that should have been mine. Joe liked to score the witnesses in my trials, as if he was scoring a boxing match or a chess match. On a score card with the two witnesses so far, it would be Papais one, Rose and Papais a draw or tie for the second witness.

"Next witness, Mr. Papais." Judge Conlon said.

"The state calls Detective Joe Matanovich, your honor." Fortunately, Joe had not only cleaned his shoes but polished them. I hadn't known polish could adhere to shoes that old. He must have taken paint to them. It was only a thirty-five foot walk to the witness stand, and though jurors may not care or notice how one was dressed, they would notice if one was unkempt, wearing soiled clothes, muddy shoes and the like. Too, they are used to watching television and seeing how smartly dressed and good looking most of the detectives are. No one would mistake Joe for any popular television detective, yet his ruggedness and sincerity befitted a real detective and not a Hollywood actor pretending to be a law enforcement officer.

After leading him through some preliminary questions, we got to the point in the investigation where he said an anonymous caller, a woman, suspected that Cantrell and Roeder could have been involved in the killing of the well known store owner. Joe had never learned the identity of the caller. Then came testimony as to the arrest of Cantrell and Roeder, as well as Roeder's short confession which we admitted into evidence over Rose's objection due to it being irrelevant and hearsay, since how can one cross examine a statement? At this point, neither of Rose's objections concerned me. As Rose well knew, I would use that confession in closing argument to corroborate Roeder somewhat, and ultimately, hopefully to show a little evidence regarding the state of mind of Cantrell—that Cantrell knowingly planned and killed Mr. Eilert Kurtz. True, it wasn't Cantrell's confession since he never gave one, but the statement along with the testimony of Roeder would have some relevancy to guilt and state of mind.

Importantly, I also had Joe detail his observations of Matthew Cantrell at the time of his arrest until his incarceration at the jail. He testified that Cantrell exhibited nothing out of the ordinary, that his appearance and behavior were not unlike that of many suspects he had arrested during his thirty year career as a homicide detective. Rose countered with how little time Joe had spent with his client, and that his main objective was to secure a confession rather than to attempt to assess any mental impairments. Joe played along and acknowledged the truth of the questions posed by Rose.

At one in the afternoon, Judge Conlon called a recess until 2:00 p.m. I noticed Cindy had left, but Angela still remained seated with the same smile she had worn earlier. I looked away knowing that I shouldn't have anything to do with her.

"Anne, let's visit our star witness and then we'll eat afterwards."

Twenty minutes later we sat before Butch Roeder in the blue room. He had a blank, distant stare that I had not seen before. I would rather have had him angry. I introduced him to Anne but he refused to acknowledge her. I could see it would be useless to have her try to question him or prep him somewhat for trial. He then looked at me with weary, unfocused eyes.

"What's wrong, man?" I asked.

"You think there's something wrong?"

"Yes, and I need your help big guy."

"I need help too," he said.

"When we leave you, I want you to immediately tell the guard you need to see a doctor." I could see that something had happened since I last saw him. Could that be fear on his face or was it a lack of concern, or worse, not even a desire to want to live. Cindy had said that a jail guard thought Roeder was becoming ill.

"Have you been eating?"

"Some sweet stuff."

"What can I do for you?"

"When do I take the stand?"

"Tomorrow," I lied, but I knew I had to get him on the stand right away.

"Didn't the trial just start today?"

"Yeah, but we're moving along fast and I thought I'd help you out by getting it over with." Again, the blank look—not at my eyes, but through them, a look of vacancy, of no one home.

"Butch, why was Kurtz killed?"

"For money."

"Sure—but, what other reason?"

"Aren't you supposed to be the great prosecutor? Figure it out."

"As I've said before, you were there. You know more than I do." I looked at my watch and knew we had to get back to court.

"Matt's mom was in the house while we wacked him." I felt every inch of my skin elevate into little bumps, a dryness in my throat, an inability to swallow and talk at the same time. I tried to convey a look of yes; of course, I knew there was something missing in this case that you had not told me before. If someone had checked my blood pressure right now, I knew I would be on the way to the hospital.

"Did she…uh…where…did she know that Kurtz was going to be killed?" I had trouble talking.

"I don't know." I looked around the small room as if its walls would give me the answers.

"So, you went to the house after the killing?"

"Yeah."

"And she was there?"

"Yeah."

"Why was she there?"

"She and Kurtz were laying pipe."

"Damn it." I got up quickly, knocking my chair over and startling Anne who drew a deep breath and tried to subtly shift her chair away from Butch and me. Her breathing became heavier and her face tightened. I couldn't help but wonder if she thought she had chosen the wrong career, and perhaps thinking what class in law school did she miss that prepares one for shocking disclosures in the middle of a trial. After all, didn't surprise disclosures only happen on television programs like Perry Mason?

"How long had this been going on?"

"Awhile, I guess."

"Why—I mean, she had severe depression, so forth."

"Sick people get it on too, you know." If Anne had been apprehensive before her first jail visit with an accomplice murderer, this certainly was going to do nothing to ease her concerns.

"Did Matt's father know about this?"

"I doubt it."

"Matt obviously knew?"

"You think?" he asked with a slight twist of his head to the right and raised eyebrows as if the answer should be obvious.

"What did Mrs. Cantrell think about Kurtz being killed?"

"Don't know." I didn't have much time to press him for explanations.

"Did she want Kurtz to be killed?" He looked at Anne, winked at her without smiling and then back to me. She immediately narrowed her eyes and fixed her gaze on Butch's face. I had no doubt that if he said or did anything else that offended her, that she would let him have it just as she had rebuked Joe in my office for calling her a word she did not find flattering.

"I think she may have suspected that Kurtz might be planning to tell her husband. You don't tell the reverend bad news. I think she knew this couldn't keep going on…somebody was bound to find out and tell Matt's old man."

"Why not kill Matt's father?" I asked.

"I don't know."

"Why didn't you tell me this stuff earlier?" I demanded to know as we got up to leave, but he said nothing and we left. I felt cold, agitated and perplexed. I fumbled for my cell phone.

"Your hands are shaking, Nick. Give me the phone. What do you want?"

"Get Cindy right away. Tell her to change the witness list with Roeder to testify shortly before lunch tomorrow. Have her also get recent cases on impeachment of witnesses." I didn't want Roeder thinking anymore. I wanted his testimony over with quickly. He could be a difficult witness—plea agreement be damned. He didn't seem to care about anything. With my hands in my pockets and looking straight ahead, I walked at a fast pace back to the courtroom with Anne trailing behind me on the cell talking to Cindy. I also believed that Roeder might be ill, very ill.

We arrived at the courtroom at 2:10 p.m. Fortunately, the judge had been delayed with an emergency request for a search warrant. Before court resumed, I told Rose that I needed to talk to him and to the judge. When the judge got back to the court, we approached the bench. I softly said to both of them that I needed to call a witness out of order.

"Unfortunately, it's my main witness," I said.

"Mr. Rose, do you have any problem with that?" the Judge asked. Rose played with his Phi Beta Kappa key and looked at the judge over his glasses, which I expected to fall off at any time.

"Well, I wasn't expecting it, but I know Mr. Papais must have a good reason for this. After all, I'm sure he wanted to end his case with the strongest witness. This helps me."

"Oh, really," I said, knowing that this further strengthened his strong case.

"No need for sarcasm, Nick," Rose said.

"Very well, let's have him ready to testify tomorrow morning," the judge said.

"I already made the arrangements your honor." Rose smiled at that and the judge wryly replied, "Yes, of course."

"Call your next witness, Mr. Papais."

"The state calls Detective Swango, your honor."

The first detective on the scene, Detective Swango testified that he and Detective Townsend responded to an emotional 911 call for help by a Mr. Eilert Kurtz, Jr and William Kurtz. After finding the body, the witness said he secured the area with police tape, took numerous photographs, and after an hour at the scene was not able to locate any weapon or any evidence other than the body, the cross and truck. Though a young detective, Swango testified in detail about his handling, labeling and securing items of possible evidence found near the body. Through Swango, I introduced photographs of Kurtz tied to the cross and even had the cross brought into court over the objection of Attorney Rose as inflammatory and irrelevant. Rose questioned detective Swango extensively about why there was no evidence linking either his client or Roeder to the scene of the crime? Why no DNA he asked. Certainly there had to be some evidence linking this crime to somebody, even if not Roeder or Cantrell. Where was the material for the cross obtained? What about fingerprints in the truck? What about the weapons? Any weapon? Certainly the questions were valid but my mind was on Roeder because my case was about to unravel if we couldn't get Roeder to testify and testify credibly. But he was sick. Why was he sick? From what Cindy had told me, no one else in the jail had taken ill. Why Roeder? I knew he was ill and my thoughts about his illness were scary. This was not a normal development.

My next witness would have been Detective Townsend, but the judge wanted to recess for the day. I wanted to keep going, perhaps to keep my mind from thinking about Roeder. I don't know if I was getting paranoid, but I had bad feelings about his health.

We were all seated at our seats the following morning at 8:15 a.m. The judge entered the courtroom at 8:25 a.m. and told me to call my next witness, detective Townsend. I wanted his testimony to end about 10:00 a.m., somewhat close to lunch time. I didn't have many questions for Detective Townsend because there wasn't much to obtain from him since little evidence existed. Rose's questions of Townsend duplicated his questions of Swango—not only was there no evidence linking his client to this murder, but Roeder as well. I knew Joe was scoring the witnesses and right now we needed some wins. If the weakness of the case wasn't apparent to a court observer earlier, it should be by now. Why even have an insanity defense? I wondered to if the Cantrell family didn't want the "best defense," but rather one that they believed was true, that Matthew Cantrell was insane at the time of the crime. In any event, right now the defense didn't need this last resort defense. This case could easily be won by a lawyer of average ability. When Rose took the case, he no doubt figured that Roeder would be a compelling witness and that there would be a plethora of physical and DNA evidence. But, right now Rose didn't know what I knew. He didn't know that Roeder was ill.

"The state calls Butch Roeder to the stand, your honor."

The judge told the jury it would probably take a few minutes to get the witness from the lockup. Arriving into the courtroom by armed jail guards, I had Butch proceed to the witness stand. He had his right hand close to his stomach as if to protect it from an assault by someone. His eyes looked worried and I could see fear in them. Gone was the unblinking, icy gaze that I recall when I first met him in the jail. Fortunately for me, no one other than Matt Cantrell knew what Butch really looked like prior to taking ill, but it didn't take a degree in medicine for anyone to ascertain that he did not appear healthy. Matt studied his friend but his expression revealed nothing. I felt everyone looking at me for an explanation but I wasn't giving any. My examination would be henceforth talked about as the quickest, shortest questioning ever of a key witness in a high publicity murder case.

After some preliminary questions and identifying his friend as the defendant, I got him to say that Matt and he had planned the murder of Eilert Kurtz the previous summer. That they had purchased the PVC pipe, wood, and various fasteners to secure the victim to the cross and dug a hole in the ground to later use in December when they would carry out the killing. Further, that Matt had disposed of their clothing, the pipe and tools used in the killing. He also testified that Matt had the inside and outside of Butch's truck power washed to remove any possible evidence. Butch was uncertain regarding whether Matt had any mental illness, but did say he was very smart and that his brother and mother had mental problems. Further, he said that he had confessed to Detective Matanovich about this killing in a statement. Roeder identified the cross that was on the courtroom floor a few feet from the witness stand. I wanted him to go to the cross and recreate for us how they went about assembling the cross and securing Kurtz to it. It took Butch a little effort to do this because he said he wasn't feeling well. I didn't want to look at Judge Conlon because I knew he had to be raising not one, but both of his droopy eyelids at me in search of an explanation for this sick witness. I also didn't want to look at the Kurtz family because I knew this had to be an unbearable moment for them. It wouldn't surprise me if they stepped out of the courtroom during some of this questioning. I have had family members who could not bear to listen to witnesses describe the killing of their loved ones.

"Butch," I asked, "whose idea was it to have Kurtz tied to a cross, sort of crucifixion style after he had already been killed?" I was hoping that he could hold on throughout my purposefully limited questioning, and Rose's questioning leading up to lunch hour. After that, I wasn't sure whether Roeder would ever testify again. I had a fear, undoubtedly irrational, that Roeder could be gravely ill.

"It was Matt's idea."

"Why the need for a cross?"

"What?" he asked. Butch shifted around in the witness chair and was looking everywhere except at me. I could tell he was having trouble concentrating.

"Why the cross, Butch?" I repeated.

"I think to upset his father."

"What do you mean?"

"Well, being a reverend, whatever."

I'm not sure everyone understood, but I didn't think I would be able to get much else out of him to explain the meaning of the cross. Butch probably didn't know much more than what he was telling us.

"How are you feeling, Butch?"

"Not too good."

I wanted to end my questioning of him with his statement that he wasn't feeling well, and thus spare him further questioning, but more importantly to make me look like I wasn't deliberately trying to limit disclosure of the evidence. My questioning lasted about twenty minutes. I didn't have to look at the courtroom to know that everyone was looking at me, looking for more testimony from the so called star witness and wondering why he appeared ill. I knew that Rose would immediately make comment about the cursory examination of Roeder.

"How did I do, Anne?" I jokingly asked in an elated, joyful but soft voice that no one could hear.

She looked at me with confusion, no doubt wondering how I could joke about something so serious. Clearing her throat, she said, "Nick, I sure hope you know what you're doing, but I have this uneasy feeling that you're not telling me everything. And, didn't that one out of state press guy ask you before the trial began about you being known for a trial surprise or two?"

"Well, if there's a surprise it will not be by my planning or design, but will be in response to something that the defense does or occasioned by some other untoward event."

"Am I going to see a surprise or two during this trial, Nick?" she asked, looking at me with curiosity and anticipation.

"I don't know," I said.

As Rose got up to begin his questioning of Roeder, his incredulous look said it all. He no doubt wondered what to make of my questioning of such an important witness.

"Well, Mr. Roeder, let's see if we can learn a little bit more about this crime than what Mr. Papais has chosen for us to know." That stung, but I knew it was coming.

Rose started out asking Roeder about his health and appearing genuinely concerned. Roeder replied that he was not feeling well, softly uttering something about a stomach flu or some bad jail food, which brought subdued laughter from a few jurors. Rose's concern for Butch's health then abruptly disappeared. He began to focus his questions on the plea agreement and his involvement with the crime, and that if what he said was true, he was equally guilty. Did Roeder understand that? Yes, he understood that because Mr. Papais told him he was equally guilty. Good job, Butch, I thought. He then probed the events surrounding the day of the crime, and the planning leading up to the killing, all the way back to the previous summer. Rose then proceeded to question Butch about the Cantrell family, and got him to admit that Matt suffered enormous physical and mental abuse. He also got Butch to talk briefly about the mental illness of Matt's mother and brother, Lenny. It was then that Butch started to become almost inaudible, head down and clutching his stomach.

Judge Conlon and Rose both looked at me as if for an answer. Fortunately, it was noon time and the judge declared a lunch recess. I knew Rose had only just begun to probe Roeder to get him to divulge serious deficiencies in Matt's mental reasoning and thought processes, and also about the lack of physical evidence. His questioning of Roeder lasted about thirty-five minutes, cut short because of lunch break.

At 1:15 p.m., Judge Conlon was informed by someone from the jail that Butch would not be able to come to the court because of worsening stomach pain, cramping and muscle weakness. Judge Conlon said that we would promptly resume the trial at 8:00 a.m. the next morning, and that he expected Roeder to be on the stand

and ready for further questioning by Rose.   His order was directed at one person, me.

    Eight a.m., the next morning.   Despite the fact that the courtroom is enclosed within a large building containing many offices and courtrooms without any windows, I could hear a siren in the distance—it seemed to get louder.   Ten minutes had gone by.

    "Nick, how many hours do you think Rose will need to finish his questioning of Roeder?"

    "Anne, I'm concerned."

    "Nick, you're scaring me.   What aren't you telling me?"

    I didn't answer her because quite frankly I didn't have an explanation for my thoughts, at least not any logical or rational answer.   Another ten minutes had elapsed.   Without looking at those in the courtroom, I could hear their murmurs and restlessness.   Judge Conlon chose not to silence them.   A sheriff's deputy came through the door used by the judge to enter the courtroom and said something to the judge's chief bailiff.   The bailiff then went over to the judge and whispered something.   The judge looked at me and shook his head.   He summoned Rose and I to the bench.   Though looking at me, he whispered to both of us,

    "Mr. Papais, I regret to inform you that your witness is dead."

CHAPTER 15

STATE WITNESS FOUND DEAD IN JAIL CELL
By Jack Asaliner

Butch Roeder, the prosecution's main witness in
the killing of Morton County store tycoon
Eilert Kurtz, was found dead in his jail cell
minutes before he was to continue his
testimony. Judge Conlon declared the trial in
recess until further notice.

Eilert Kurtz, Jr., speaking for the victim's
family, expressed concern about the state being
able to obtain a conviction against the
defendant, Matthew Cantrell who has pleaded not
guilty by reason of insanity. Cantrell's
attorney, renowned criminal lawyer Howard Rose
has told this reporter that he doesn't need any
defense for his client, since other than
Roeder's brief testimony, there is no other
evidence linking his client to the crime. Some
court observers wishing to remain anonymous
believe this unexpected development to be a
serious setback for the prosecution.

Others point out that more evidence has yet to
be presented. Those familiar with Papais,
including insanity defense expert University of
Chicago Law School Professor Reginald Horowitz,
told this reporter that Papais has a keen
understanding of the state's insanity law and
mental illness.

Veteran defense lawyer, Thomas Riley said
he has never seen anyone who had the
ability and experience to question
psychiatrists for hours without looking
at notes or taking notes.

It is believed that Roeder's death was a
suicide. An autopsy will be performed as
soon as possible. Roeder's death shocked
many, since he had a plea agreement to
serve only a few years in prison in
exchange for testifying against his
childhood friend, teenage genius, Matthew
Cantrell.

It is interesting to note that Papais
must have felt some concern about Roeder
since the accomplice was not scheduled to
testify until the end of the case.
Usually the state has its best witness
testify either first or last. What
Papais feared is not yet clear, but
suffice it to say he had concern, since
he told Judge Conlon and Howard Rose that
he wanted to call Roeder to the stand
earlier than planned—what trial lawyers
refer to as calling a witness out of
order.

I read Asaliner's article, though seldom do I completely read
any articles about my cases. What for? Often they were a little
inaccurate and obviously there's nothing I'm going to learn about
my own case.

I still had a tough time believing Roeder was dead though I did
believe him to be seriously ill. Occasionally, trials move relatively
fast and there isn't much time to reflect on similar cases from the
past, but Roeder's symptoms had reminded me of a case I

prosecuted years ago, a homicide caused by poisoning. I had had a few homicide poisoning cases, but one was especially poignant and relevant. Most poisoning cases are slow in causing death. When looking at Roeder the last time in jail with spider, that homicide poisoning case suddenly materialized in my head. Believing that Roeder could die, and if he did without testifying, the judge upon motion from Rose would have to declare a mistrial. As a result, our office would dismiss the case. The legal reasoning for a mistrial and dismissal would be because Rose would have no opportunity to cross examine the only witness who had any evidence against his client. Simply, hearsay. What other evidence existed? To date, there was no DNA and I hadn't been informed nor encouraged to believe that any would be forthcoming. I figured if I could get Roeder on the stand for just a little testimony, enough to implicate Matthew Cantrell, it might prevent the granting of a directed verdict or dismissal of the case. Yet, I knew on Friday morning, the first thing Rose would do, would be to move for a directed verdict, if the state had nothing else to link his client to Kurtz's death. And, I also knew that Judge Conlon would have to give it serious consideration, perhaps dismissing the case.

The thought briefly crossed my mind that if the Judge dismissed the case, then I'm done with it. Admittedly, I felt some momentary delight at that thought, albeit brief, though with more consideration, I had one thought in mind, convict Cantrell. I knew Cindy wanted him incarcerated because she was scared of him. Myself? Well, according to the phone call a while back to Cindy, he, in effect, personally challenged me to convict him. Was this all a game to him?

I thought back to the judge's astonishing disclosure to Rose and myself that Roeder was dead. That explained the sirens I had heard. I started to walk away, head down and with many thoughts in my mind.

"I'm not done, Mr. Papais," the judge had said in a low but decisive voice. I returned to the bench.

"This isn't your fault, Mr. Papais. These things happen. Apparently he committed suicide and because of the unusual circumstances, I'll give you a couple of days to resume your case." These things happen, he said? I reflected on that comment. Not in my thirty years has anything like this happened.

"Suicide?" I asked, "I think he was killed." Rose took off his glasses and his back seemed to straighten. With his mouth opened it looked like he wanted to challenge and protest what I had said, but he said nothing.

The judge explained to the jury what had happened. I looked over at the defense table while the judge talked. I squinted trying to make out Matt's expression. He looked at me and our eyes met. Was that a smile on his face? Quickly, I looked at the jury to see if any had looked at Cantrell. It was quick, but it looked to me like the Russian history teacher might have seen him.

The phone rang and it was Angela.

"Yes."

"How's it going? I feel bad for you."

"I feel worse for Butch, his family and the Kurtz family because I now have a case that could be dismissed, and if not, what's left is very weak."

"Sure, but..."

"But what, I interrupted."

"Nick, he's a murderer." I wanted to say aren't we all, but didn't.

"What have you been doing?" I asked.

"The usual crimes and misdemeanors." I reflected on that, unsure of a response, but suspecting some truth to it. I told her I was expecting Joe and Spider, but reluctantly agreed to see her on

Saturday at 6:00 p.m.   A few minutes later the phone rang again, but I didn't answer it. The caller persisted. It was Dr. Loh, the pathologist. It's even more difficult to understand Dr. Loh over a phone than when he is on the witness stand; however, I had no difficulty comprehending his conclusion. Roeder died of heart failure secondary to ingestion of a poisonous substance, as yet, not precisely identified. Thus, voluntary ingestion, no force, suicide.

"Couldn't he have been poisoned?"

"In a jail, Mr. Papoos," he countered and went on, "how that possible, Papoos?" He still couldn't get my name right. I said nothing but waited for him to elaborate.

"Anything possible…lot of sweet stuff, maybe some mushrooms and other tainted food in stomach," he said after some reflection.

I hung up and realized I hadn't said goodbye or thanks.

I called Cindy to tell her to have Joe and Anne come to my place as soon as possible, but not to tell anyone.

I rarely drink during the day, but I haven't really experienced a normal day lately. Instead of days they might be more accurately described as events or periods of wakefulness during which something eventful happens. I grabbed a glass of Greek Metaxa.

I heard unfamiliar knocking at the door and figured it had to be Anne.

"Come in Anne," I yelled. I don't think I had ever seen her wear blue jeans and a shirt before. Yet, what did I expect on short notice. Did it matter? I motioned her to my study. She managed what appeared to be a smile.

"Where's Joe?" I asked.

"I didn't know he was coming. Nick, the boss wants to see you and so does Eilert."

"When I'm ready."

"Of course, Nick, what else would I expect you to say?" she said with a sarcastic tone.

Next came Joe who just walked in, made his way to my study, and took a seat next to Anne, while I sat at my desk chair.

"I think Roeder was killed," I said. Anne wrinkled her forehead and showed a doubtful look. She looked uncomfortable—probably wondering whether this disclosure would mean an assignment for her. Joe started jingling change in his pocket. I'm not sure if he agreed with my conclusion.

"How do you know he was killed?" Anne asked, throwing her hands up for an explanation. "After all, the autopsy results aren't in yet."

I told them about my conversation with Dr. Loh, and that though I wondered about his findings, nevertheless, he is a competent pathologist and I have never disputed his conclusions prior to this case.

"I think it's that damn jail food," Joe said, looking at no one in particular. I might have laughed if it hadn't been my case.

"Why not suicide?" asked Anne, ignoring Joe's comment.

"I guess I like to think that my witnesses don't commit suicide. Sure, there's always a first time, but Butch was too macho for a poison. Usually, if an inmate commits suicide it is going to be by hanging. And, even if it was suicide, how did he obtain any poisonous substance? Joe, I want a list of all visitors to Matt and Butch from the last five days? Please get it to me as soon as possible and let's keep quiet about this. If possible, find out about any contact between visitors to Butch and jail personnel. Also, whether Butch had any contact with other inmates." Joe didn't give me a nod of approval, just occasionally furrowed his brow as he listened to me; but, I knew he would try to get this information despite being busy lately.

Not wanting to let go, Anne said, "I hear about inmates having access to drugs all the time."

"That's usually in prisons and not short term jails or detention facilities." Redirecting her attention, I asked her how we should proceed. "There are two keys to trial success. The first is preparation. I make it my job to know more about the case than anyone. That gives me the advantage, doesn't it? Yet, I'm still lacking information or evidence. What do we do?" I asked with eyebrows raised, wanting a response after a short time—but getting none. I wasn't going to let her off the hook.

"If no comments, at least what questions should we consider?" I looked at my watch as if to note the time and see how long before she answered. It may have seemed inconsiderate or disrespectful, but I didn't care. We didn't have time—the case resumed on Friday. She closed her eyes for what seemed like a minute, her lips curved upwards in a forced smile. Anne narrowed her eyes trying to read my face, knowing that I expected an intelligent response.

"We get another witness," she said. Joe stopped jingling his change.

"Go on," I said pleased, but not wishing to convey my delight.

"Who? There is no one else," I said. I figured she would not come up with who I thought would be an excellent witness—Mrs. Cantrell.

"Mrs. Cantrell," Anne said without hesitation. I turned my head as if to ponder her choice.

"Explanation, please."

"There's no better witness than a mother testifying against her son."

"No way we could secure her cooperation," I said, "How many mothers have you known who have testified against their sons in murder trials?" I looked at Joe shifting in his chair. He resumed jingling the change in his pocket and had the look of someone wanting to say something. Anne countered with the impossibility of winning without a significant witness. I could only nod, knowing the truth of her assessment. We needed time too, and

Anne had some good news in that regard. She said the judge had extended the recess until Monday.

"Joe, I thought your people checked Kurtz's house. Can't the Bureau of Identification tell if two people had sex in the same bed. Bonnie Cantrell's prints must be all over that house."

"Sorry Nick, we didn't find anything conclusive."

I just looked at him, a look that he knew I wasn't pleased with that part of the investigation.

"Why was she having an affair with Kurtz? Why would she and Matt want Kurtz killed? Who would want Roeder killed? Feel free to speak at any time on these questions, either of you. Please limit your responses to at least five minutes per question."

Anne spoke first, "Nick, I don't need your sarcasm. I'm sorry I don't have your experience and knowledge. I'm learning a lot from you and regret that I can't be of more help. Evidently you don't know the answers either, so how should I or we be expected to know?"

"Sweetie, I mean Anne, believe me, Nick knows the answers to those questions or at least most of them," Joe said.

I thought I knew the answers, but I wanted to see if their thought processes correlated with mine.

We discussed a few other issues and then they left, but Anne walked back in.

"What is it, Anne?"

"You never mentioned the second key to trial success."

"Oh, it's also preparation, always more preparation."

She shook her head, no doubt thinking, why did she even bother to ask me a question knowing that the answer would not be what she had been looking for.

It may have been a little premature, but I called Angela and cancelled our date for Saturday. I told her I believed Roeder was murdered, and I needed time to think about adding a witness or two and ponder who might want Roeder murdered. Perhaps more significantly, how did he, or they, accomplish it. Before slamming the phone, she replied that I should leave that up to the police.

I had begun to believe that a conspiracy existed to kill Roeder. At least two people had to have been involved in his death. How could they have done it without leaving any evidence? Did they care, since the trial would be over and the defendant acquitted before they could be indicted. Still, who wants to be indicted, even if their main objective had been accomplished. There would have to be no trail of evidence linking them to Roeder.

CHAPTER 16

Monday morning. Despite having been in this courtroom for three decades and scores of trials, I didn't know it could hold so many people. With all that was on my mind, I thought it odd that I would be wondering whether any local fire code regulations had been violated. Shortly after taking our seats I asked to approach the bench. I told Judge Conlon and Rose about my phone call from Dr. Loh. Of course, Rose had also been informed about Dr. Loh's findings. I also told them that I had planned to call Ms. Cantrell to the stand. As expected, Rose quickly indicated he would object on the grounds of no previous disclosure of this person as a witness, competency due to her severe mental status, and a host of other objections. I took Rose by surprise when I said in fact, we had listed her along with "everyone" as possible witnesses; nevertheless, Judge Conlon's face said it all: It was a look of exceptional skepticism. Further, I disclosed that for some reason she had not been attending the trial and thus could not have been influenced by any testimony or evidence. The Judge asked if I knew what she was going to say, but I'm sure what he really wanted to ask was did I know what I was doing. Had he not been familiar with my prosecutorial background, he no doubt would have questioned me in greater detail. I told both of them that I had not yet talked to her and did not know if she would even cooperate, but I felt compelled to ask her to testify. He indicated that under the circumstances he would allow her to testify, but that he would give Rose the opportunity to take her deposition if he so desired before she testified. A deposition is a discovery tool which allows one side to learn or "discover" information under oath about a person or potential witness. Obviously, I was in no position to object, so that would be done sometime before she testified. Neither the judge nor Rose had to tell me that what I was contemplating was risky. Even if she took the witness stand, she could be very uncooperative and hostile, or say things that would destroy my case, but what case I thought to myself. I didn't have much of a case and I knew that Rose was going to ask the judge to dismiss the case after I had rested, particularly on the ground that he did not have ample opportunity to question Roeder.

I decided to start this day's testimony with witnesses who had spent a lot of time with Matt when he was young—school teachers. Having talked to these witnesses before their testimony, I did not expect anything significant. Yet, what they had to say was important on the issue of his mental state. For these witnesses, I wanted the jury to hear answers to questions such as:

-anything unusual about Matt Cantrell
-anything different about him compared to other students
-how was his cognitive ability, intelligence and concentration
-any discipline or behavior problems
-his interaction with other students and faculty
-anything unusual about how he dressed
-any indication that he had ever been abused or beaten
-any indication of drug usage
-and, anything bizarre or odd about him.

The grade school teachers testified in summary that Matt was very intelligent, an introvert, didn't play sports and had a friend, Butch Roeder who also helped fend off a couple of bullies that liked to target Matt. No teacher indicated anything bizarre or out of the ordinary. The teachers also mentioned that though the mother would show up for many parent teacher conferences, Mr. Cantrell never appeared. Rose's inquiries focused on psychological testing and social interaction which yielded nothing that was not already known.

After several hours of testimony Judge Conlon called a recess for lunch. I needed time alone in my office to think. Often during trial recesses, I would retreat to my office and try to relax and not think about anything, sort of a yoga meditation routine. My effort was short-lived as Cindy came in and said Butch's sister wanted to talk to me.

"You know what to do Cindy," I said. She knew I didn't like to talk to anyone during brief court recesses unless it was very important or a witness whom I had not yet talked to.

"Normally, I would Nick, but not now because she has been waiting here all morning." I let out a sigh and motioned her to let them in.

Vernonica Roeder was accompanied by her husband who chose to stand. Butch's sister's eyes were red and moist. She stared at me as if looking for some explanation.

"What can I do for you?" I asked.

"Mr. Papais, I don't believe my brother committed suicide."

"Any evidence other than your beliefs?"

"He wouldn't do it," she replied, "especially when he had so much to look forward to."

What he had to look forward to I wasn't sure, but I chose not to pursue it. Her eyes swelled with tears. I pushed a box of tissues towards her. I told Veronica that I had a trial that must go forward, and her brother's death was being briefly looked into since I also had some doubts. I also told her that we might call her as a witness. After a little consoling, they left.

Back in court that afternoon, Judge Conlon told me to call my next witness to the stand. I proceeded again with teachers, but now Matt's high school teachers. Like their grade school counterparts, they testified to Matt's brilliance, with two of them saying he was the smartest student they had ever taught. Their testimony portrayed a loner, someone who didn't cause any trouble, but had some problem with absenteeism. He seemed to be inattentive, yet, if called upon, he always knew the answer to any question. Again, he didn't play in any sports, though he excelled in the chess club, and dropped out after not finding it challenging enough.

On cross examination Rose questioned the witnesses briefly about Cantrell's absences, vacant staring and lack of interest in his studies. Though not mental health specialists, the witnesses agreed Rose's client had some emotional, mental or behavioral issues that strayed at least moderately from normal.

I called to the stand a couple of Matt's neighbors and none could recall anything that they considered unusual or out of the ordinary for a boy his age.

Judge Conlon recessed court for the day and Joe took me home.

I needed a break from the case, so early in the evening I called Rog, my attorney friend from Indianapolis, and then Tom in northwest Indiana. While talking to Tom, Joe came over and so I hung up to find out what if anything Joe had for me about Roeder's death, and other issues.

Joe was sweating, causing me to wonder when he last saw his doctor. He cleared his throat then said, "I've looked at the jail guard's visitor list and there are a few names on it. Obviously, mostly family members, but there is a recent doctor visit, well specifically a psychologist."

"A psychologist?" I asked. "What's his name?"

"I can't quite make it out."

"What was the time and date of his visit, Joe?" Joe told me, but I was thinking more about the visitor right now, and not the time aspect.

"Who was the guard on duty?"

"Novotony."

"Thanks, partner."

"Oh, it's partner now?"

"We've been partners for a long time, Joe. You know that."

"Why do I feel my partnership status comes and goes depending upon whether you need something or I get something for you?"

"You're the best Joe. Oh, what about my missing gun?"

"Well, the bureau of identification dusted your place for prints, and well, of the prints that we were able to lift, all were of people we know and people who have frequented your place with your consent."

"How come I wasn't told about their visit, Joe?"

"Nick, come on, you know, you're busy and no one wants to bother you. I was present so it was all professional. No snooping of your personal stuff or anything like that."

I began to wonder why I even had a door to my condo. Perhaps, I should have it removed so that anyone desiring to enter would not be inconvenienced by having to use a key or turn a knob to gain entry.

In any event, I was tired and ready for bed. I had just one more phone call to make. I called Cindy, but her husband answered. He must not have had the phone covered when handing it to her, or maybe he wanted me to hear.

"It's that damn Papais. I've got a feeling he's going to be bothering us a lot more with this trial."

"You jerk, he probably heard what you said. Give me the damn phone."

"Hi Nick."

"Sorry for calling at this time."

"It's all right. What can I do for you?"

"I just got done talking to Joe and he told me that a psychologist visited Roeder a couple of days before he died. He couldn't make out the name on the visitor list. Were you aware of this?"

"Yes, Nick. I assumed it was the same defense psychologist that had previously questioned Roeder and just wanted to get a few follow up questions."

"Yeah, you're probably right. Cindy, I can't remember if I asked Joe, but could you obtain from the jail kitchen their menu for the several days preceding Roeder's death, and then give that to Dr. Loh to see if those foods are consistent with any samples he might have kept that were obtained from the autopsy?"

"Sure."

"Well, I'm not going to keep you. It seems like your husband is a little perturbed."

I was awakened an hour later by Judge Conlon who also had Howard Rose on a party line hookup. "Nick, I'm sorry to call you and Mr. Rose at this time, but I felt I needed to alert both of you about this possible piece of evidence that Dr. Loh neglected to bring to our attention."

"No problem, judge," I said. "What do you have for us?"

"I'm informed that Dr. Loh neglected to say that on Butch Roeder's person was a handwritten note purportedly written by Roeder on a piece of newspaper, that reads and I quote, " Mr. Prosekutor, Matt said at time of Kurtz killing that there were five reasons why he was being killed. It's initialed B. R with the date and time."

CHAPTER 17

After Judge Conlon's call last night, I immediately called everyone and told them to be in my office at 7:00 a.m. for a briefing and discussion. I didn't sleep well, yet I felt wide awake as I always do for my trials because adrenaline and anxiety kept me going. For me, exhaustion would occur not one, but two days after a trial.

With everyone in my office the next morning, I told them of my plan to seek an agreement with Rose to get Roeder's writing into evidence, and that if he would not agree or what we call "stipulate" to this, that I would use expert witnesses to identify the writing as Butch's and through a long process accomplish the same result.

Additionally, I wanted us to figure out what were the five reasons or motives that Cantrell had told Roeder about. Maybe Roeder never even knew what the five were, but now it was our task if I wanted the writing into evidence which I did. I wanted every little bit of evidence that I could get because we had so little. We discussed the motive issue and were able to identify three plausible reasons or motives for killing Kurtz. Of course, robbery was the easy one. The second was killing Kurtz before he told Clinton Cantrell of the affair. Three was what I believed to be the killing of a good friend to indirectly inflict pain, suffering and sorrow on the surviving friend.

If we didn't get the additional reasons or motives, then I figured Rose would argue to the jury how we had not presented all the evidence for the jury's consideration. Even without Rose's argument, the jury would wonder what were the five reasons, and I didn't want them wondering about anything.

So, in summary, we got some additional evidence that we needed, but as a result, we were now stuck with giving the jury additional explanations for the killing. A double edged sword some might argue. While we were all still in my office and debating the reasons or motives, I emailed Rose and asked if he would have any objection to my getting Roeder's writing into evidence. He immediately replied that he did not.

Next, was a call from the judge's office to get started, so we all proceeded to the courtroom. At our table in court, I quickly emailed Rose asking if he had any witness, specifically a doctor or psychiatrist or psychologist see Roeder a few days before his death? He looked at me with an open mouth and questioning eyes that seemed to say, no. If there was any doubt about his facial expression his reply on the computer answered my inquiry: No.

With that, I quickly got up and went to Joe and whispered to him to quickly question the jail guard Novotony about this doctor or psychologist or whoever, and get a detailed description of this person and any other information about the visit or visits.

"Mr. Papais, call your next witness." I told the court that we had an agreement with regards to admitting Roeder's writing into evidence, so that was done, and the jury now knew that Roeder had indicated that Cantrell had more than just one motive for killing Kurtz. Whether they believed the writing or five reasons or motives was another matter that I would have to discuss or argue in my closing argument.

Rose had planned to take Ms. Cantrell's deposition soon. Sometime after that I would call her as my last witness and then rest the prosecution's case.

I called Butch's sister Veronica to the stand. She was dressed in tight blue jeans and blue denim shirt. Veronica was strong like her brother, but with black hair that looked like it had not been attended to for a long period. She seated herself, but looked like she would be more comfortable sitting on a chopper at a biker gathering in Sturgis, South Dakota than in a criminal court witness chair. I figured she probably did drugs like Butch and was probably on something now, legal, illegal or both, despite my admonition when I interviewed her a couple of weeks ago to be drug free and look "presentable." I couldn't help but wonder what not presentable meant to Veronica.

She testified that she had known Matt "forever," but wasn't too sure what her brother or anyone saw in him since Butch and Matt were dissimilar physically and mentally. Yes, Matt and Butch did drugs, "once in awhile." I knew Rose would ask so I figured on minimizing the damage now. "Veronica do you or have you done illegal drugs?"

"Yes."

"How often," I asked.

"Occasionally."

"What do you do or have you done?"

"Marijuana, hash, crack a few times."

"Do you work?"

"Yes."

"What's your occupation?"

"I'm a hair stylist."

I didn't scan the courtroom, but I'm sure most people were trying to suppress a laugh or had quizzical, doubtful looks. In any event, she worked so she couldn't be that screwed up with drugs.

"Have you ever observed anything unusal about Matt, anything out of the ordinary or bizarre."

"Well, he's shy…he likes animals."

"How do you know that?"

"He and Butch own a hunting dog together. Matt loves the dog."

"Matt ever tell you anything about his home life."

"It was tough for him."

"How so?

"He never got much attention. Mother and brother mentally ill, father gone a lot. You know, a cold house."

"Figuratively speaking you mean?

"What?"

"It wasn't cold temperature wise?"

"Oh, the house is cold, dark, creepy you know."

"Veronica, when did you last see Butch?"

"The day before he was killed."

Rose quickly objected and asked the court to strike the part about Butch being killed as it assumed a fact not in evidence, called for a conclusion and the witness was not competent to testify on such a matter. The court sustained the objection.

"Veronica, how much education do you have?"

"I have a GED." I asked that question so that the jury would appreciate that this was not an educated woman, and that some of her answers might reflect that fact.

"Veronica, if I may, let me ask you this. Were you surprised by your brother's death?

"Yes."

"Was it unexpected?"

"Yes."

"Would it be out of character for him to do something like that?"

"Yes."

"Your witness, Mr. Rose."

Rose's questioning focused on what she did not know about Matt, about the fact that she was ten years older and didn't really spend that much time with him. He asked her whether she was on any drugs now to which she replied no, and to which I quietly exhaled a sigh of relief. He asked a few more questions designed to show the jury that her contribution to this case was limited and then ceased questioning.

The Judge recessed for lunch, but before getting up I looked at those in attendance and saw the usual familiar faces, including Angela, and of course, Kurtz, Jr. and his uncle. They haven't asked to talked to me, and I preferred it that way. I learned early in my prosecutorial career that you can never talk enough to grieving families. If you convicted the killer of their loved one, then you've done your job and they're grateful. If the killer goes free, as sometimes happens, you have to hope that they believe you did the best you could.

Back in the office, I summoned everyone while I ate lunch.

"God it stinks in here, Nick. You eating that Greek garbage again, those "jirohs?" Joe asked.

"They're gyros and phonetically pronounced, 'year rohs,' not 'jirohs' or jive'.

"Whatever, they stink. Did Plato eat that crap?"

"You often ask that, and I continue to tell you that as I recall, he did," though doubtfully thinking that any such sandwich existed over two thousand years ago. "Any developments from anyone on visitors or mental health professionals seeing Roeder? What about bribed jail guards? The nature of the poisoned food? Anything?" I asked. No one looked at me which told me there was nothing new. "And, Joe get me those materials you found in the Cantrell crawl space, too. Anyone have any thoughts on calling the school psychologist to testify, Anne?"

"He didn't do much," she said, lightly touching her thick dark hair with her right hand, and smoothing out her light tan skirt with the left hand, "but he did do the depression test. Of course, he believed Matt to be heavily into drugs. The risk is cross exam."

"Joe?" I always liked to include everyone's opinion to make them feel like I believed and valued what they had to say, even if I had already decided on a certain course of action, as I had with the school psychologist.

"First, boss, did you say something about a bribed jail guard?" Joe asked, looking at me with a questioning stare. "That's a good crew there, Nick."

"I'm not ruling anything out Joe," I said, "now your opinion on the school psychologist?"

"Call him. You have no expert witnesses."

"What do you think, Cindy?" She still hadn't smiled much lately, but looked resplendent in a light blue dress which matched her summer blue eyes.

"He's in the reception room, Nick."

I just nodded, thinking that she was the best paralegal this office ever had.

"Ok, let's get him in here." I introduced him to the "team" and asked if he had any questions. He didn't. I told him to be prepared not for what he did in his examination of Matt, but for what he did not do. He understood.

"Ok, let's go upstairs."

It was after 1:30 p.m., and the judge told me to call my next witness.

"The state calls Dr. Tyrone Williams, your honor."

I took him through some preliminary questions, got him comfortable and then got more specific.

"How did you come to see Matt Cantrell?"

"The social worker for the school or district told me that a teacher or a couple of teachers expressed some concern about Matt."

"What did you do?"

"We notified the parents, the child, and set up appointments."

"Eventually you saw Matt?"

"Yes."

"Did you take notes of this interview?"

"Yes."

"What did you observe about Matt?"

"He was appropriately dressed, hygiene was adequate."

"What did you talk about?"

"Well, I was interested in his life inside his home and outside."

"What did you learn?"

"He seemed reluctant to talk, but he did relate to me what I would call a chaotic home environment. I felt he was introspective and detached."

"Before we break some of this down Dr. Williams, let me go right to the conclusion. Do you have an opinion to a reasonable degree of psychological certainty as to a diagnosis for Matthew Cantrell?"

"Yes."

"And what is that opinion?"

"I believe Matthew Cantrell has mental illness, specifically depression with a history of drug abuse, legal and illegal."

"Did you administer any test?"

"Yes, two tests designed to evaluate and measure depression."

"These tests confirmed depression?"

"Yes."

"The severity, doctor?"

"Moderate to severe."

"You mentioned a chaotic home environment, doctor. I'm sure half this courtroom or more are thinking that description is applicable to their families." I could hear some murmuring and whispering in the courtroom, some joking about similar dysfunction in their homes. More of that, and I knew Judge Conlon's gavel would loudly resound throughout his court.

"If I may," he continued, "the Cantrell home environment is more like a place where people gather, but do not have much in common, other than say, to eat and sleep there. It's a place with no direction or guidance, and no appreciable evidence of anything cohesive and loving."

"Yes, unfortunate, doctor, but how does all this impact on Matt?"

"This contributes to a negative impact on his life, his social functioning and adjustment with others."

"Doctor Williams, was he oriented to reality, time and place?"

"He seemed to be. There was nothing to indicate to me that he was incapable of feelings or lacked a conscience, if you will."

"Did he appear to be a threat to himself or others at school?"

"More to himself than others."

"Doctor, obviously we have the benefit of hindsight—would your answers or conclusion be any different now knowing that he participated in the brutal killing of someone?"

"I found nothing to indicate that he would be a danger to anyone...nothing to indicate a capacity for killing."

"Nothing further, your honor. Your witness, Mr. Rose."

"Yes, Mr. Papais, thank you."

"Doctor have you ever examined anyone who later killed someone?"

"I don't know since I have not done any follow-ups with students who have graduated or left the area."

"Are you familiar with this state's insanity laws?"

"Vaguely, since I'm not a forensic psychologist."

"Has your conclusion of Matt changed since the killing? In other words, were you wrong, doctor?"

"I saw him months before the killing, so I didn't have the benefit of any new or later developments or information."

After a few more questions, Rose replied he had nothing further with this witness.

Before the court recessed for the day, I told Rose and the Judge that I was still concerned how Roeder died, since I was not ready to blindly accept Dr. Loh's findings. Neither had much concern since they accepted the doctor's conclusions, and that even if Roeder had been killed, any arrest would occur after this trial had ended; thus, no relevance to the trial at hand.

Court recessed for the day and we returned to my office.

"Well Joe, how did you score that witness or round?" I asked.

"Nick, Dr. Williams testimony was not the most favorable. I score it a draw."

"Yes, I agree, but interesting since I didn't see you in the courtroom much today?" I asked.

"Yes, we need to talk, Nick," he said, looking only at me and not Anne and Cindy.

"Talk, Joe, we are a team, remember?"

"As you wish, Nick. Angela has your gun," he said, voice lowered and looking as serious as I had ever seen him. I wanted to say something about him snooping again, but didn't. Strangely, I didn't even hear him jingling change in his pocket.

"Also, there evidently has been a person who visited Roeder on at least two occasions before his death. The person has been described as a woman with long, black hair and..."

"Veronica Roeder," I said, interrupting him.

"Let me finish, Nick—first, all the guards know Veronica—no, this person purported to be a psychologist. She's been described as older and good looking, a fox."

"Darn it, Joe. How could an unauthorized visitor get access to an inmate in a secure facility with strict visitor regulations?"

"It gets worse, Nick. Other than you and Anne, it's difficult to tell who may have visited Roeder the last several days before his death."

"I don't believe any of this. What about visitor jail logs, etc?"

"They seem to be missing or tampered with."

"What about the cafeteria staff? Maybe one of them had something to do with Roeder's death? Joe, I made an off hand comment recently to you about the possibility of a bribed jail guard, and you had replied something like the jail staff was, 'a good crew,' or something like that?"

"Well Nick, you know they're a good crew," he said, without conviction.

"Wait a minute, didn't you earlier say something about jail guard Novotony telling you about a psychologist visit to Roeder?"

"Sorry Nick, my fault. That wasn't entirely accurate information."

"You're right, Joe. It's your problem, isn't it?" I said, slamming my leather portfolio down on my desk, scattering pens, papers and notes everywhere. "You wanted me to take this case and I took it, but I can't be involved in the investigation of a jail scandal. I've got enough to do with trying to prosecute a young murderer." I could see fright etched on the faces of Anne and Cindy. "See you all tomorrow. I'm going to Angela's to get my gun back," I said, moving quickly to the door.

Cindy bolted out of her chair, "Like hell you are, Nick...that woman is a nut job, Joe do something."

Anne squirmed in her chair and pulled at her thick hair with both hands, no doubt wondering how the three of us had ever managed to work together.

"Anne, Cindy, go!" Joe yelled, gasping for breath. "I need to talk to Nick."

After they left, Joe and I paced my office for a few minutes, refusing to look at each other.

"Nick, I'll work mainly on this jail situation and not the trial, if that's all right with you? As far as Angela, go ahead, but we're going to do it my way."

Two hours later, doing it Joe's way, I let myself in to Angela's place with a key she had given me. I could hear the shower running. The living room was dark and the only light came from her open bedroom door. I quickly turned on a light and opened the curtains to the patio door. The place was a mess with two open suitcases lying in the middle of the living room floor, and piles of clothes everywhere. It appeared she was planning to leave for somewhere or perhaps to vacate the place permanently.

I picked up some clothes to remove them from the seat of a chair. A black wig fell from between the clothes and onto the floor. I bent down to pick up the wig for a closer look.

Still holding the wig, I sensed her presence. In the open bedroom door Angela stood tall, wet hair dripping water down her shoulders and chest. Her porcelain skin was a ghastly pale against the large dark, blue towel she held wrapped around her body in her left hand. Her face and narrow, looking eyes showed no expression, no emotion, much like Matthew Cantrell.

"What's going on?" I asked.

"Shouldn't I be asking that question?"

I held up the wig in my left hand and gestured towards the open suitcases that lay on the floor.

"Did you visit Butch in jail?"

She removed her right hand from under the left, revealing a Glock 45 revolver, mine. I knew it to be loaded with deadly hollow point bullets.

"He had to die," she said, as simply as if she was placing a phone order for pizza delivery.

My heart was pounding, my throat was dry and I couldn't talk.

"Having trouble talking, Nick? The great orator, the state's great prosecutor who always has something to say, who can rebut anything, and who seldom loses?"

"Angela, I want to help you. I care about you."

"All you care about is your trial, your last trial…and Cindy."

"Give me the gun, my gun," I said in a voice that I knew didn't sound very demanding.

"I didn't kill Roeder, Nick; but, I keep my promises. I could have loved you. We have so much in common, except for your lack of understanding of severe mental illness. Oh, and aren't we all killers? Yes, I know about the boy you killed in Nam. You underestimated my ability to do things, to find out things."

Her accusations enraged me and brought my voice back. Too, I didn't want to be killed by my own weapon, nor did I want to end up on Dr. Loh's autopsy table.

"Angela, did your research about the 'boy,' as you call him, in Nam disclose that we snipers almost always had a backup…." No doubt instantly realizing the implications of what I had just said, she sharply turned her head to the right towards the patio door as a loud explosion shattered the sliding door. Angela fell sideways to the floor, blood and life pouring out of her head and blending in with her scarlet colored hair. I looked down at her opened green eyes and could feel my own quickly well up with tears, and wonder if there could have been a life with her.

I may have heard a door open, perhaps people rushing in and someone lightly placing a hand on my shoulder, but unsure of which shoulder.

CHAPTER 18

SWAT TEAM KILLS WOMAN WHO ATTEMPTED
TO SHOOT PROSECUTOR.
BIZARRE STORE OWNER KILLING
TRIAL TO BE DELAYED AGAIN.

By Jack Asaliner

Early yesterday evening, the county
police SWAT unit shot and killed Angela
Bedford, occasional companion of
prosecutor Nick Papais, the lead
prosecutor in the ongoing trial of
Matthew Cantrell, the alleged boy genius
mastermind in the killing of wealthy
store owner, Eilert Kurtz.

Just a few days earlier, Papais's main
witness, Butch Roeder died in his jail
cell shortly before he was to continue to
testify against his friend, and co-
defendant, Matthew Cantrell. The county
coroner's office has indicated that
Roeder died because of the voluntary
ingestion of some poisonous substance.
Papais contends that Roeder's death was
neither accidental nor a suicide.

Papais went to Ms. Bedford's place to
retrieve his handgun, which he had
learned from detective Joe Matanovich,
the lead detective in the Kurtz killing,
that Ms. Bedford had earlier stolen, for

reasons which are unclear. The
detective's special unit, the Bureau of
Identification along with assistance from
the FBI,wired Papais and monitored his
conversation with Ms. Bedford
approximately twenty yards outside her
condominium.

When it appeared that Ms. Bedford was
going to shoot Papais with his own
weapon, the SWAT unit instantly shot and
killed Ms. Bedford.

Upon learning early this morning of
yesterday's tragedy, Judge Melvin Conlon
once again postponed the trial for at
least two days.

Attorney Howard Rose was scheduled to
take the deposition of the defendant's
mother upon learning that Papais intended
to call Ms. Cantrell to the witness
stand. The move to call Ms. Cantrell to
the stand was seen as risky and a
desperate attempt by the prosecution to
bolster a weak case. According to
prominent defense lawyer Jake Hardwicke
of Los Angeles, Papais has little choice
since even the court appointed mental
health professionals are prepared to
testify that Matthew Cantrell was insane
at the time of the crime.

After reading the article, I quickly tossed it in the garbage can.
News of the incident spread quickly to relatives and friends. After
talking to my sons, then Mary and a few short chats with some of
the more important well wishers—thank God for caller ID—I took

the phone off the hook and placed my cell phone in a drawer. There were simply too many phone calls for me to respond to, and my ears still hurt from the loud noise of the gun shot and door shattering.

Too, I still had a headache from the shock of the incident and trying to sort out what had happened, and feeling troubled by thinking myself to be a good judge of character. How could I have been so wrong about Angela? Maybe I was so desperate to be in a relationship with someone who had a few qualities that I liked, that I overlooked something about her personality, an understatement to be sure. She said she didn't kill Roeder. But, why would she steal my gun? And what had she meant by, "I keep my promises." What promises? I knew she hadn't made any promises to me. If she didn't knowingly kill Roeder, who did? She said "killed," so I assume she knew, like I believed, that his death was not accidental or a suicide. What did she know? What she knew was that someone else was orchestrating events.

"Nick, wake up. You alright?"

Opening my eyes to what I believe was the morning light, I saw Joe and asked what day it was.

"It doesn't matter. We're in recess until Monday. I didn't want to just enter your place, but I called a couple of times and you didn't answer. I thought you were a light sleeper."

"I don't think I thanked you yet, Joe"

"Well, Cindy and I would have hated to go through a lengthy Greek funeral service."

"Yes, myself included."

"Nick, Cindy told me to tell you that Ms. Cantrell wants to talk to you."

"Sure, please have Cindy reset the deposition time."

"Sorry, Nick, I know you've been through a lot, but here's her phone number. Cindy said there was a real urgency to her voice."

"I'll call her, Joe."

"Anything else I can do for you before I leave?"

"You've done enough Joe, and I never seem to ask, how's your health? You know, lungs, breathing, so forth?"

"I'm in great health, Nick."

"Yeah, right, get out of here my friend. I'll see you in court next week."

"Bye, Nick."

"Mrs. Cantrell, this is Nick Papais. As you know, we have rescheduled your deposition to, I believe, Monday morning in one of the attorney conference rooms adjacent to Judge Conlon's court."

"Yes, I know, but it's very important that I talk to you before then." I understood the urgency that Joe mentioned, but urgency wasn't the correct word, rather fear defined her voice.

"How about meeting me at my office in an hour?"

"Not the courthouse."

I knew I had to try some other location. "Ms. Cantrell, what about the public library on Cedar Street, the magazine section in the back of the main floor, twenty minutes."

"Fine," she said in a voice so low, I could barely hear.

As I proceeded to the back of the library, I could see a petite, middle aged woman dressed in a black blouse and long, black skirt with no makeup. Her long, blond hair was styled tightly into a bun on the back of her head.

"Mrs. Cantrell, I'm Nick Papais."

"I know. I have seen many pictures of you in newspapers, magazines and television over the years. I'm sorry for what happened to you the other evening and for Angela, as well. I feel responsible," she said, head looking down towards her outstretched hands which revealed very short, jagged, uneven fingernails, probably from biting her nails.

"Well, it's not your fault, Mrs. Cantrell. So, what did you want to talk to me that couldn't wait until the rescheduled deposition date."

"I knew Angela quite well, Mr. Papais. I think you are going to need to sit down." I can't believe what I was thinking. The hair on my arms and legs instantly perked up as if in a response to the flick of a switch.

"Mrs. Cantrell, it just occurred to me. I can't believe I didn't recognize it, the photo of you…"

"Yes, Mr. Papais, the photo with me and a woman, the photo you evidently found in my closet…that was Angela. Angela and I were roommates for several weeks in the Morton County Mental Hospital," she whispered, dropping her gaze from mine as she spoke.

"Go on," I said, feeling the goose bumps prominently at attention on my arms and legs.

"At first I didn't think I was going to be able to get along with her. She seemed so distant and suspicious of me. Then one night, something happened that changed our relationship forever. It was late, past midnight, I think. A terrible thunderstorm erupted that seemed to last forever. I tried to sleep but couldn't. I don't know if Angela was awake or not. Our bedroom door opened, and as I opened my eyes I could see the silhouette of George, the night attendant approaching Angela's bed. Leaning over her, he grabbed her around the throat. She tried to let out a scream as he put his other hand over her mouth, then he tore off her nightgown and climbed on top of her. I could see her struggling and kicking, and I knew I had to do something. I jumped out of bed looking for something to hit him with. I grabbed the table lamp and swung its base at his head as hard as I could. That did it. He fell off of her, confused, stumbling and looking for the door. Angela told me I had saved her life and from that time forward, she was determined to somehow pay me back.

She waited on me hand and foot after that night, even visiting with Matthew and Lenny when they came to see me. Angela told me Matthew reminded her of her younger brother, who died of a drug overdose years ago. At the time of her discharge, she told me she would never forget me nor what I had done for her."

Perplexed and stunned, I said nothing because I didn't know what to say or ask. She sensed my shock and said that evidently Angela had never gotten all the treatment that she needed.

"Mrs. Cantrell, tell me about your relationship with Matt."

"Matthew was a difficult pregnancy, unlike Lenny. As he grew up his physical stature was more like mine, small. Lenny and his father are big, broad shouldered. Matthew is smart, loves to read, like myself, and loves animals. He was very caring towards me during my episodes of depression. His behavior changed about the time he entered his senior year of high school with his grades falling and not wanting to attend school. He became withdrawn and we were no longer close. I suspected he was doing drugs, especially since he began to spend a lot more time with Butch Roeder. He became defensive and belligerent. There were times he went out and would not come home at night. Maybe we should have gotten treatment for him. It's been tough for him with an absent father and me with severe depression. He's still my little boy, Mr. Papais. Can you understand that, sir?"

I nodded. I started to feel uncomfortable and a little understanding. Her wrinkled hands were stretched out on the table, her eyes looking away from mine. We touched hands and I looked into her eyes, hoping she would look into mine. Presently, I wasn't a prosecutor but a parent, both of us parents. Hardship, loneliness and emotional abuse were etched into her face. I would have thought her to be much older than forty or early forties. She didn't smile. Why should she? Who gave her cause to smile? From what I knew, probably not her husband. And across the table from her was a man who was seeking to put her boy in a maximum security prison, a place with bigger, stronger, violent men, men who would probably violate her son. I felt like walking out, dismissing the case and shredding my license to practice. Yet, I had to remind myself of the brutal killing of Eilert Kurtz.

Whatever happened, I wanted to know a little more about the Cantrell family.

"Mrs. Cantrell?" She was not focused. I repeated, "Mrs. Cantrell."

She just looked at me. Her expression could have been one of not caring whether she lived or die.

"Yes?"

"Matt…Matthew and his father?"

"They were never close, particularly after grade school. Later when Matthew's behavior changed, he refused to go to church and Sunday school. My husband was incensed and felt if he wasn't going to church, he wasn't going anywhere. And, of course, not doing well at school, the same school where Clinton was the principal was too much. He would grab Matthew by the neck with his huge hand, pull him down the basement stairs and tie him to one of the support poles. It broke my heart as I and Lenny would hear Matthew yelling from the basement."

She put her head down on the table and began to softly cry. I reached out and touched her hand.

"Mrs. Cantrell, there's been some difficulty finding or interpreting the jail visitor log, but my understanding is that your husband visited Matthew many times. Has there been any improvement in their relationship?"

"I hope so, but don't really know."

"If I may, how long have you and your husband been married?"

She seemed to sink down in the chair as she replied, "Too long, Mr. Papais."

"How were the early years?"

"We didn't have much money, so Clinton would work odd jobs and help out Eilert on his property. I would do some babysitting, some odd jobs, and also help Eilert. Once Clinton became principal, he was very involved with school functions, PTA, sporting events, budget matters, and so forth. Also, he was the assistant pastor at our church and was involved in many church activities."

"How did the both of you get along?"

"I could never seem to do anything right to please him. The children and I could never be ready on time for church. My voice wasn't good enough to sing in the choir, and of course, I was often too sick to be involved in many of the church activities."

"How did he feel about that?"

"Over the years he started to resent me, and I often wondered if he still loved me."

I've interviewed thousands of witnesses over the years, but Mrs. Cantrell's story touched me, and reminded me that in many cases, there's another story to be told other than the victim's family. I didn't want to, but I knew I still had to ask her a couple of tough questions.

"Mrs. Cantrell," I whispered. I looked up into her tear filled eyes. "Were you at Eilert Kurtz's house the morning he was killed?"

She covered her face with both of her hands and began to cry again.

"Eilert and I were special friends for many years, even before I met Clinton. We grew up together in the same neighborhood. As a child, Eilert would often say that he could sell anything to anyone, and would challenge us neighborhood kids to give him items to sell, and he would do it." I could see it was difficult for her to answer my question, but I think the answer was obvious.

"I haven't forgotten your question, Mr. Papais. Yes, I was there, and yes, we were close. It started many years ago. Eilert was kind to me, a wonderful man and I loved him, despite many people believing he was odd and unusual. As you know, he had considerable wealth, yet he chose to live in an old country farm house, haunted, as Lenny was fond of saying.

"Mrs. Cantrell, how did Mr. Cantrell get along with his congregation or school administration."

"The school did not like him and felt he was responsible for their declining enrollment, and overall academic decline comparable to other high schools in the area. The church? That's where Clinton belongs, that's his home and the members would do anything for him."

"Mrs. Cantrell, I should tell you something. Some of what you have said could be incriminating to you. I will not seek to charge you and would resist any efforts by my office to do so, but I just feel it is my duty to tell you. Generally, what we tell people in your situation is to talk to a lawyer."

"Mr. Papais, I only have the truth to tell. God and the jury will decide my son's fate. I'm a believer, sir, and God will determine my ultimate destination, but shortly my fate will be determined..." I raised my eyebrows and looked to her for more explanation, but I chose not to pursue it, and she didn't offer to elaborate.

"Mrs. Cantrell, could we do your deposition this afternoon?"

"Perhaps," she said almost inaudibly.

"Again, if I may, one more question. Kurtz's killing to some extent was solved by an anonymous tip from a woman...." She pulled out a tissue to wipe her eyes and some movement by someone behind the magazine rack and bookcase caused her to turn her head in that direction. I could see sudden fear in her eyes and I knew this interview was over.

CHAPTER 19

Arriving at the court house after a brief lunch with Joe, I proceeded directly to the conference room adjacent to the Judge's chambers for the latest resetting of the deposition of Bonnie Cantrell at 1:30 p.m. Rose was already in the room when I arrived along with a court reporter who would record the deposition proceedings.

Standing as I entered, he had a concerned look on his face, not having seen me since before the incident with Angela.

"Nick, I hope you're all right?"

"With ten years of therapy, I should be fine, Howard."

"Glad you still have your sense of humor, Nick," he said, looking like he meant it. It was 1:50 p.m. and Mrs. Cantrell was not here.

"I was just with her a couple of hours ago," I said.

With his cell phone Rose called the Cantrell residence but got no answer. He sent someone to look for Clinton Cantrell who might have some information about his wife. Thirty minutes later, one of Rose's attorneys arrived with Mr. Cantrell. Like his wife today, the principal was dressed in an all black outfit which, if possible, made him appear even taller. He looked at me with no effort to smile or greet me. Rose wasted no time.

"Do you know where your wife is, Reverend?"

"What do you mean?" he asked. The crevices in his face widening.

"Well she was supposed to be here 1:30 p.m. for a deposition. We called your home and there was no answer." It didn't go unnoticed by me that Rose called him Reverend. I had no doubt that if he called him as a witness in the trial, he would address him as such.

The "Reverend" looked at me with his granite colored eyes then back to Rose.

"Well, when I left for school this morning, she was still in bed."

"Could she have gone to someone else's home, perhaps a relative?" I asked.

"She doesn't tell me where she goes. I'll get Lenny and we'll go look for her." He turned abruptly and headed for the door.

"Mr. Cantrell," I called out to him. "Are you aware that your wife had a meeting with me this morning?"

"No," he called back, not even turning around. I could hear his footsteps as he headed down the stairs.

Two court days later.

"Next witness, Mr. Papais."

"For the record your honor, the state calls Mrs. Cantrell to the witness stand. Unfortunately, no one seems to know where she is. She was to be my last witness and without her, I'm prepared to rest the State's case, but reserve the right to call her later."

"Mr. Rose is the defense ready to proceed?"

"Well, your honor, my first witness was to be Clinton Cantrell, the father of the defendant, but he has been gone a lot looking for his wife."

"Well, call someone else then Mr. Rose," the judge said in a voice that reflected irritation and exasperation with the delays and unique problems of this trial, especially since his calendar of other cases was being pushed further back.

"Yes, of course, your honor, but first, I would like to make a motion outside the presence of the jury."

"Let's proceed, Mr. Rose," the judge said, motioning with his hand as if to put an exclamation point on his desire for speed after having the jury removed.

What Rose did for the next ten minutes was to eloquently lay out a motion for a directed verdict, which means asking for the court to basically dismiss the case since there was so little evidence on each element of the charged indictments. I knew there was little evidence and the possibility that the judge would dismiss the case. But, also, Rose strongly argued that he was deprived of adequately cross examining Butch Roeder because of his unfortunate death. Without looking at Judge Conlon, I knew he was raising not one eyebrow as he was occasionally prone to do, but both eyebrows in my direction, as if to indicate I had better have a good argument why this case should not be dismissed. Rose also pointed out something I didn't think he would catch or mention. I should have known he was too good of an attorney to overlook the fact that I might have known Roeder to be gravely ill, and timely scheduled his testimony knowing that he would become more ill after the lunch recess, and by the next morning be totally incapable of testifying. He skillfully avoided mentioning any impropriety on my part, but the implication, albeit slight, was there for the astute listener.

My turn. This time I looked at the judge and his glare told me he wanted a very good explanation as to why this case should not be dismissed. Though my argument wasn't as long as Rose's, I attacked what I figured was the defense's strongest argument, and that was the lack of ample opportunity to question Roeder, thus a deprivation of the right for meaningful cross examination. First, I stated that I wasn't a doctor and not in charge of the medical unit of the jail, and thus could not have known the gravity of Roeder's illness. Further, that Mr. Rose did have the opportunity to question Roeder, and that there is no case law indicating how many minutes or hours are required for a meaningful examination. Additionally, Rose's questioning of Roeder covered all the essential aspects or elements of the case. In regards to the amount of evidence on each element of the murder indictments, I argued that admittedly the case was not the strongest, but that there was enough evidence for the jury's consideration.

Judge Conlon's turn. I was glad he was in a hurry to continue with the trial because he didn't say much, other than to agree that my case was weak, but enough for a jury to decide the outcome, even though he told me not to be overly optimistic about a favorable verdict. He admitted strong concern about the limited length of time for Rose's cross examination of Roeder, but said he thought it was enough, albeit barely, and would leave that issue to the state supreme court, should Rose appeal an unfavorable verdict.

I think Anne and I both simultaneously exhaled long held, deep breaths. A small victory for us, but as the judge reminded me, don't be optimistic about the conclusion.

Rose proceeded with the defense case by taking some testimony from a couple of school teachers, neighbors and relatives, all of whom testified basically that Matthew Cantrell had significant social, drug and behavioral issues.

Rose's next witness was the Cantrell family doctor who also was a faithful member of the reverend's congregation. He testified that he believed Matt to be very sick, possibly even psychotic from the use of drugs. I could feel Anne next to me wanting to tear into this family doctor and destroying his conclusion. With a lot on my mind thinking about where Bonnie Cantrell could be, and her statement about her fate in the short term, I was happy to let Anne cross examine the doctor. I cautioned her to be friendly with the doctor so as not to alienate the jury or create sympathy for him, but destroy his conclusion of insanity.

She did just that. Anne orchestrated a nice series of questions designed to render the doctor's conclusion useless, doing an excellent job of bringing out from him that he had no training in psychiatry or illegal drug usage, and very little opportunities to observe Matthew other than a few times in church. Further, his clinical observations of Matthew were limited to the routine physical examinations before the start of every school year. Too, if he suspected severe mental illness or drug usage, why was this not reflected in any of his medical chart notes.

It was ironic hearing witnesses talk about Cantrell being inattentive, because I was not attentive either. It was good to have Anne helping out with witness questioning because she knew I wasn't focused due to recent events. My mind constantly drifted to wondering where Mrs. Cantrell was. Could she be with an attorney discussing her testimony? Could she have gotten in an accident? Did she get cold feet and leave the area? And then, Angela. I guess she wanted to kill me to prevent a successful prosecution of Matthew, for a debt if you will, that she felt she owed Bonnie Cantrell. She didn't want Matt to go to prison, evidently likening him to a younger brother that had died of an overdose of drugs.

Judge Conlon adjourned court because of the unavailability of essential witnesses and other pressing court matters. I thanked Anne immensely and returned to my office to get my briefcase before leaving. Joe opened the door just to remind me that Aleisha's wedding was tomorrow afternoon. With so much that has happened, I had completely forgotten that Joe's daughter was getting married.

"Of course, I remember Joe," I lied. "Is it going to be a Polish 'CBS' reception?"

"Of course." I was glad of that since I liked chicken, beef and sausage.

I reflected on Joe, who for over thirty years has worked two and sometimes three jobs to help get some financial security for his family. Joe was shocked a few years ago when his wife filed for divorce, but the time spent since then with his daughter, Aleisha and her fiancé has helped.

I left the door open and Cindy walked in.

"Here's a wedding gift card for Aleisha. I figured you wouldn't have time…"

"Cindy, I want you to listen to me."

"Please don't say anything right now, Nick."

"I assume you'll be at Aleisha's wedding and reception?"

"We'll be there."

Almost near my condo, I instinctively decided to turn around and head towards the library. Shock gripped me as I pulled into the parking lot and saw what I knew to be Bonnie Cantrell's car still parked in the lot. This can't be right. Quickly running inside, I was pleased to see the same librarian, a Mrs. Winthrop according to her lopsided name tag clipped to a blue cotton blouse. She stood behind a large semi-circular counter with raised eyebrows in a questioning glance.

"Mrs. Winthrop, correct?"

"Yes."

"Do you recall seeing me the other day towards the magazine section with a woman in a black outfit?" I asked, quickly.

"Please slow down and talk quietly, sir. This is a library and not the courtroom, Mr. Papais."

"Do we know each other?"

"I read the newspaper and watch the news, sir."

"Yes, fine."

"I recall seeing the both of you."

"Did you see her leave?" I asked.

"I wasn't paying close attention sir, but shortly after you left, she also left with a gentleman."

"Could you please describe him?"

"As I recall, I was distracted because it was the pre-school story hour and the toddlers were acting up."

"What about size, clothing?"

"A big man, khaki pants and a blue shirt."

"Did you hear any conversation between them?"

"No."

"Did she appear to know him?"

"I think so, but..."

"Yes?"

"She appeared a little shocked, perhaps frightened a little."

"As they were leaving, was he ahead of her, next to her or ..."

"I think next to her."

"Why would her car still be in the parking lot without being towed away?"

"We have had a problem with people leaving or abandoning cars, sir."

Her short precise answers reminded me of the difficulty I had months ago in trying to get the reporter, Randy Denny, to answer questions about whether I had become cold and insensitive after years of prosecuting.

"Thank you." I started to leave.

"One more thing." This is the first thing she said that I did not have to initiate.

"Yes."

"I'm not sure it's the same man or not, because I couldn't quite see from my angle here at the counter, and I didn't want to seem nosy, but he sort of hung around behind the both of you at the magazine and book rack; you know, as if he was eavesdropping."

CHAPTER 20

When I got home I called the detective bureau to have someone check the area near where Bonnie Cantrell and I sat in the library for possible prints and any other evidence. I also wanted her car looked into for any possible evidence it might yield. I didn't want to bother Joe with these requests because he was no doubt busy with the wedding. I knew I could be overreacting with regards to Ms. Cantrell's disappearance, but I couldn't help think something ominous, something macabre, a kidnapping, a felony of some sort. Why not? The course of the trial was not following a typical script; yet, it made more sense that she left so as not to have her deposition taken or to testify against her son. But, why didn't she take her car? And who was the big man that led her out of the library? The obvious suspect is Mr. Cantrell, but the clothes that Ms. Winthrop described were not the same as the all black outfit worn by Mr. Cantrell that afternoon in the deposition room. I needed Mrs. Cantrell as a witness—with her testimony I would have a good chance for a favorable verdict.

Less heat and humidity greeted Aleisha's wedding day. With so much to do, plan and think about, I didn't want to go, but knew I had no choice because it was Joe's daughter and most of the office would be there; and, of course, my absence would be conspicuous.

It occurred to me that this would be the first wedding and reception I have attended by myself. No wife, no date. It would also be the first time in church for me in months. Thinking of my family, I called and briefly talked to my sons, then my friends, Rog and Tom. I needn't have been to concerned about being without a family connection. While on the phone with one of Joe's colleagues answering some follow up questions on my library requests, my ex-wife, Mary dropped off Mackenzie, our Yorkshire terrier, which we agreed she should have following the divorce. She asked if I could watch her for a few days while she went on a several day trip with her boyfriend. Sure, no problem, I said while still on the phone. I'm not doing much these days, but I think she left before hearing my sarcastic response.

The wedding was a Catholic High Mass which was delayed for thirty minutes by the priest's absence. Even with air conditioning the church was unpleasantly warm. The brief programs made useful fans. Aleisha looked beautiful. Frankly, I enjoy weddings about as much as lengthy commercials preceding movies at the theater. I try to tune them out. No one was seated next to me, so I closed my eyes and thought about many of the troubling aspects of my case. I still couldn't think of what additional motives Matthew Cantrell could have had for killing Kurtz.

I realized that I had fallen asleep for a few minutes. Hopefully, no one noticed. No such luck. I caught a glimpse of Joe's ex-wife and she appeared to be glaring at me. We never cared for each other. She likes to think that I'm the cause of her breakup with Joe, particularly the many requests over the years to pursue leads and do other investigatory tasks. She was now married to Mario, an owner of a small, but excellent restaurant in town. I got along with Mario, "Mediterranean brothers," as he liked to call us. I would often have dinner at his restaurant where his chef would prepare for me an excellent seafood salad.

I went over to Joe who was with detective Townsend and told him congratulations.

"Thanks, Nick. I have something here for you," he tapped the inside pocket of his tuxedo. The tux fit Joe nicely, but he appeared a little pale and his face glistened with sweat.

After the wedding, the crowd began to disperse and I proceeded to the reception hall, specifically the bar, facing the entrance of the hall and giving me a view of those walking in. For the first time in a while, I felt like I could relax. I had left Mackenzie in the company of a neighbor. The guy next to me was named Jack, though not in a suit, he looked comfortable in a sports coat and shirt with no tie. I think Jack pursued women for a living since that is mostly what he talked about. He had heard of me and of the case I was prosecuting, though his interest appeared minimal. I learned that Jack was a doctor, a family practitioner. I felt like saying he should have been a gynecologist, but thought better of it.

"Hey Nick, check this one out."

In walked a woman and a man. The woman wore a bright colored, mid length flowered dress, kind of airy at the bottom, reminding me of the famous photo of Marilyn Monroe. She had a V-cut neckline adorned by a gold necklace and earrings. Her hair was pulled up elegantly, some of it dangling down the sides with bangs. Her wide smile revealed white, straight teeth. She had dark, sleek legs, almost a sheen to them. I couldn't tell at first if she had on hose since her legs were so beautifully colored and sculpted. Matching nail polish on her fingernails and toes with open toe, high heeled shoes completed the ensemble.

I was too far back, but I'm sure she had on a perfume which cried, "sexy." Simply, this woman was stunning; yet, she had class and reminded me of a Greek Goddess with the facial composure and walk of a confidant woman. This was a woman from antiquity, a woman that poets wrote about.

I was so caught up in her beauty I didn't realize that the martini I had ordered was tilted to the right and spilling over until nudged by Jack. He too was fixated. She looked at me and smiled. I smiled in return.

"Do you know her?" Jack asked.

"No."

I couldn't quiet my heart. I had seen Cindy look beautiful so often for almost thirty years, but never like this. I had to loosen my tie. I was so fortunate to work with such a beautiful, talented woman. I didn't want to share this fact with Jack. With my Greek heritage and the strong martini, I believed her to be Helen of Troy. I knew a better looking woman would not come through those doors tonight. I quickly ordered another martini with feta cheese, stuffed olives.

"Make it strong, bartender."

"So, Jack who do you know?"

"Come again?"

"The wedding party?"

"Oh, Mario. I helped him out a little when he opened up the restaurant and we became kind of close after that. Nice restaurant with an ethnic atmosphere, you know, everything Italian, including the waiters, the music and murals. Say, Nick, what's going to happen with that Cantrell boy? Seems like a trial with some strange happenings?"

"Yes, not a typical trial. 'Strange happenings.' I'm sure they're over," I said, wondering if I really believed that.

"I have never had a trial like this." Looking towards the doctor, I realized that he had left and I was talking to myself. "It will make me appreciate retirement more, I guess," speaking to no one. "What will happen to the boy?" I started to enjoy a dialogue with myself. "Obviously, I don't know."

Hoping no one had noticed my talking to myself, but then not really caring, I decided to wander around with my drink in hand, not really wanting to talk to anyone. In fact, not content with my life right now, I wanted to leave. I knew my life was lacking closeness with someone, spiritually lacking also. Maybe the wedding and reception symbolized something other than two people getting married. It was about people being together and celebrating and enjoying themselves. My life had been in courtrooms where lives were "torn asunder," where conflict, tension, lies, theater or drama prevailed rather than closeness, unity and truth. Ironically, trials were to get at the truth, but often the truth was manipulated and distorted. The jury was besieged with two different tales and told to sort it out and find the truth. To construct a puzzle was the mission of a jury. If most of the puzzle was completed, then perhaps this would be enough to find a defendant guilty.

How do I get out of here without upsetting people? Do any of them really care? I figured I needed to at least see Cindy and Joe, then Aleisha and Erik. Everyone had to understand that I was busy and had been through a lot lately.

With the drinks and an old lens prescription in my glasses, I couldn't see that well in the distance, but it appeared to me I could make out Cindy's husband talking to a woman near the men's bathroom with his arm around her, below her lower back.

Cindy was at a table with a few other people. I took the seat next to her.

"Hi, Cindy."

"Nick."

"You look like Helen of Troy"

"Is that good? Something I suppose from your Greek history?"

"It's good. Where's Todd?"

"I don't know. Did you enjoy talking to yourself?"

"You could see?"

She nodded. Oh great, I quickly searched around the area hoping not to see faces looking at me and laughing.

"Cindy, I...."

"Nick, I just hate the way you sometimes start out your sentences."

"I was just going to tell you that I want to leave after I see Joe and Aleisha. I'm not feeling well and I've had a few drinks."

"Leave, Nick."

"Something wrong?"

"No," she said, a little too loudly. I could see the others at the table look up at me. Fortunately, I didn't know any of them.

"Sure, I'll leave." I got up and left without looking at her. I proceeded towards the men's room where Todd was still there with this woman. I went up to him and he quickly took his arm off her.

"Hi Nick," he said, with a face showing surprise and shock.

"Get back to your wife before I find some reason to prosecute you."

I had to go to the men's room, and there I found Joe sitting on the floor, back up against a wall under the towel dispenser, looking pale and sweat pouring off his face. With his right hand clutching his chest, he seemed to be struggling for air. A man and what I believe to be his son were tending to him. I quickly ran out to find the doctor. Of course, he was talking to a woman.

"Jack, I need you quickly."

"What? You damn lawyers always want something." He wouldn't move, so I grabbed him by the arm and started pulling him towards the men's room, explaining about Joe en route.

"Wait for me," he yelled back to the woman, "I'll be back."

As we arrived, Joe sat there staring blankly, unable to talk. Reaching for his cell phone, Jack stepped out of the restroom presumably to get better reception for his phone. I could hear him giving instructions to the hospital emergency room and a 911 dispatcher. I stood there helplessly, praying to God to let Joe live.

Jack came back in and shouted orders, "Everyone out. Nick, direct the EMT to this room when they arrive." I could already hear the ambulance.

"I'm not leaving, Jack."

"You're going to have to because I need you to get his wife, family, and that priest that's walking around out there."

I wanted to say Joe didn't have a wife, but I quickly realized this was not the time to be discussing Joe's marital status.

"Now, Nick!"

I quickly left as Jack instructed, but not before grabbing the papers from the inside of Joe's tuxedo jacket, which Jack had immediately taken off of Joe as soon as he entered the bathroom.

After locating everyone, I proceeded to go home to pick up Mackenzie from my neighbor. While driving home I couldn't wait to find out what was in the papers, so flicking on the overhead light in the car, I quickly scanned some of the contents.

What first caught my eye was the fact that Angela was right when she said she didn't kill Roeder. A receipt found in her purse showed that she had purchased the wig just a few hours before my visit. If there had been any woman posing as a psychologist to see Roeder and to kill him by poisoning, it couldn't have been Angela—or so I thought.

CHAPTER 21

STATE WITNESS MISSING IN STORE
OWNER KILLING
LEAD DETECTIVE SUFFERS MASSIVE
HEART ATTACK

By Jack Asaliner

Bonnie Cantrell, the mother of Matthew
Cantrell who is on trial for the murder
of prominent store owner, Eilert Kurtz,
has been missing since Thursday
afternoon, when she was to give a
deposition to defense attorney, Howard
Rose. She was last seen Thursday morning
at the Morton County library where she
was being interviewed prior to her
deposition by lead prosecutor, Nick
Papais.

Papais was surprised by her failure to
appear for the deposition. Upon
returning to the library later for
any information about her whereabouts
Papais discovered that her car was still
in the parking lot.

Mrs. Cantrell's husband, Clinton
Cantrell, principal of Westin High
School, and an assistant pastor, could
give no reason for her absence or
disappearance. Looking for an

> explanation and perhaps suspecting foul
> play, Papais has asked the FBI for
> assistance.
>
> The trial has been standing room only
> since it began with local and national
> news coverage. Many people eager to
> watch some of the trial have camped
> outside the courthouse…

I didn't need to read anymore. Asaliner had written a couple of paragraphs about Joe's heart attack, but I was being kept well informed on Joe's condition by Aleisha who had put her honeymoon on hold.

On my way to the courthouse the next day, my cell phone rang and I could hear Cindy crying at the other end.

"Talk to me, Cindy."

"I can't."

"Take your time." She did, a few minutes elapsed.

"He…has been seeing another woman for years."

"Are you sure?"

"He told me, Nick."

"I'm sorry, Cindy. Anything I can do?"

"What can you do?"

"I wish I could do something…like maybe have him killed?" Normally, she would laugh at such a comment.

"Bye Nick, I have to go."

"Don't bother to come into work. I'll tell Ron you're sick," I said, but knowing that she had already hung up.

Anne and I were seated at the prosecution table, waiting for the defense to call one of their star witnesses, Dr. Tom Glowacki to the witness stand. As always, I was a little anxious before the testimony of a significant witness, a witness whose testimony could be outcome determinative. Glowacki had impressive credentials, graduating from Johns Hopkins University medical school with a distinguished residency at a teaching hospital in Chicago. A few years later in Indiana, he was made director of an inpatient psychiatric unit for children and adults, a position he still holds. Though not prolific, he had written a few articles on mental illness and the law. He was board certified in psychiatry and a member of the American Psychiatric Association.

If I was a defense lawyer looking for a psychiatrist to examine my client and come to the conclusion of insanity, Glowacki would be my choice. He spoke well and juries liked him.

Though competent, I considered Glowacki a "hired gun" for defense attorneys. He never testified for us because we simply did not pay enough. Also, I thought he took shortcuts in making diagnoses, severe diagnoses like schizophrenia and other psychotic disorders, ones most likely to come within the purview of this state's definition of insanity and mental disease or defect. He not only understood a fee and where it came from, but also had a good understanding about future referrals. These were dependent upon a diagnosis of a psychotic disease and a finding of insanity.

Standing at the defense table with his smile fixed in place, Rose glanced at the jury as he spoke.

"The defense calls Dr. Glowacki to the stand your honor." One might forget Glowacki's name or how it was pronounced, but never his appearance. He had long, white hair that rested comfortably upon his shoulders and complemented his pale, white face. His thick, white moustache was more like a braided cord or rope extending down the sides of his mouth to below his chin where they met.

With his legs crossed, back pressed into the witness chair, he appeared relaxed and exuded confidence, as well he should, having been a veteran of many trials. Dr. Glowacki testified he examined Matt Cantrell at the county jail on four different occasions for a total of ten hours. Besides his clinical exam, he administered a few psychological tests.

Rose then asked, "Doctor, based on all of that do you have an opinion to a reasonable degree of psychiatric certainty about the sanity or insanity of Matt Cantrell?"

"Yes, I do."

"And what is that opinion?"

"I believe he was insane at the time of the crime."

I glanced at Cantrell as the doctor spoke. His hands were folded in his lap, looking straight ahead at nothing in particular. He gave no reaction or indication that he had even heard the testimony.

"How did you come to that conclusion?"

"I believe Matt suffers from schizophrenia."

"I think most of us have heard of schizophrenia, but can you briefly tell us what it is?"

"It's a severe mental illness or disease usually characterized by delusions or hallucinations, difficulties in reality perception, thought or communication disturbances, and a decline in social functioning.

"What in your examination of him corroborates or substantiates this diagnosis?"

"He clearly had a decline in functioning at school with thought processes inconsistent with normal reality thinking. He denies that his father ever abused him, yet my understanding is that he was abused psychologically and physically. His communication is faulty at times or nonexistent. He has had episodes of stupor or near catatonia, that is, sitting almost motionless, staring vacantly, as he is doing now."

Everyone tried to get a look at Cantrell to verify what the doctor had said.

"What could have brought this about?"

"We don't know. There is a suspected hereditary component along with possible environmental factors, but certainly a physiological abnormality in the brain."

"What about the killing of Mr. Kurtz, Dr. Glowacki?"

"Can you rephrase that?" asked Dr. Glowacki, looking puzzled.

"Of course doctor," Rose's smile widened, "and if at anytime I ask a question which is unclear, please let me know. My question is did he know what he was doing the day of the killing?"

"On that morning he was irrational, distressed, had taken some downers with wine, and had an argument with his father. Couple that with profound, disturbed reality thinking and insight, he could not have appreciated what he had done."

As I often do, I made glances towards the jury, most of whom looked attentive, with two leaning forward as if not to miss anything.

"Did he ever appear to you as manipulative, as lying?"

"No."

"Could this tragedy have been prevented doctor?"

"I don't think anyone can answer that."

"Was he able to appreciate the consequences of the killing?"

"At the time of the killing, no. Young, severely mentally ill children, especially if also on drugs, alcohol, whatever, rarely think about consequences." Rose asked a few more questions of Dr. Glowacki then turned the witness over to me.

The Judge looked at me and said, "Your witness Mr. Papais." I came from behind the prosecution table and walked to the left center of the courtroom, positioning myself between him and the jury a few feet away.

"Doctor, how many times have you testified for the defense?"

"I don't know."

"My research indicates this is the twenty-sixth time you have testified for the defense, doctor. Any reason to doubt that figure?"

"Without knowing for sure, I will assume you are correct."

"Have you ever testified for the prosecution?"

"No."

"Is that because we don't pay enough?"

"I have a standard fee which your office finds unacceptable." I wasn't going to press him any further on that issue. I just wanted the jury to know that he was testifying because he was getting a nice fee.

"Dr. Glowacki, prior to examining the defendant, Mr. Rose's office provided you with a lot of information about the defendant, his family and the killing, correct?"

"I was given all the information I needed."

"Perhaps too much information, doctor?"

"I don't understand." He folded his arms across his chest as he answered.

"As you are aware many forensic psychiatrists prefer to interview a defendant first, so as not to be biased by reports and information from others. You do not subscribe to that practice, doctor?"

"I feel I can stay detached and objective."

"Objective, despite reports by others?"

"That is my practice, Mr. Papais."

"Let's talk about your practice. Doctor did you know that your diagnoses in twenty-four of the twenty-six cases was schizophrenia?"

"I couldn't possibly remember."

"Twenty-four cases of schizophrenia diagnosed by you starting four years ago, when you first started to testify for defense teams."

"I don't know that for a fact."

"Any reason to doubt my research on that point?" I started to move towards the prosecution table and Anne had a stack of papers bulging out of a manila file folder preparing to hand them to me.

"In any event, Mr. Papais…"

"Doctor, any reason to doubt those figures?"

"Again, I don't know. I will assume you're correct."

"Have you ever changed a diagnosis, doctor?"

"I don't think so."

"Could you have made a mistake in the diagnoses of any of those twenty-six cases that you testified to?"

"It's possible."

"Wouldn't you agree doctor that other psychiatrists could come to a different diagnosis about Matthew Cantrell and those twenty-six cases you testified about?"

"Of course."

"In other words, doctor, your profession is not that precise of a science to exclude the possibility of errors, mistakes and misdiagnoses?"

"Yes. Just like yours, Mr. Papais." That remark surprised me because Glowacki usually kept his cool demeanor. Well, if he thought I was getting to him now, he would be in for a huge shock because the worst was yet to come.

"Doctor, would you agree that there have been studies shown which indicate that many in the mental health field have reached a diagnosis or conclusion within the first several minutes of an interview with a patient?"

"Yes."

"That they in effect become focused or fixated on that diagnosis and first impression?"

"Yes."

"Let me ask you Dr. Glowacki, did that happen here?"

"No."

"No? Well, let's look at your diagnosis of the defendant." I glanced at the jury to see how things were going and then back to Anne. I couldn't tell much from the jury at this point. At least they were awake and seemed to be listening. Anne occasionally wrote down some of the doctor's responses for my closing argument. I walked to the jury box and leaned my hand on the rail.

"Doctor, let's first make it clear to the jury that though a person may in fact have a diagnosis of schizophrenia, does not mean that that person commits murder or any crime for that matter, would you agree?"

"Yes."

"As a matter of fact doctor about one-third of people with schizophrenia work full time and one third work part time. Any reason to dispute that statistic, doctor?"

"That sounds about right."

"Isn't it also a fact that schizophrenia is often misdiagnosed, particularly in younger people?"

"It's misdiagnosed, but I don't know the frequency."

"And the reason for mis-diagnoses are other causative factors that were not considered or inadequately considered, true?"

"It's possible."

"Some of these other factors are the person's overall health, the use of illegal drugs and side effects of medicines, right?"

"Yes."

"Doctor, I believe you mentioned earlier that there is often a hereditary component to schizophrenia?"

"Not necessarily often."

"Now doctor, you interviewed the defendant's family?"

"Briefly."

"Did you inquire or look for any history of schizophrenia among them or their families?"

"Yes."

"Result?"

"I could find no evidence of schizophrenia, but again my focus was not on the rest of the family."

"Doctor do you believe Matt had or has experienced any delusions or hallucinations?"

"Hallucinations more than delusions."

"Did you consider other factors that can cause hallucinations?"

"Yes."

"Notably the use of illegal drugs and or prescription drugs…can these not also cause hallucinations?"

"Yes, I considered them, but discounted their significance due to what I believe was minimal ingestion of these substances. And yes, they can cause hallucinations."

"Minimal ingestion, doctor?"

"Yes, he stated his drug use started a couple of years ago and was infrequent."

"How much drug use is needed to cause hallucinations, doctor?"

"It would depend upon the drug, the amount, the frequency and the individual."

"Doctor can you deny that drugs did not cause the defendant's hallucinations?"

"No."

"Doctor, many psychiatrists before diagnosing schizophrenia or other mental illnesses will have their client undergo a CAT scan of the brain, MRI or EKG to rule out any physical or chemical irregularity in the brain or nervous system, correct?"

"Yes."

"And would you agree that it would be the better practice to have one or more of these tests done."

"Yes."

"And I'm sure you have often had your patients undergo these types of tests correct?"

"Yes."

"Did the defendant have any of these diagnostic tests done?"

"No."

"Now as far as psychological tests doctor, would I be correct in believing that one of the more significant test to administer, especially when one suspects a psychotic illness is the MMPI?"

"Yes."

"Doctor, could you please tell the jury what that test is and what it stands for?"

"It's a lengthy psychological test that has been in existence for over fifty years and consists of over 500 questions that ask for a yes or no answer. The MMPI stands for Minnesota Multiphasic Personality Inventory test and it's meant to provide an in depth analysis of personality and emotional makeup."

"So, doctor it can be helpful in revealing conditions like depression, anxiety and schizophrenia?"

"Usually."

"Now, doctor were any of these diagnostic procedures or tests done or administered to Matthew Cantrell?"

"No."

"So, what's left doctor? What, if any, tests did you administer to the defendant?"

"I administered the sentence fill-in, Rorschach inkblot and drawings."

"With all due respect doctor, those tests are useless and..."

"Objection, objection, your honor."

"I only need to hear the objection once Mr. Rose, but I would like the reason for the objection."

"Argumentative and it doesn't give the witness a chance to answer."

"Sustained."

"What I meant to say doctor is that those test are referred to as subjective tests, are they not?"

"Yes."

"Isn't it true that they do not have the objectivity, the reliability of objective testing?"

"Generally," he said, reaching for a glass of water, as his voice softened and the pauses between his words lengthened.

"Doctor, if I may by analogy, would it not be better for an orthopedic surgeon who is about to open up a patient's back in the operating room to relieve severe low back pain, have objective testing done like an MRI, CAT scan, etc., rather than just the patient's description of his back pain and a little probing by the doctor in his office?"

"The mental health profession works in a little different way, Mr. Papais."

"Well, but you can certainly increase the objectivity and reliability with MRIs, CAT scans of the brain, and psychological tests like the MMPI, can you not?"

"It is my opinion that the conclusion or diagnosis I reach with a patient would not be significantly aided by other test measures."

"Doctor, would that opinion be shared by your colleagues?"

"You would have to ask them."

"I think we both know the answer, don't we doctor?" I knew it would be difficult to get him to answer some of my questions, but I was confident that the jury would know that he was being evasive and unwilling to answer questions that he easily could have. Yet, it was my nature and perhaps stubborness to not totally let him off the hook. I left the jury area and walked to the podium. I was in a good comfort zone and felt I was making some dents in his neatly put together façade.

Dr. Glowacki uncrossed his legs and leaned forward. His face had become more stern, less relaxed and less confident than three hours ago. I wasn't done and I could see most of the jury looked interested, particularly the history teacher who I believed would be the foreman or foreperson. There may have been over three hundred people in the courtroom, but the only noise came from

reporters and their note pads and electronic devices. My throat
was getting a little sore and dry. As I headed towards our table,
Anne extended a glass of water to me. We had been at it for
almost three hours.

"I think a recess would be in order, Mr. Papais," the Judge said.

"If I may have just a few more minutes with this witness, your
honor?" I didn't want a recess. I felt I was making good progress
in lessening the value of a key witness. It was unrealistic to expect
him to change his diagnosis and I wasn't expecting that, but I
wanted to substantially destroy the foundation on which that
diagnosis or conclusion was made. And, most importantly, I didn't
want Dr. Glowacki to get reinvigorated. I wanted to wear him
down and destroy his credibility. There needs to be an objective
with every witness, especially with cross examination. To cross
with no goal in mind is meaningless. One might as well ask
nothing. Cross examination cannot be just a series of questions, or
clarifications. It must have a target. Each cross examination of a
witness should be looked at like a chapter in a book that inevitably
leads to the conclusion or final chapter that the author wants.

"Proceed, Mr. Papais."

"Doctor would you agree this was not an isolated or random
killing?"

"Can you rephrase your question?"

"Well, wouldn't you agree that the defendant had the ability and
the means to kill anyone that morning?"

"I suppose so."

"But, he chose to kill Mr. Kurtz?"

"I suppose so."

"Well, did he kill anyone or was Mr. Kurtz the target?" I was
going to continue to hammer him with simple, direct questions
until he answered the way I wanted.

"He and the other boy killed Mr. Kurtz."

"Doctor, how soon after the killing did you get to see or interview Matt?

"At least a few weeks."

"Ideally, of course, it is best to examine a defendant as quickly after the crime as possible."

"Well, sure."

"Doctor weren't you hired much earlier and told by someone from Mr. Rose's office to see the defendant as soon as possible?'

"Yes."

"As soon as possible was three weeks later, was it not?"

"I had a full calendar."

"Did that full calendar include a five day getaway to Cabo San Lucas with a female patient?"

"Objection, your honor, irrelevant."

"Overruled." I owed Joe for that bit of information which was located in the inside of his tuxedo jacket pocket while he sat slumped in the washroom floor suffering a heart attack.

"Your answer, doctor?"

"It's not what it seems."

"Oh, they never are, right doctor?"

"Objection, your honor."

"Sustained." I didn't need the acute hearing of some animals to hear the murmuring going on in the courtroom. The defense table showed no reaction which is standard protocol after a devastating blow to a star witness or any witness for that matter. Most of the jury was hunched forward. Even Matthew's gaze wandered from its fixed stare. The doctor's eyes were focused on the courtroom doors and beyond, to another place, no doubt wishing he was back in Cabo San Lucas. I wanted to go on but the Judge called a recess.

I made my way to the prosecution table where Anne's huge smile and brown eyes, normally without expression, but now lit up, said it all. I had forgotten that she once wore glasses, nondescript, of course.

"Almost four hours of relentless cross, Nick. No notes, nothing. I could never…"

"Stop, Anne. You'll get better over the years and develop your own style and technique. It doesn't have to be like mine."

"That's not style, Nick. Even the Kurtz family was smiling and they never smile. Are you going to pursue this romantic tryst?"

"No. The damage has been done." I wanted to smoke a cigarette even though I had quit smoking over twenty years ago.

"Let's grab a smoke, Anne."

"Nick, you don't smoke," she said, looking puzzled.

"I used to. Can I watch you smoke?"

"You've been through a lot, Nick. Can I help somehow?"

"I wonder how much Dr. Glowacki would charge me for about a few years of therapy." We both laughed at that and went outside to a secluded area behind the court building where she smoked a cigarette.

"It's refreshing to see you smile, Nick, especially with all that you have been through lately."

I said nothing, but thanked her for letting me inhale some of her smoke, and then we left to grab a quick lunch.

Back in court and after two more hours of questioning Dr.Glowacki, and a brief mid afternoon recess, I resumed my examination of him.

"Let me ask you this doctor, are there any set of facts that I could throw at you which would cause you to change your mind?"

"Probably not." Leaving the lectern, I slowly moved a little closer to him. Gone from his face was the confidant demeanor of early this morning.

"You say that doctor," I raised my voice, "despite the delay in interviewing him, despite your not using the most recognizable test in the world to diagnose him, despite no idea of his health, despite his use of drugs which you minimize, and despite your admitting that other psychiatrists could come to a different conclusion than you, correct?"

"Yes."

"Doctor with your belief about the defendant did you then immediately tell the family doctor and jail personnel that he should be put on psychiatric medicines and separated from other inmates because of the possibility of violence?"

"No, and I did not say he was a violent person."

"Wasn't he violent that cold December morning?"

"Yes, of course."

I knew I had to wrap this examination up, but not before asking one or two more questions that I knew would draw an objection and be sustained by the judge. Lawyers often ask certain questions knowing that there will be an objection, and a sustaining of that objection, solely to plant a seed in the minds of the jury about something that the lawyer wants them to hear, though perhaps technically irrelevant and or prejudicial.

"Dr. Glowacki did you ever interview Mr. Cantrell and Mrs. Cantrell together?"

"Yes, briefly."

I could see Howard placing his hands on the table, getting ready to leap out of his chair and voice a vigorous objection. I suspect he knew my intentions. Out of the corner of my eye, I could see Judge Conlon who seldom moved in his chair, lean forward.

"Dr. Glowacki, certainly in your practice you have observed the interaction and behavior of hundreds of parents of children, or the interaction between husbands and wives, have you not?"

"Of course," he said, with a questioning look.

I went to the prosecution table and Anne handed me a file folder with papers in it. Unbeknownst to the doctor and probably everyone—except perhaps Rose—the papers inside the file folder contained only blank sheets of copy paper. I was gambling here on a belief that the doctor noted that Mr. & Mrs. Cantrell did not get along well, that she may even have been afraid of being in his presence.

"Is it not true doctor," I asked, glancing inside the folder, "that you noted in your observation of the Cantrells, that Mrs. Cantrell appeared to be afraid of being in the presence of Mr. Cantrell?"

"Objection, your honor, and I want that stricken from the record."

"Sustained."

CHAPTER 22

Though a little tired from yesterday's questioning of Dr. Glowacki, the cross exam went better than I had expected. I had looked at the jurors before returning to my table, and a few had smiles, a good sign for trial lawyers. Though Joe might not have scored it a knockout win, it had to have been close, particularly considering a strong, entrenched, steadfast witness. It's always a pleasure too, to get compliments or "job well done," from those observing the trial, especially defense lawyers who while in the court building on other business, sometimes drop in on trials to watch the proceedings. Truth be told, many defense lawyers don't mind prosecutors winning trials, just as long as it's not against their client. After all, when one of their colleagues loses, that's one client who will likely not return to that attorney for any future business, nor be a source for future referrals. Before leaving for the day, I told Anne to be ready tomorrow to question Dr. Leiser, Rose's next witness. I also left her to answer questions from Randy, the AP reporter, Asaliner, and from mental health organizations.

Tuesday morning. It seemed odd in the mornings without Joe to announce his presence by playing the piano or to question me extensively about some facet of the case. I also missed him driving me to work but not his malfunctioning air conditioner. I have often told people that though I didn't consider myself materialistic, if I had enough money, I would hire someone to drive me around. I would rather be in the backseat reading something or closing my eyes and listening to music than driving, an activity which I believed to be overrated. Fortunately, Mrs. Youngman, my elderly neighbor, watched Mackenzie when I was gone for long periods.

Back in my office, I summoned Anne. "Are you ready?" I asked. She looked apprehensive, but I believe it was not because of how she expected to do, but rather how I might think she did. I told her to expect Dr. Leiser, though a psychologist, to testify much like Glowacki, though he would add an additional diagnosis of PTSD or post traumatic stress disorder, which Glowacki only briefly mentioned.

"I'm ready, Nick."

"Anne, agree with Dr. Leiser on the PTSD diagnosis depression, anything except a psychotic diagnosis, unless its origin is drugs."

"Got it, Nick." Anne had never looked better. Though her pink skirt may have hugged her a little too tightly, she seemed comfortable in it. Wearing some makeup, albeit minimal, the contacts, and discarding the glasses seemed to give her a whole new appearance. I told her to go upstairs and I would join her shortly. What I needed to do was talk to Cindy and find out how she was doing. It must have been devastating to find out about Todd's years of betrayal. She entered with a forced smile, but it was good to see her. I thought about asking her why she told me to leave her table at the wedding reception, but I didn't have to.

"Sorry Nick, about telling you to leave at Aleisha's reception."

I waved it off with my right hand, as if no explanation necessary. "Is he out of the house?"

"Yes."

"You going to be all right?" I asked, and without giving her a chance to answer, "Didn't I tell you to take some time off work, you know, sick?"

"I'm going to be all right, Nick. How's Joe?"

"According to Aleisha, he's going to make it, though it will be awhile before he can return to work."

"And Mackenzie?"

"Well, thank God for Mrs. Youngman, my neighbor who helps out when I'm gone for a long while."

"Nick, you'd better get up to court."

"Any word on Ms. Cantrell?"

"Detective Townsend or Swango, I can't remember who, says he wants you to know that they have no idea where she could be. Also, her car yielded no clues or evidence."

"Cindy, tell Townsend to discreetly and quietly keep tabs on DeVechio, Lenny and Mr. Cantrell. Certainly, they have to be persons of interest."

"All three, Nick?" she asked with a skeptical look.

"You're right. After all, the librarian talked about a big guy, but then too, DeVechio is kind of big. Well, just Lenny and Mr. Cantrell. I'm thinking, we know so little about Lenny. Would he try to help his mother avoid testifying?"

"Nick, you're rambling…you don't know what you want," she said forcefully.

"You're right. Let's have Townsend or whoever, question Lenny and Mr. Cantrell about their whereabouts on the day she was to have her deposition taken."

With a determined look, she said, "Get up to court, Nick." I ran up the stairs and quickly seated myself next to Anne.

"Your honor, the defense calls Dr. Leiser to the stand."

Dr. Leiser testified as expected, corroborating what Dr. Glowacki had said, but with emphasis on the PTSD. I figured even with a loss as Joe might score it, the case would be decided on the next three or four witnesses: The two court appointed mental health experts, Mr. Cantrell, and Ms. Cantrell, if she appears. I now felt certain that Mr. Cantrell would testify, since he had now become—even though the police or press had not said so—a "person of interest," in the absence, or rather disappearance of his wife. I figured we had a shot at a favorable verdict with a draw from one of the court mental health experts and Mrs. Cantrell.

Anne questioned Dr. Leiser for five hours, not counting a lunch break and two other short recesses. Most of the time, I looked at the jury trying to fathom how they evaluated her questioning and the truth or substance of the witness. I believe they welcomed her intervention and the sincerity of her questions.

Judge Conlon looked like he had all that he could absorb and called a recess until tomorrow morning, when the two court appointed mental experts would take the witness stand.

"Anne, I'm proud of you."

With raised eyebrows, a large smile, and smoothing her blouse, she said, "I believe you mean it."

"Of course, I mean it," I said, curious by her choice of words. "Go home to your husband. You deserve to get out of here early."

"Sure Nick, whatever."

Quickly her smile disappeared, and I noticed a sudden change in her voice, her tone, but I didn't follow up with asking her if anything was wrong.

Returning to my office, still somewhat taken aback by Anne's facial transformation, I listened to a voice mail from Aleisha, saying that I could make a very brief visit to Joe when I had time. Why wait?

Arriving at the hospital and to Joe's unit and bed, I stood there looking at him, uncertain what to say, which lately seemed to be part of my repertoire.

"Hi Joe," I said, "I'm sorry, but you don't belong here. Isn't this place for sick people?" I asked, sounding trite, but doing my best to humor him.

His mouth curled into a slight smile and then he softly told me about the good job I had done with Dr. Glowacki.

"How did you find out?"

"I may be a little sick, but I still keep in touch with the guys via texting."

"Well, your information on Cabo San Lucas helped a lot. So, when are you getting out?"

"Doctor says hopefully in a couple of days."

"Sounds good, Joe. Well, I've got to go, because I was told I could only have a couple of minutes with you, and I've got to pick up Mary's dog, Mackenzie, from Mrs. Youngman."

"Semper fi, Nick."

"Semper fi, Joe." Semper fidelis or semper fi is the Marine Corps motto meaning, "always faithful".

I went to bed that night but had trouble sleeping, thinking about the loose ends in the case and the work yet to be done. I couldn't get comfortable, but after what seemed like hours, I started to get tired. Good, because I needed to sleep, but then Angela came into the room with a towel wrapped around her body, and then it fell to the floor revealing her nakedness. She told me to look at her face and head, and I did, but there was no face because it was torn apart by a bullet. I screamed and bolted up right in the bed, scaring Mackenzie who leaped out of her dog bed, jumped into my bed, and licked the pouring sweat off my face.

Next morning. I was feeling tired and drained from little sleep and the nightmare. Getting into my car, I couldn't help but notice the sunrise, another masterful work. This time, dark blue clouds, hundreds of them, clearly defined, yet nestled against each other. Through these clouds were angled shafts of sun, like thick lasers penetrating the earth. The forecast was for another ninety degree plus day.

Instead of going to my office as I normally did, I decided to go directly to the courtroom and took my seat next to Anne, who gave me a polite smile and a sheet with a few questions she thought would be of benefit for the court appointed psychiatrist and psychologist. It had been previously decided that the two remaining witnesses, namely Bonnie Cantrell and Clinton Cantrell would testify after the court appointed mental health experts.

I couldn't resist asking Anne whether everything was all right, to which she replied yes, and queried why wouldn't everything be alright? I decided not to engage her in any further questioning about her welfare.

While waiting for Judge Conlon to appear, I thought it ironic that at the beginning of the year before getting this case, how often I had thought about retirement. And, now with retirement just a few days away, I hadn't thought much about it. Of course, being busy with the trial snatched away thoughts and images of retirement.

I hadn't paid much attention throughout the trial to whether any of the extended Cantrell family members may have been attending. I knew their family was small, consisting of a few relatives in neighboring counties and a few in the southern states. I hadn't even noticed if Lenny had been attending, but he was here today. He looked like he had the day I entered his house for the search and bore a very close resemblance to his father. I still wondered whether he could have been the one who eavesdropped on our conversation at the library.

The judge asked Rose and I to approach the bench. At the bench, I didn't have to see his irritation. I could feel it. While looking intently at us, he softly but firmly said that this trial would be over with this week, even if it meant going into Saturday. He told us that he did not want to hear any more about missing people, sick people, dead people, calling witnesses out of order, whatever. The remainder of the trial would be Dr. Rice, Dr. Catlin, Bonnie Cantrell, and last, Clinton Cantrell. There would be no variations and no substitutions. Did we have any questions? Neither of us dared ask any questions. Judge Conlon looked like he would rather have a colonoscopy than be involved any longer with this trial.

The judge then briefly explained to the jury about the court appointed mental health experts, and the state law that required him to appoint such people to testify where the issue of insanity has been raised.

Dr. Michael Rice, a court appointed psychologist took the witness stand. He was simply dressed in a nice sport shirt and dress pants. Dr. Rice looked young, but had been a psychologist for almost twenty years. Like Rose's two previous expert witnesses, Dr. Rice believed that Matthew Cantrell was insane at the time of the crime and had a diagnosis of schizophrenia. Though Dr. Rice wouldn't budge from his diagnosis, he admitted that other diseases or mental illnesses can masquerade schizophrenia's core symptoms of hallucinations or delusions. I continued to question him.

"Doctor, Matthew Cantrell's major crime was the morning of December 22nd, this past year when he and a friend brutally killed Mr. Kurtz and tied him to a cross, crucifixion style. Would you agree?"

"Yes."

"To speak in the vernacular of young people, he was 'stoned' or 'high' that early morning, would you agree?"

"Perhaps, but he was also psychotic."

"Doctor, you know as well as I that even if he was psychotic at the time of the killing, does not mean that he could not appreciate the wrongfulness of his conduct, am I correct?"

"Yes, though some might disagree."

"Well, of course, doctor, there are those who will disagree about anything. If we may move on, as you are aware, the law says that his mental illness must be so severely abnormal as to grossly and demonstrably impair his perception of things. In short, is that basically a fair statement of the law."

"Yes."

"Doctor, this defendant planned this killing months in advance, drove out to not anyone's house, but a certain identifiable individual that he had known most of his life, killed him and tied him to a cross, the wood of which had been purchased months in advance. Are you prepared to tell this jury that the individual seated next to Attorney Rose had such a gross and abnormal illness that impaired his perception of things on that fateful day?"

"That's consistent with my testimony, Mr. Papais."

"And, that he could not distinguish between right and wrong?"

"Yes."

"Doctor, don't you believe that what really happened was that the defendant 'snapped' on that day. An isolated, violent act not the result of a long term psychotic disease, but an instantaneous rage fueled by the voluntary consumption of drugs, liquor and an argument with his father. Isn't that what happened, doctor?"

"With all due respect, Mr. Papais, that is not my testimony."

Rose didn't need to do much with this witness, since the testimony was consistent with his defense. It was 1:15 p.m. and Judge Conlon wanted a recess, but only until 2:00 p.m. Anne and I returned to my office where a hot pizza awaited us, compliments of Eilert Kurtz, Jr.

"What do you think, Anne?" Looking at her, I remember my dad often saying how women, more so than men, can dramatically change and enhance their appearance. Anne corroborated my dad's observations with the light blue dress that I never recall her wearing.

"Nick, you need to do some damage with Dr. Catlin, and you'll have to destroy Mr. Cantrell." I just nodded, knowing that she was correct. I too, felt that the case would come down to the last witness, Clinton Cantrell, if we did not get Mrs. Cantrell here in time to testify, and time was running out.

"You look nice, Anne." She looked away, perhaps a little uncomfortable with the compliment. Maybe she wasn't used to getting many praises at home or elsewhere. I figured I would break the awkward silence by calling Chuck, a FBI agent I had worked some cases with, and inquire about Mrs. Cantrell. Responding from his car via cell phone, he told me that they had nothing—it was as if she had vanished. I told him I assume that Mr. Cantrell or Lenny had to be targets, or at least persons of interests. He told me that the bureau and Joe's department were doing all they could.

We were back in court with Dr. Mildred Catlin on the witness stand.

Dr. Catlin has testified many times as a court appointed psychiatrist. "Milly," as we liked to call her in the prosecutor's office, had long, black hair with thin streaks of gray through it. Cosmetic companies no doubt liked Dr. Catlin because of her excessive make-up usage. No one had any idea of Milly's age, but her birth certificate and appearance were of little concern to the prosecutors office. What we liked was that she seldom ever believed any defendant to be insane. Such was not the case with Matthew Cantrell, and now it became a dilemma for me, because as Anne said during lunch, I had to inflict some damage on Milly. I didn't like doing that because she had been an ally for us for years; yet, I didn't believe Matthew Cantrell insane at the time of the crime. I was in a trick bag, as we often used that term in the Marine Corps.

"Schizophrenia, doctor?"

"Yes, Mr. Papais."

"Interesting," I paused, "we must have an epidemic of schizophrenia in the area. Maybe we should alert the Center for Disease Control in Atlanta."

"Objection, your honor."

"Sustained. The jury will disregard the gratuitous comments of the prosecutor. I want no more of that, Mr. Papais."

"Yes, your honor." I left the table and moved towards the front of the podium or lectern, and eventually situated myself between the witness and the jury section, my favorite location. With her posture erect and her hands folded in her lap, I continued.

"Doctor, it seems to me that the defendant can follow rules, laws and regulations if he wants; after all, he did it in school, did he not?"

"Well, he had unexcused absences and distractions. Too, I suspect they did not want to expel the son of the high school's principal."

"Well for an expulsion, doctor, there would have to be some serious infractions, wouldn't you agree? I mean he wasn't causing trouble, starting fights, bringing weapons into school, things of that nature?"

"True, but as you no doubt know, while in jail the guards made many references to Matthew's odd behavior, sounds, voices, crying, talking in what some guards described as another language. This is a very ill child, Mr. Papais."

"Well, he speaks several languages, so that may very well be true," I said, my words trailing in volume and without conviction. And, also knowing quite well, that what she said the jury was believing. And, I knew something else: I was losing the case. I felt panic, despair. I looked to Anne, but not sure why. I'm the expert. I don't need her or anyone. I paused a little, more than a little. I sensed an uncomfortable silence in the courtroom, everyone waiting for me to do something. I knew that I had to do something dramatic. I needed a win with one of the four mental health experts. This case could very well rest on the next couple of questions. I had to gamble, something I seldom do. I looked again to Anne. She sensed my predicament, my fear, my gamble. She nodded. She read my mind: Do it, Nick. You have no choice. I discreetly looked at the standing room only court room searching for Eilert Kurtz, Jr. He was in a seat in the area usually occupied by Angela. His face showed worry and anticipation.

"Dr. Catlin, what did the defendant tell you about the killing of Mr. Kurtz?"

"He sees the killing of Mr. Kurtz in a detached way, dream-like, if you will."

"He knows he killed Mr. Kurtz?"

"It's not that simple. He believes that Mr. Kurtz died as a result of a physical action by himself and his friend, but that he was an unwilling or rather unknowing participant in the killing. Let me explain it this way. It's as if he is a few feet away and watching his body kill this man. He's immobile, frozen and can do nothing to prevent it."

"Interesting doctor," I said, "but that's not what happened. For the benefit of the jury what you are describing is known or characterized by some as depersonalization is it not?"

"Yes."

"And that may not necessarily be symptomatic of schizophrenia, doctor. It's where a person is sort of detached from the situation, an onlooker, if you will. But, I'm going to tell you and everyone why Mr. Kurtz died. We have terms, too. Only this one is a lot simpler. It's called motive. In this case, five reasons or motives."

I could see Milly's hands clasped tightly in front of her. No juror dare cough or make any noise so as not to miss anything. The jurors seemed tense, some leaned forward. Matthew was attentive and looked at me waiting for my next words. The courtroom was quiet with no one even shifting or adjusting in their seats. I deliberately waited before speaking again. I wanted everyone's attention.

Dr. Catlin looked at me as if she had made a mistake.

"Motive," I said to the jury rather than Dr. Catlin, but not too loudly because I wanted them to strain to listen.

I looked back at Dr. Catlin. "Detachment didn't kill Eilert Kurtz, doctor. On the contrary, attachment killed him…attachment to Matthew Cantrell's mother and the desire to commit the perfect crime."

CHAPTER 23

With evening approaching, Judge Conlon recessed for the day and told everyone to be back at 8:00 a.m. for the prosecution to resume its questioning of Dr. Catlin.

While driving home, I took little delight in knowing that the trial would end soon, because a few loose ends begged to be resolved, chiefly, the fifth motive or reason for killing Kurtz. Rose would raise the issue as an unanswered piece of a complex puzzle that would cause the jury to wonder and thus create a doubt. In fact, I'm sure he would say that the fifth motive was the main motive for killing Kurtz. I agree. I also believed, though not completely sure, that the Cantrell family knew that motive, but Roeder probably didn't.

I was in my office early the next morning. It had been one week since Bonnie Cantrell's disappearance. I strongly sensed that she was dead and conveyed that thought to FBI agent Chuck Fennert, who called me late last night to tell me that he talked to Mr. Cantrell, but the conversation yielded nothing. In his words, "for a preacher, he doesn't say much." Well, I told him that I expected him to say a lot at the trial. Fennert also said that the Reverend declined to take a lie detector test, saying that he was a believer, a man of faith, a man of God, and not a believer in man made, unreliable mechanical machines.

With Anne and I at our seats in the courtroom, waiting for the judge to tell me to resume my questioning of Dr. Catlin who was seated in the witness chair, I glanced over at Matthew Cantrell. Admittedly, he looked detached and introspective, his glistening, green eyes focused on some destination outside the courtroom, and his orange-brown hair cut short, parted on the left. Every day, he wore either a blue blazer or a brown sport coat. His gaze was never at a witness, but rather to either side of the witness's head.

"Dr. Catlin, during your questioning of Matthew Cantrell, did you ever ask about his interests, and hobbies?"

"A little, yes. He indicated mostly reading."

"Such as?"

"Everything, including the study of languages."

"Did everything include books and articles about crime detection, DNA, and committing the perfect crime?"

"No."

"Doctor, are you familiar with the names, Nathan Leopold and Richard Loeb?"

"Yes, Mr. Papais," she said with some irritation to her voice.

"Doctor, on the prosecution table are numerous books and articles about crime scene evidence, and the Leopold and Loeb case, all taken from the crawl space of the Cantrell home. If I may doctor, briefly summarize for the benefit of the jury, Leopold was a brilliant young man, a linguist, who in the early 1900s in Chicago, devised a plan to commit the perfect murder, along with his friend, Richard Loeb. Would that be a fair and accurate statement, doctor?"

"I think so."

"Did any of your examination of Matthew Cantrell focus on this extensive interest of his life?"

"Only minimally."

"If I may move on, doctor, you once wrote in a psychiatric journal years ago that you believed Hitler to only have a personality disorder. Do you still have that opinion?"

"As you know, Mr. Papais, that was a very long time ago."

"So, your opinion would be different now?"

"I never examined Hitler, Mr. Papais."

"But that was your opinion at the time, was it not?"

"Yes."

"Doctor, do you know why Matthew Cantrell put Eilert Kurtz on the cross?"

"I believe it was for retaliation against his father's strong religious beliefs."

"Unfortunately, doctor, you are only partly correct."

CHAPTER 24

Judge Conlon wanted a recess before starting the testimony of Clinton Cantrell, the last witness. Even the most optimistic of court observers held out little hope for Bonnie Cantrell to appear. I had gotten a text from Aleisha that Joe had been released from the hospital and would probably be in court, despite his cardiologist's advice and warning to the contrary.

With the weekend near and my retirement imminent, on my desk were cards and gifts from well wishers and friends, some of whom I hadn't heard from in awhile, like Keith Medved from Dyer, Indiana, my cousin Mikki from Hobart, Indiana, and a childhood friend, Frank from Katy, Texas. I only had a few minutes to read some of the cards before going upstairs for Rose's direct examination of Clinton Cantrell. My phone rang at the same time that Cindy walked in. She closed the door and gave me her card which was handmade and handwritten. I didn't answer the phone.

The card read:

Nick,

I wish you well in retirement and your new life. I'll never say good bye because I want to see you, to talk to you, to have you make me laugh like you have all these years, to get mad at you for leaving, and to hear your lies about my beauty.

Love,

C.

I wanted to say things to her, but I got choked up. We looked at each other, both of our eyes straining to avoid crying. I would miss looking at her reddish gold hair and light, summer blue eyes. I reached for her and we hugged. The phone rang again, no doubt Judge Conlon's secretary summoning me to court.

"Nick," Cindy said, with her voice soft, but controlled and steady, "you go up there and show everyone why you're the best. But, the best, Nick, doesn't always mean a favorable verdict. I want you to strip that religious facade off Clinton Cantrell and have the jury see him as ungodly, as a sick man, as the devil. I expect your cross examination to be difficult because he will be hostile, and his answers short and noncommittal. Nick, I don't condone what Matthew Cantrell did, but I can sense why the killing happened. I recall you telling me about going through the house and thinking something like, if love ever occupied this place, it was of short duration and quickly left with no reminders and no forwarding address."

"Cindy, they weren't lies."

"What are you talking about, Nick?"

"Your card," I said as I left to go upstairs to court.

"Your honor, the defense calls Clinton Cantrell to the witness stand." With his glasses ready to fall off and fingering his Phi Beta Kappa key, Rose went to the podium, and led his witness through some preliminary questioning, including his educational background, and his role as an assistant pastor, and the principal of Westin High School.

"First, Pastor," Rose said, leaning a little to the right because of his ailing back, "we need to tell the jury why you haven't been in the courtroom."

"I've been spending a lot of time looking for my wife," he said, with his granite colored eyes focused on the jury.

"If I may, this has not been the first time she has been gone or missing is it?"

"Correct, she has been gone many times, but always returned."

"Has she ever been gone this long?"

"No."

"And your wife has been ill has she not for a long time?"

"She has severe depression."

"If we may move on, Pastor, how would you describe your relationship with your son, Matthew?"

Looking at Anne and me, then at the jury, Mr. Cantrell said he had not been a good father to Matt. He said he had been gone a lot with his pastoral duties and school principal functions. Further, he said he had high expectations for his son, and that when he didn't do well in school or didn't participate in church, he would mete out harsh punishment, such as had been inflicted on him as a child by his father. He reasoned that since he was successful in life, that the same punishment would be of benefit to his son. Rose then told his witness to look at the jury and that as painful as it may be to speak the truth, tell them what he meant by punishment.

"I would tie him to the pole, the support beam downstairs," he said, placing his huge right hand over his wedge shaped face, covering the dark crevices.

"What do you think now about what you had done over all these years to your son?"

With his head down, looking apologetic and barely audible, he muttered, "I made a mistake. I was wrong."

Rose then questioned Mr. Cantrell about Butch Roeder and the influence he had on his son. Then, appearing as if he was done with that line of questioning, Rose went back to Bonnie Cantrell.

"Pastor, I know this is tough for you, but while you were gone," he paused at the podium to grab a cane from his seat at the defense table to steady himself, presumably because of his back condition, "there was testimony about your wife's attachment to Eilert Kurtz. Were you aware of this affair?"

"Only recently."

"Pastor, how long have you known Eilert Kurtz?"

"Many years."

"How well did you know him?"

"Evidently, not well enough."

After about twenty more minutes with this line of questioning, Rose ended his direct examination of the pastor. Judge Conlon then ordered a fifteen minute recess for which I was thankful, because I needed this short break to go back to my office, close my eyes and rehearse my strategy for questioning Clinton Cantrell. Anne understood that I needed this time alone. Unfortunately, the time alone amounted to less than five minutes, when Anne rushed in and told me about some updated information she had just gotten from Detectives Townsend and Swango outside the courtroom. I read it and then we talked about it, or more precisely we differed as to what to do with the new information. I told her to immediately tell Rose about this information. With her face constricted and mouth clenched shut, Anne quickly made for the door, not acknowledging Cindy who brushed past her coming into my office. It reminded me of the behavior Cindy and Angela had displayed towards each other.

"A lover's quarrel?" Cindy asked.

"Excuse me, but I have no idea what you're talking about."

"You don't know much about women, do you, Nick?"

I paused, wondering how to handle this useless inquiry. "Well, let's look at the evidence. In one year, I've had one woman divorce me, one try to kill me a couple of weeks ago, and oh yes, you, telling me at Aleisha's wedding in front of a crowd of people to leave your table. And now, Anne storming out of my office. Oh, and last night, Mackenzie bit me. So yes, I guess you're right, and very quickly because I don't have time for this nonsense, what does all this have to do with Anne?"

"Spider likes you. I think she dresses up every day mostly because of you."

"Anne is married."

"She and her husband are separated, and if you ever bothered to read a newspaper you would see where they have filed for a divorce."

Back in court, thinking about Cindy's disclosure, I felt a little uncomfortable next to Anne, but my discomfort would soon disappear as I began my cross examination of the pastor, the principal, the father of Matthew Cantrell.

I started out with about ten minutes of general questions for the pastor. Though, it was my understanding that Clinton Cantrell was not an ordained minister, but not wanting to look disrespectful, I reluctantly decided to address him as pastor, as Rose had done.

"Pastor, you told Mr. Rose that you had been looking for your wife, correct?"

"Yes."

"By yourself?"

"I and Lenny, my son."

"Where did you look?"

"All over, and we called relatives in neighboring counties and in the south, where we have some family."

"Pastor, when did you last see your wife?"

"About a week ago."

"Objection your honor, all this line of questioning about his wife has little if any relevance on the guilt or innocence or mental makeup of my client," Rose said, standing up and leaning on his cane.

"Overruled," said Judge Conlon.

"Pastor, you knew she was to give a deposition to Mr. Rose prior to testifying later for me, correct?"

"Yes."

"And you knew she was to see me that Thursday morning at the Morton County library prior to the deposition, did you not?"

"I know nothing about that."

I was now going to gamble again, but I needed to inflict some damage on this witness.

"Pastor, was it a coincidence that you were at the library that morning at the precise time I was interviewing your wife?"

"I haven't been to the library in a while, Mr. Papais."

Gamble failed, rearrange the questioning and keep at it, I thought.

"How tall are you pastor and how much do you weigh?"

"Six and a half feet, about 260."

"Do you occasionally get mistaken for someone else?" I asked.

"It has happened."

"What if someone said you were there that day and time that I was questioning your wife? Would that person be lying?"

"Maybe not lying, but mistaken."

I was getting a little concerned as to how I was going to prove he was there. Keep trying, I told myself, but I knew another objection from Rose would be sustained. I looked over at Anne, who like with an earlier witness, seemed to sense my gamble and predicament, but giving a slight nod to go forward. "Tell me Pastor, how likely is this. A parishioner of your congregation, sees you behind a book shelf in the library, not looking at any books, but with your ear to the books, eavesdropping on my conversation with your wife? Further, that you were dressed in khaki pants with a blue shirt?" I recall the librarian, Mrs. Winthrop describing the clothes of the person who escorted Mrs. Cantrell out of the library.

Seldom during his testimony either with Rose or myself, did the pastor look away from the Jury, but now with his eyes glaring at me, and then looking at his son, he said, "Yes, I was there. What husband wouldn't be concerned about his wife who had often left without disclosing where she was going?"

An important small victory for me, I thought, yet he had a good follow up response. He was proving to be the tough witness that I had figured he would be. I now wanted to switch to Roeder before coming back to Mrs. Cantrell.

"Pastor, did you ever believe your son would harm or kill anyone?"

"No."

"Ever think he would kill your best friend?"

"No."

"Pastor, a life was taken. Do you agree there should be some punishment?"

"As I believe Dr. Catlin said, Mr. Papais," his granite eyes looking at mine, then his son, " 'he's a sick or ill child.' He's been punished enough."

I occasionally looked towards Matthew who never really looked directly at any witness, but throughout his father's testimony, his eyes seldom strayed from his father's face. From where I was standing, I couldn't see Matthew that well, but it looked like his pale green eyes had a glassy appearance to them, perhaps showing some emotion which I had never seen before in him.

"Did you ever ask him why he killed your friend?"

"He said he didn't know why."

"Pastor, you of course, knew Butch Roeder was to testify for us?"

"Yes."

"Did his death surprise you?"

"I was shocked."

"Were you?"

"Yes," he said, in a loud, authoritative voice.

"Pastor, you didn't want Butch Roeder to testify against your son did you?"

"I have no control over who testifies. That's up to you and Mr. Rose."

"Did you have any control over whether Butch Roeder lived?"

"Objection, your honor."

"Overruled. Answer the question, Pastor."

"Only the Lord…only God has that control."

As if on cue, and wanting to be heard on this matter, the loud crack of lightning rumbled through the courtroom, causing some people to be startled and scared.

"But in your congregation don't you often speak the words of the Lord."

"I had nothing to do with Butch Roeder's death," he said, as he reached inside his black suit coat and took out a bible and cross, placing them both on his lap.

With the court's permission, I approached the witness and decided to try a sympathetic, compassionate, non-prosecutorial approach. And, I wanted to get back to questioning him about his wife.

"Pastor, when you were at the library and listened in to our conversation about many things, including Matthew, and your wife's many year affair with your best friend, that understandably enraged you, did it not?" Again, the loud boom of lightning caught everyone's attention.

"Yes."

"You no doubt knew then why she had been gone so much from home?"

He nodded.

"Pastor, can you answer?"

"Yes."

I moved closer to him, his gaze and face had lost its authority. He looked hypnotized, submissive, his big hands fingering the cross like Rose fingered his key. It was judgment day and lies would do no good. I looked at Anne who no longer looked upset at me, and who nodded her head towards the front of the courtroom doors. There with a light blue sport coat on sat Joe next to Cindy. I felt the examination of Mr. Cantrell was not over, but I believed I could get him to answer some nagging questions or resolve some loose ends. I placed my hand near his hand and the bible and cross.

"Pastor," I said, looking at the jury, particularly the former Russian history teacher, who I still believed would be the foreperson, "your wife is sleeping, isn't she?"

"Yes," he said, not loudly and with no commanding voice, but rather, sounding like he was in a trance or hypnotic state. "She's where she wants to be."

I quickly thought about his answer and realized where she must be. "Your honor, we need an emergency recess. I believe I know where she is."

"Granted."

I quickly gathered Joe, Cindy and Anne in one of the attorney conference rooms and told them what needed to be done right away. Of course, I told Joe, that I didn't want him doing anything, that he was to have Townsend or Swango do the work.

Judge Conlon resumed court with the Reverend Cantrell back on the stand. I felt that I had accomplished most of what I wanted, but I wanted to try to get the pastor to admit to a conspiracy to kill Roeder. Again, I was going to bluff and take a risk.

"Pastor, I know about the intent to poison Butch Roeder, but why…"

"Objection, your honor, calls for a conclusion, hearsay, and assumes facts not in evidence. Also, this witness is not competent to testify to such matters."

"Sustained."

"Very well. Pastor, I have a witness outside the courtroom, a faithful parishioner of your congregation, who says he helped you by putting poison in Roeder's food, thus killing him. Do you want me to bring him in or do you want to tell us about the killing of Butch Roeder?"

Perhaps not believing me or not hearing me, the pastor said in a voice so low that everyone had to lean forward to try to hear what he said, "My son is not responsible for what he did, and I don't want twelve strangers who don't know him, to make the possible mistake of finding him guilty and spending the rest of his life in prison. I don't want you or the jury or anyone to steal my son's future."

"But, he knowingly killed a man, pastor…a man, who you as a pallbearer, helped carry his body to the mausoleum." I got real close to the pastor as I further said or rather asked, "Isn't the family of Eilert Kurtz entitled to some kind of justice?"

The pastor's demeanor changed again, gone was the somnolent, hypnotic responses he gave a short while ago about his wife. "Don't steal my son's future!" he said defiantly.

"Pastor, you stole his future, a brilliant boy's future, his childhood, his adolescence by your verbal and physical abuse, and…"

It happened so fast, I never saw the swiftness of his huge right hand as he seized me by the throat. I couldn't breathe and struggled to free myself from his grip with both of my hands as the two courtroom bailiffs jumped on him, subduing him and releasing his hold on me.

With chaos in the courtroom, I think I remember the judge yelling for additional help and for everyone to clear the courtroom.

CHAPTER 25

ANOTHER STATE WITNESS DEAD IN STOREOWNER
KILLING. PROSECUTOR ATTACKED BY DEFENDANT'S
FATHER.

Jack Asaliner

The continuing bizarre trial of genius, Matthew
Cantrell, who prosecutor Nick Papais says tried
to commit the perfect crime in killing wealthy
store owner, Eilert Kurtz, took another
dramatic turn yesterday. With the boy's
father, Principal Clinton Cantrell, on the
witness stand, Papais in a subtle,
compassionate approach asked the pastor whether
his wife was sleeping. Cantrell said yes, and
that his wife was where she wanted to be.
Papais, believing he knew what that meant,
asked Judge Conlon for an emergency recess
which was granted.

Papais's hunch was correct. Detective Joe
Matanovich, who had just been released from
hospital yesterday, quickly sped to the
home of Eilert Kurtz, ran upstairs to the
master bedroom and found Bonnie Cantrell dead
in the bed of her lover, store owner, Eilert
Kurtz. Dr. Loh, a pathologist, said he
believed that Mrs. Cantrell had been dead for
at least one week. His preliminary
report indicated cause of death due to
strangulation.

Shortly after the recess, Papais had resumed his examination of the principal, when suddenly the witness reached out...

While occasionally touching my throat, I read most of Asaliner's article, but not the related stories on the other pages. Assuming I was all right to do closing argument, Judge Conlon told everyone to be back in court at 1:00 p.m. for jury instructions and closing arguments. After Joe returned from the Kurtz home, he arrested Clinton Cantrell for the murder of his wife, Bonnie Cantrell. Suspecting that Pastor Cantrell had help in his scheme to poison Roeder, Joe had Detective Townsend get the congregation membership list from pastor's church to see if any member also worked at the county jail. It turned out that a woman with long black hair worked in the jail kitchen. Joe had her taken into custody for questioning in the death of Butch Roeder. I recall Bonnie Cantrell telling me that the congregation members would do anything for the reverend. I suspected further investigation and evidence would warrant indictments against Mr. Cantrell and his parishioner for murder and conspiracy to commit murder in the death of Butch Roeder.

Mary arrived home late last night from her vacation to pick up Mackenzie, who she thought looked a little on the thin side, and inquired about whether she had been properly fed. After abruptly dismissing her and her concerns about Mackenzie's welfare, I went to bed.

It was a little after noon, and I was in my office with Anne going over key points to include in the closing arguments. In a criminal trial, the prosecutor has the opening and closing arguments, with the defense having their argument in the middle. Anne looked comfortable and relaxed sitting opposite me in my office. I had become very proud of her and all that she had done for me in the trial. Though her face looked tired and her eyes struggled to stay open, she looked attractive and professional in a black dress and high-heeled shoes.

"Yes I know, Nick, I probably look tired, don't I?" she asked.

"You look nice, Anne," I said.

"Nick, there's something I've been wanting to tell you," she said, looking down at the floor, then out the window, everywhere but at me. "No, darn it, I can't do this now. I'm so sorry, Nick for bringing this up right before your closing argument."

"I'm not leaving this room until you tell me, Anne"

"I didn't know you had such a strong interest in mental illness," she said, as if reading from a prepared script, "obviously, this trial has had to be very difficult for you."

"Anne, I've been judging people and their credibility for thirty years. If I may, I've gotten fairly good at knowing when people are not speaking the truth, or are not saying what they want to say. What do you want to tell me?" I asked, staring directly into her brown eyes.

"I've been seeing Eilert Kurtz."

It shouldn't have bothered me, but it did, and I don't know why. I quickly grabbed my suit coat, closing argument notes and left without looking at her or saying anything. Getting this trial over with, getting out of this place, and promising myself to never look back was what I wanted.

My opening closing was a typical prosecutor's summary of the evidence and why we believed that Matthew Cantrell was guilty. I scanned the courtroom and saw Eilert Kurtz, Jr. Our eyes locked for a few seconds, and then I looked at Anne, who turned her face away from me. For a crazy instant, I thought how easily I could purposely lose this case. It happens in sports, doesn't it? But, then usually there's a payoff or bribe, or some inducement to throw a game, or a boxer agreeing to lose a fight for a big paycheck. Why was I even thinking like this? The jury was likely to find him not guilty anyway.

Rose's argument lasted one hour. Though oddly his smile had disappeared, he spoke eloquently and convincingly, reminding the jury about the minimal evidence in the case, and how little we heard from Butch Roeder, the only witness who says his client was involved in the murder of Eilert Kurtz. Further, he said the jury must remember that Butch Roeder testified because he got a plea agreement, a slap on the wrist in exchange for a few minutes of testimony. How fair was that? Rose asked. He then told the jury that there were gaps in the case and weak links. To emphasize that point, he pulled out a chain about two feet in length, stretched it in front of him causing it to snap and break in the middle. The state, he said, had failed to present a continuous chain of evidence linking his client to the killing of Eilert Kurtz. Weak links are reasonable doubts, he said. The state he added, presented no evidence of fingerprints, no DNA, no blood samples, no clothes, no vehicle, no weapon, nothing. Despite the vast resources of the state, all the prosecution could present was a body tied to a cross. Further, he said, tapping his cane on the floor, and looking at me for the answer, and then at the jury, where's the fifth motive that the prosecution had promised? And, he asked, what was the additional reason or main reason why Eilert Kurtz was tied to a cross. After all, he reminded the jury, didn't the prosecutor tell Dr. Catlin that her explanation for the victim being tied to the cross was only partially correct.

He then said, if by some unfathomable reason, the jury felt that the state had proved Matthew's guilt beyond a reasonable doubt, he be found not responsible by reason of insanity at the time of the crime. He reminded the jury that all the mental experts believed his client insane at the time of the crime. Specifically, he recalled Dr. Catlin's testimony that his client was an "ill child." As a final remark, and before I could object, he thanked me for my years of work with organizations dedicated to helping people with mental illness. Yes, he knew how to work the jury, I thought. I could see why he was so successful defending insanity cases throughout the country.

My turn. After twenty minutes into my final closing, I told the jury that I had compassion for Matthew Cantrell, and believed he had depression and Post Traumatic Stress Disorder as the result of a harsh upbringing by an abusive father, but that did not justify a cold, calculated killing.

"Ladies and gentlemen of the jury, this was not a spontaneous event or a random killing. It had been planned out months before that cold December 22nd day, when Matthew Cantrell left Butch Roeder in the truck and began his long march to Kurtz's home to lure him out of the comfort of a warm bed and the pleasure of Mrs. Cantrell's company. All of this reflected a rational thought process, and not one encumbered by psychotic delusions or hallucinations. This was not a warped or deranged mind. The law on insanity in this state is not a suggestion or advice, and it's more than unlawful or antisocial conduct. There is no indication that what he did reflected an inability to distinguish right from wrong. Quite the contrary, as I have already said, and as we will discuss shortly with his efforts to dispose of evidence.

This was not a young man without emotion. He had a friend in Butch Roeder, obviously, not one's choice for citizen of the year, but it shows that he is capable of having a friend. Also, you will recall Butch Roeder's sister talking about his love of animals, and how he loved their jointly owned dog, the black lab, Buck. And, of course, he loved his mother, but her infidelity disturbed him; however, more traumatic would be Kurtz telling the Reverend about the affair. No one wanted to incur the Reverend's wrath. They knew what he was capable of, and we all witnessed it a short while ago with the assault on me. Matthew did not want anything to happen to his mother, yet ironically, what he did not want to happen inevitably happened. The killing of Kurtz set into motion a violent sequence of events leading to the deaths of three people, Butch Roeder, Angela Bedford and Bonnie Cantrell."

Grabbing some water to ease my sore throat, either from talking too much or from the assault by the pastor, I continued.

"Ladies and gentlemen, what followed was a methodical plan to dispose of incriminating evidence; and, it was successful. As Mr. Rose said, and I agree, there was no DNA, no blood samples, nothing. Why would there be? Matthew Cantrell is smart, a genius, if you will. He had read the books on crime scene analysis and forensic evidence. You can't expect the state or prosecution to present evidence if the defendant destroys or removes that evidence. That doesn't mean he didn't commit the crime. It simply means he was smart enough to dispose of the evidence.

As regards the mental health experts, the judge will instruct you that you may disregard or discredit all or some of the mental health expert testimony. Yes, that is correct. Their testimony is to be evaluated just like any other witness. Please keep in mind that none of them had done any of the nationally recognized testing to rule out other causes for the defendant's behavior, such as drugs, legal or illegal, or a physical disease process."

"Significantly," I continued, "no one mentioned about treatment or help or medication. After all, many schizophrenics, even assuming a correct diagnosis, are successfully managed by medicine and therapy. Too, many people with a schizophrenia diagnosis are people who break no laws and function well in society, with many of them working. Thus, a diagnosis of schizophrenia is not necessarily a precursor to criminal behavior." I paused to look at the jury and drink a little more water before continuing.

"Mr. Rose challenged me to tell you about the fifth motive and the significance of the cross. I gladly accept the challenge but not before I show you something."

I went to the prosecution table where Anne pulled out of a box a thick chain, about three feet in length. This was the chain I had asked Joe months ago to get for me. I didn't know if I would need the chain, but having researched some of Rose's closing arguments in prior trials throughout the country, I read where he occasionally would use the chain to show weak links in a prosecutor's case. I looked over at Rose whose face showed no expression or surprise. Of course, I would expect nothing less from such a skilled attorney, but I knew inside he had to be experiencing regret for using the chain, now knowing that I had researched his closing arguments, just like a coach preparing for a game by reviewing films of the opposing team.

"This chain, ladies and gentlemen of the jury, does not break." I stretched it out in front of me as hard as I could and then placed it back on our table.

"This chain cannot be broken because there are no weak links in it, no reasonable link of doubt. If there is a reasonable doubt, I ask, what is it?"

Let's briefly review the four motives. Again, please keep in mind that I do not, I repeat, the state does not have to prove any motive, but I have no problem doing so because they are true and believable. If you will recall, we admitted into evidence a piece of paper Dr. Loh had found on the person of Butch Roeder wherein he indicated that Matthew Cantrell had told him that there were at least five reasons for killing Kurtz. Let's briefly review four of them. First, robbery. The boys took over $300.00 from Mr. Kurtz. Second, the concern that Kurtz was going to tell the reverend about the affair; and, of course, one doesn't tell the reverend or the principal of Westin High School bad news. Third, Matthew wanted to hurt his father. What better way than kill his best friend? The fourth was the desire to commit the perfect crime, which was almost accomplished, but for an anonymous call from a woman that resulted in the arrest of Matthew and Butch Roeder. It wasn't until months later that we learned that the anonymous caller was Bonnie Cantrell. Why did she do it? We will never know...we can only speculate. I assume she no longer could live with the thought that her son who occupied her house had killed someone, not just anyone, but Eilert Kurtz. Of course, she knew her son killed Eilert Kurtz because she was at Kurtz's home on the morning of December 22nd., when her son knocked on the door to ask Kurtz for help in starting his friend's vehicle. That would be the last time Bonnie Cantrell saw Eilert Kurtz alive.

Before we get to the fifth motive ladies and gentlemen of the jury, what is the significance of the cross? Dr. Catlin said something like defiance or retaliation of his father's strict religious beliefs. That's partly true, but there's more. Actually, the cross and the fifth motive are inextricably woven together."

Approaching the jurors, I said, "Let me explain. For millions of Christians throughout the world, the cross is indelibly stamped in their minds with the image of Jesus Christ. For believers, the cross is a symbol of remembrance of Christ and what his death represented and meant. Matthew Cantrell and Butch Roeder did not hide the body. On the contrary, they wanted the body to be found. What they didn't want was to be caught. But a killing without a cross would be just that, a killing, no different than many killings throughout the world every day. Matthew Cantrell was too smart and too different to do something ordinary. A killing should be one that is remembered. Many crimes are remembered because of the nature of the killing or doubt as to who committed them. People still speculate about who was Jack the Ripper? Who killed the Black Dahlia? Was there a conspiracy to kill President Kennedy? Matthew Cantrell wanted his crime to be immortalized, to live on, just like the Leopold and Loeb case, but there's something else.

What bothered Matthew Cantrell was that he was not remembered by Eilert Kurtz. He was treated as a stranger by Kurtz. Yes, the reverend was a strict disciplinarian and abusive, physically and mentally, but he never forgot Matthew. He wanted Matthew to do well, to become successful like himself, and not associate with the likes of people like Butch Roeder."

I looked at the jury, all of whom were attentive, particularly the Russian history teacher who gave me a slight wink and what looked like a smile, as if in agreement with what I was saying.

"So what you ask, that Eilert Kurtz paid no attention to Matthew Cantrell and treated him like a stranger, like nothing, while also enjoying the favors of his mother. The defendant no doubt believed what better symbol for remembrance of a crime than a cross, but the remembrance would not be for the victim, but for the mastermind behind the killing.

Ladies and gentlemen, among the photographs we introduced at the beginning of the trial, along with the photos showing the destroyed face and head of Mr. Kurtz, was a full length photograph of Mr. Kurtz shortly before his death. In the jury room look at the pale green eyes, the coarse, orange brown hair, the jutting jaw, the small stature. Now look at Matthew Cantrell.

Eilert Kurtz deserved to die because he was not just anyone. He was Matthew Cantrell's father."

CHAPTER 26

It was late Wednesday night of the following week. I had just arrived in Greece, specifically Chania, Crete, to vacation and visit with my Greek relatives. Summer is not the best time to visit Greece because of the extreme heat, but I had to get away, far away. As far as I knew, the jury still had not reached a verdict. I knew this was a complex case for them to decide.

Immediately after the trial, I thanked Joe and Cindy for their work on the case and wished Anne well in her relationship with Eilert Kurtz, Jr. I told Anne to fax the verdict to me at my cousin's real estate office in Crete. Cindy didn't look too happy at my leaving, and I had a tough time trying to say goodbye to her without choking up.

On Thursday morning, my cousin Menolis called from his real estate office to tell me that I had a fax and did I want him to read it. I thanked him, but said no, since I already knew the contents. He then laughed and said there were no contents, just a big letter, "G."

I had already figured the jury would find Cantrell guilty when I saw the wink of the eye and slight smile from the likely foreperson, the former Russian history teacher, and from nods by many of the jurors during the final few minutes of my closing.

Late Friday night, my cousin Katia told me there was someone at the door to see me. It wasn't just anyone. This woman looked to me like a Greek goddess or like Helen of Troy must have looked like, a face from history, from antiquity. She looked like she did on the night of Aleisha's wedding, but weary and tired, as if having travelled for many hours. I looked at my cousin for an explanation. She said nothing, but smiled and nodded the look of an accomplice to this get together.

"Is there something you want to say, Nick?"

"I want to say so much, but I'm kind of in shock."

"You don't know much about women, do you Nick!" she said with a huge grin.

"I seem to recall you recently telling me that. I'm thrilled and ecstatic to see you. Please come in and welcome to Greece."

THE END

Judge Peter Caras is a former trial prosecutor, Lake County,
Indiana Magistrate, and retired U.S. Administrative Law Judge.
He and his wife make their home in Illinois.